Falling Home

Book One in the Buckeye Falls Series

Libby Kay

ISBN: (ebook) 978-1-958136-30-0
(print) 978-1-958136-31-7

Inkspell Publishing
207 Moonglow Circle #101
Murrells Inlet, SC 29576

Edited By Yezanira Venecia
Cover Art By Fantasia Frog

DEDICATION

Once again, for Curly.
Your love and support make all the difference.

CHAPTER 1

Ginny Meyer glanced at her phone for the third time in two minutes. Was time standing still? From her spot in the rental car line, she knew it would be another five minutes before she got to the front. An elderly woman in an ugly Christmas ensemble stood perched on the edge of the counter, explaining all the reasons she could not drive a stick shift. Once again, Ginny looked at the time and grimaced. She promised her dad she'd be on the road an hour ago.

After taking a cleansing breath, Ginny took in her surroundings. Despite the fact that most people were still digesting their Thanksgiving leftovers, the rental store had already decked the halls. Piney wreaths hung in front of each kiosk and tinny Christmas carols filtered through the overhead speakers. As a girl, Ginny had loved Christmas. The traditions, the movies, the presents, the cookies covered in edible glitter—Christmas brought back some of her favorite childhood memories.

Christmas also brought one of the most painful memories of her life. Especially since she was mere hours away from facing her past head-on. Nope, she would save the soul-searching for the road to Ohio. Right now, in New York, she had enough to handle, starting with the festive troublemaker in front of her.

"You see, dear," the woman said over the barrier at the kiosk, "I asked for a different car."

The clerk bit her lip and forced a professional smile. "Yes, ma'am. As I said, we can give you a compact car, but it won't be in the evergreen color. All we have available is black."

The elderly woman leaned back on her heels, as if driving a black car was grounds for a nervous breakdown. "But, dear, it's Christmas time. I can't show up to Pennsylvania in something that isn't festive." To punctuate her point, she waved down at her dress. Santa himself couldn't have designed a more festive frock. Red and green stripes covered the older woman from neck to knees. A candy cane wrapped in twinkle lights would be more tasteful.

Ginny stifled a groan as the clerk nodded and asked a manager to assist her. Ginny didn't see what all the fuss was about; a car was a car—who cared if it was green, black, or purple? Behind her, another customer cleared his throat and gestured at his watch with an expression that was anything but jolly. "We all have places to go," he mumbled loud enough for the older woman to hear.

Pulling herself to her full height of barely five feet, the older woman stomped back to the man and pointed with a gnarled finger. "Young man, I would appreciate some patience and kindness. You will get your turn as soon as I'm finished. There's no need to be rude this close to Christmas." She nodded at her words and turned before he could respond; his jaw was still cemented to the floor after his dressing-down. Ginny hazarded a glance over her shoulder and saw the man was as red as the woman's sweater. Apparently, no one wanted to get scolded by Mrs. Claus in public.

Fifteen minutes later, Ginny was behind the wheel of her rental car. It turns out the rental company didn't have evergreen cars available, but the woman got a sedan in cherry red. Ginny took the black car and was happy to be out on the road. Living in New York City meant she rarely drove herself anywhere, so she relished the feel of the open road and minimal traffic once she made it to the highway outside city limits. Granted, she couldn't get to Indy 500 speeds, but Ginny settled for going above 55 mph.

Pushing the controls on the steering wheel, Ginny tried to find a radio station that wasn't playing Christmas carols, but it was no use. Every station had a jingle bell, Rudolph, or a crooner lamenting his blue Christmas. She had enough and stabbed the radio off with her thumb. "I don't need any music. It's only a—" Her words stalled as she calculated the length of her solo journey. "Um, ten hours?" she asked the empty car. Clicking the car's GPS alerted her that nearly ten hours waited for her. It might be impossible to avoid the holiday hoopla on the airwaves.

By the time she reached her first toll booth, Ginny had given up the fight. She plugged her phone into the console and found a true crime podcast to fill her time. Who needed Old Saint Nick when you could have serial killers and nightmarish tales to fill the void? When she was halfway through Pennsylvania, Ginny's stomach growled so loud she barely heard the details of the investigation. With a pat to her rumbling belly, she pulled over to a small diner for a quick bite to eat.

As soon as she stepped out of the car, she realized her mistake. While the building didn't look anything like her ex's restaurant, it had the same smell and atmosphere. Ginny shuddered as she opened the door and inhaled the aroma of fries, stale coffee, and bleach.

A chipper hostess in a blue uniform and holding a handful of menus greeted Ginny. "Hiya," she beamed, "just one today?" Pinned to the young woman's uniform was a Grinch pin and a Christmas wreath flashing green and red. Ginny thought about the older woman from the car rental store—these two were quite the festive pair.

Ginny bobbed her head. "Can I order something to go?"

The hostess nodded and handed her a menu. "Have a

seat at the counter," she said over her shoulder. "I'll swing by for your order in a second." Ginny did as she was told and perched herself on the end of a stool. Her jeans slid on the vinyl material, and she felt her feet stick to the floor.

Flicking the menu open, Ginny decided a wrap would be the easiest thing to eat while driving. "Miss, I'm ready to order." She waved at the girl as she walked past with a pitcher of coffee. "Can I have the chicken wrap and a large coffee?"

Nodding, the waitress sashayed past to place the order. "Want a piece of pie with that? We make the best shoofly pie you'll ever have." Ginny didn't doubt it, but her appetite wasn't ready for sweet desserts. Over two years living in the city had shown her that her pants size varied greatly when home-baked desserts were available. She declined the pie and turned her attention back to her phone.

There were a few texts from work, enquiring how long she would be on leave. Another text from her dad, saying he was excited to see her and would have a late dinner ready. Ginny replied that she was five hours away and dinner would be great. Her father loved to cook when she was in town, and she knew he was waiting to flex his culinary muscle.

Her texts from work were harder to answer. Ginny didn't have an end date for her visit back to Buckeye Falls, and that scared her to death. Since moving away, she had made a point to plan her visits around an event. In this case, it was her father's hip surgery. He wouldn't be able to take care of himself for a few weeks, and Ginny couldn't stomach him relying on strangers for help. He was her father; it was her responsibility.

The biggest reason she wasn't ready to go to Buckeye Falls had everything to do with the diner she was currently sitting in. Well, not this place specifically, but another one. Max, and his beloved diner, were in Buckeye Falls. The diner, which didn't even have a proper name, was the focal point of her hometown's food scene. Her hometown was so small, its most popular restaurant didn't even need a name. The diner, which some days felt like the real love of Max's life, was going to taunt her. Deep down, Ginny knew she shouldn't begrudge her ex's success, as he likely wouldn't begrudge her hers.

While tapping her fingers on the countertop, she battled a metric ton of roiling emotions. Frankly, she wasn't sure how far to delve into these thoughts. It seemed dangerous, like poking a hibernating bear. But through Ginny's musings, one fact stuck out to her the most—she was curious how Max was doing. Was he happy? Was the diner the success she assumed it was? Did he miss her? Had he met someone? Wait, she certainly didn't care if he did. That changed nothing in her mind. And yet …

Yes, she was so not ready for a Buckeye Falls reunion. "Ready or not, here I come." She sighed to herself.

Aside from wanting to avoid a certain dining establishment, Ginny's palms slicked with sweat for a bigger reason as she grew nearer to her destination. She hadn't reached out to tell Max she was coming back, even if only temporarily. Despite her plans to avoid the diner, word traveled fast, and she'd be outed in no time. She knew she couldn't hide forever, but damn did she want to. After they divorced, the pair hadn't stayed in touch. It felt foolish to reach out with her plans after all this time. Her plans weren't his concern.

Practicing her breathing exercises, Ginny leaned back and inhaled deeply, centering herself. Even though it was foolish to think she could control the outcome of her visit, she tried to picture the perfect, stress-free trip home. She would avoid Max at all costs and would focus on her father. There was no reason to open old wounds and check in with her ex. Nope, Max was none of her business anymore. Now, she just had to convince her heart that he was old news.

Max Sanchez wiped his brow with the corner of his apron. The dinnertime rush was murder on Sundays. Take-out orders for family dinners were his biggest business, which kept him up to his elbows in pie crusts and roast beef. "How much chili do we have left?"

"About six cups, four if Evan is serving," CeCe yelled over the din of the bustling kitchen. She was also sweating in the heat of the cramped space, but her eyes were laser-focused on the orders in front of her. Max could always count on her.

Evan, his newest waiter, stumbled into the kitchen and slammed his tray on the counter. "I heard that," he grumbled as he dipped the ladle into the bowl. "It's not my fault that I want to give the customers generous portions."

Max bit back a grin and shook his head. "I wouldn't worry about us being too generous, but it's our busiest night, so try not to give out bowls when customers order cups." Trying to be diplomatic with Evan and CeCe was difficult because Max liked them both so much. CeCe was a trained pastry chef, and Evan was just getting started on his own. Max strived to keep the peace as often as he could, especially in his own kitchen.

When Evan was out of earshot, CeCe leaned over the counter toward Max. "We better get out the soup we made for tomorrow. Helen said there's a line out the door, and that's not counting the take-out orders."

Max agreed with her but turned his attention back to his station. Dozens of plates waited for their meals, but Max was slow on his feet tonight. When Harold called that morning, it threw Max for a loop. He knew his ex-father-in-law was having surgery soon, but he didn't know who would be coming to take care of him. Of course it made sense that Ginny was coming home to help. Harold was her only family. It surprised Max how much it gutted him that she hadn't reached out on her own.

Much like the dwindling pot of chili, Max's relationship with Ginny needed attention before there was nothing left to salvage. He missed her, deep in his core, but he didn't know how to reach out and tell her. Deep down, he knew it wouldn't make a difference. There were ample reasons they were no longer together, all of which Ginny would happily recite to him as soon as they saw each other.

But that was the problem; they never saw each other. Over the last two years, Ginny had avoided Buckeye Falls like the plague. He'd heard through the local grapevine when she was visiting Harold, but she never stopped by the diner, never even called to see how he was doing. There wasn't even so much as a birthday text. Max never asked Harold, but he was sure that Ginny didn't know her father and he were still close.

Even after all this time, Max couldn't believe how little he knew about the most important woman in his life. A rough year in their marriage erased years of friendship and love. If he allowed it, Max knew he could stay up for days obsessing about what went wrong, who was to blame, and how he'd missed the cues that he'd been on thin ice. He wasn't too proud to admit he'd bored his former father-in-law one too many times on the subject. *Poor Harold.*

Tuesdays, when they were closed, Max would go to Harold's and make dinner. They would watch whatever game was on TV and talk about the good ol' days. Even though Ginny wasn't around, Max could see her in the details of the old house. From pictures on the mantle to the stories and updates Harold would share, Max knew enough to feel like he still knew his wife. Well, his ex-wife.

The most important thing he knew was that she was still single. That tidbit shouldn't put Max at ease, but it did. Knowing there wasn't a special man in Ginny's life let a tiny kernel of hope bloom in his chest. It didn't matter what the Ohio courts said, Ginny still felt like his wife. Of course, he'd tried going on a couple dates. Those stilted outings were awkward and uncomfortable, and he always felt like he was cheating. It was taking far too long for his heart to get the memo that his brain had accepted long ago. Much like that last serving of chili, Max was flying solo.

"Did you hear what I said?" CeCe asked, a pair of tongs pointed toward Max's torso.

Shaking his head, Max cleared his throat. "No, sorry. What was that?" He tossed a handful of parsley onto a plate and slid it to the edge of the counter for Evan. "Make sure you add an extra pat of butter for Mrs. Henderson," he ordered.

CeCe put her hands on her hips and stared down at her boss. "I said we're almost out of hash browns. Do you want me to start new ones or tell folks it's home fries?"

Max wiped his hands on his apron, stalling. Things were getting too busy for his head not to be in the game, and he hated to waste time on chopping potatoes. "Let's go with the home fries. Tonight, potatoes are potatoes."

CeCe nodded, but she arched an eyebrow at Max. "Will do." Before she stepped away, she lowered her voice and asked, "Do you want to talk about it?"

Max stopped chopping, his knife raised in the air. "About hash browns?"

Groaning, CeCe shook her head. "No, about the real reason you're not listening. I heard a certain city slicker is headed back to Buckeye Falls. If you don't mind me saying, it's messing with your mojo tonight."

Max wouldn't give CeCe the satisfaction of admitting defeat. "I don't know what you're talking about. And why are you talking like we're in an old-time Western?"

CeCe rolled her eyes and pulled a bin of hash browns from the chiller drawer. "If you want to play coy with me, that's fine. You're the boss. I think it would be healthier to talk about your feelings, instead of not chopping enough potatoes at the beginning of our shift."

Max knew she was right, but his pride got the better of him. "If Ginny is back in town, that's her business. It hardly has anything to do with me." As soon as the lie was off his lips, his knife skidded and nicked his thumb. Mumbling a slew of obscenities, he ran to the sink and the first aid kit.

The cut was tiny, but the lack of focus frustrated him. "This was nothing, an honest sl-sl-slip up."

Damn, now he was stuttering. Max closed his eyes and tried counting back from ten. Frustrations were high, and that's when his old nemesis liked to come out and play. His stutter was hardly a well-kept secret, but he had been so good at controlling it. Fortunately CeCe was familiar with his problem and was kind enough to change the subject.

"If you're okay, I'll go help Evan take orders." She hitched a thumb at the now-full prep station. "We're set here for now."

Max met her gaze and smiled, truly happy in that moment to have such a good friend on his team. CeCe and Max didn't always see eye to eye in the kitchen, but he knew she had his back. "Thanks," he said, pulling his attention to his bandaged finger. "Tell the Martins that their steaks are almost ready."

With a nod, CeCe disappeared into the dining room, leaving Max alone with a throbbing thumb and a million racing thoughts. Could he survive a visit from Ginny? More importantly, could he survive *not* seeing her while she was in Buckeye Falls? They had been a couple for over a decade and friends for a lot longer than that. It seemed so cold and hurtful to avoid each other now.

Harold was going to have surgery, and Max knew his friend was worried. Recovery time, prepping the house for his recovery—there were a lot of moving pieces. Back when there were family emergencies during their marriage, they were a team. If Ginny zigged, Max would zag. Now it felt all wrong, like he was watching his old life play out without him. He liked to help the people who were important to him, but he knew he wasn't welcome anymore. That stung. It shouldn't after two years, but it still did.

"Come and see me," he muttered to himself. "Don't be a stranger, Gin." Squaring his shoulders, Max went back to the matter at hand and finished searing steaks. The diners were counting on him, and he would never let them down.

CHAPTER 2

The tires of the rental car crunched down the gravel driveway as Ginny parked behind her father's pickup. To say the trip was long would be an understatement. She'd dealt with podcast fatigue, indigestion from one too many cups of coffee, and a little road rage as she merged onto I-70. But she arrived in one piece, so overall it felt like a victory.

Before her feet were on solid earth, she heard her father on the porch. "Ginnybread!" he called, opening his arms for a hug. She left her things in the car and sprinted toward him. After over ten hours behind the wheel, her legs felt stiff and awkward. Her father's arms enveloped her, and suddenly her throat was tight.

"It's good to see you, Dad." She breathed into his cable-knit sweater. He smelled like the holidays, piney with a hint of cinnamon. From over her shoulder, Ginny heard the TV blasting ESPN. In addition to needing new hips, her father could probably stand to get a hearing aid, but she wouldn't press her luck right now. *One medical issue at a time, please.*

Harold Meyer kept his arms around his daughter. "I guess that's the good thing about you living outside Buckeye Falls—the hugs are longer." Just as Ginny opened her mouth to argue, her father's chest rumbled with a laugh. "I'm only teasing you," he promised. "You think I don't like bragging about my hotshot daughter at the community center?"

Ginny stepped back and ran her fingers through her hair. "I'm not sure how much your neighbors care about my marketing career."

Harold shrugged. "They're your neighbors too. Plus, they're proud of their girl making good in the world." Taking a step forward, he leaned on the railing to catch his balance. His lips dipped down as he tried to cover a scowl.

Splaying her hands in front of her, Ginny stopped him. "Oh, no you don't. Get back inside. I'll get my stuff."

With a dramatic eye roll, Harold took another step down. "What's the point of having this surgery if I can't wear out my hips helping my daughter?" He eased down onto the driveway and followed Ginny to her car. She knew he wouldn't leave it alone, so she handed him her cosmetic bag and purse. "Either you're packing light, or you're insulting your father's manhood."

Ginny shook her head. "I've got the rest. Go inside and pour me a glass of that eggnog I know you have simmering." While she wasn't the most festive person in Buckeye Falls, Ginny knew her dad's eggnog was legendary. When their family was cut down to two, certain traditions remained in the Meyer home. Eggnog throughout December was one of them. Ginny promised herself she'd check the medicine cabinet for her father's cholesterol pills. She was here to play nurse, and she'd own the role.

Harold beamed, the skin around his brown eyes crinkling at the corners. "I already have your favorite mug ready." He turned and started lumbering up the porch. Ginny took a moment to watch him, feeling her heart pull in her ribcage. As much as she hated to admit it, they were both getting older, and time was precious. During her time in New York, she'd made sacrifices in the name of her career, ones she didn't regret but still gave her pause.

After dragging her two suitcases into the house, she wheeled them toward the stairs and met her father in the kitchen. The tiny space was a time capsule to Ginny's childhood, complete with the old wooden table and chairs, almond-colored refrigerator, and aging stove. She hung her coat on the back of a chair and helped with pouring a mug of eggnog.

"This smells heavenly." She slurped from her mug and raised an eyebrow. "You changed the recipe." It wasn't a question.

Harold lowered his gaze and gestured toward the living room. "Uh, yeah. I added a little mace. Let's have a seat and catch up before dinner." Ginny's father wasn't usually cagey, so she knew something was up. She perched on her side of the couch and looked at the fire roaring in the stone fireplace, knowing if she gave him time, he would come clean with whatever he was thinking.

Two stockings hung on the mantel; a third nail still sat empty. Ginny wouldn't think about the owner of that third stocking. Well, technically, there were two owners, but she wasn't going there either. Despite the booming sound of sports TV, Ginny could hear the ghosts of Christmases past if she closed her eyes: the gentle laugh of her mother and the low rumbling chuckle of Max. So much for not going there. The ghosts of her past would need to wait.

"The fire feels amazing." Ginny leaned back and surveyed the Christmas cards on her father's bookcase. The cheery cards ranged from nativity scenes to plump snowmen wishing glad tidings. Her mind flashed to her apartment back in New York, and she tried not to grimace at the thought that no Christmas cards waited for her return. She hadn't even bothered with decorating the tiny space, as she knew no one would see it. *Way to bring down the mood*, she chastised herself.

Forcing herself to stay in the moment, Ginny surveyed the rest of the shelf. Situated front and center sat a framed photo that caused her breath to catch. "Why is my wedding picture up?" She rose and slowly walked toward the offending object, as if the memories would bite her. Racking her brain, Ginny struggled to remember if that picture had been up during her last visit home. She'd bet good money it hadn't been, and it bothered her to see it now.

Harold eased onto his cushion and winced before adjusting his back. "I'm sorry, Ginnybread. I was pulling out old decorations and found it. You look so beautiful and happy. I meant to put it away before you got home."

Ginny spun on her heels so quickly, she nearly spilled her eggnog. "I'll take care of it later." She gingerly flipped the frame face-down with her index finger, as if touching too much of the image would scald her. Divorce, either hers or her parents', was not a popular topic of conversation in the Meyer home. Harold knew the basics of why Ginny left, but she'd purposely kept the details to herself. It was no one's business why she made the choices she did. Well, she supposed Max deserved an honorable mention on why their marriage ended. *There will be plenty of time for soul-searching (with or without) Max later … she mused.*

Standing in the living room, Ginny searched for something to pull her back to the here and now. Her bags weren't even unpacked, and she was falling back into memories and overthinking all the reasons she'd left. First—and her personal favorite—she and Max were workaholics. Two workaholics could not possibly live happily under the same roof. One of them was always busy, and the other resenting them for not being available. She'd seen it happen one too many times, and she'd decided to move on before things got too ugly. *It was so easy taking each other for granted.*

The other reason for the dissolution of their marriage was a little more nuanced … and a lot more painful. As Ginny spun around and surveyed the rest of the photos and knickknacks, a certain person was missing from everything. There were no mementos linked to Ginny's mother. No old wedding snapshots of Harold and her, not even a family photo documenting their early years. Her mother had made a choice to move on, and both Ginny and Harold had respected it in their own way. Or she should say, they *eventually* respected it.

Desperate for a distraction from thoughts of Max and her mother, she pointed to a tray of cookies on the coffee table in front of him. "You're baking now?" Ginny laughed, taking a sugar cookie and shamelessly dunking it in her mug. It was universally known that sugar could temporarily solve all problems—even the emotional landmines of divorce.

Her father chuckled and sipped from his mug. "No, the ladies' church group brought these over. You know, the women from St. David's." Of course, she didn't really know, but Ginny dutifully nodded and nibbled on the treat. "Susan Windom, you might remember her son, Greg, she brought them over this morning when she heard you were visiting. And my friend Mona dropped off some cinnamon bread for us to have for breakfast." Something shifted in her father's expression at the mention of Mona, but she was too absorbed in his words to register what it meant.

Ginny's hand froze in front of her mouth, a cookie crumb plopping into her mug. "You told people I was coming back?"

"Sure. Everyone at the community center was asking who was going to take care of me. Is that a problem?" His tone was casual, but Ginny didn't miss the glint in her father's eyes. He was up to something.

Ginny recovered, downing the rest of her eggnog and nearly choking on the lost piece of cookie. "Nope, all good." She put the mug on the coffee table and paced to her suitcases. "You mind if I unpack a little before dinner?" When they were in the kitchen, Ginny had seen the slow cooker and smelled her father's chili. Her stomach rumbled at the thought of the spicy stew.

Harold nodded and turned his attention to the blaring TV. "Take your time. You know chili; it'll last forever." Ginny listened to the dueling sportscasters until she reached the top of the stairs and closed the door to her childhood bedroom.

Being back in her hometown always brought a mixed bag of emotions. Ginny was happy to see her dad, but there were so many painful memories housed in these four walls. Sometimes Ginny would lay awake and replay some of the defining moments of her life, over-analyzing each second of heartbreak. Shaking herself, she tossed her suitcases on the bed and started unpacking.

Considering what she usually wore in the city, Ginny knew she'd packed light. Power suits and sky-high heels were still in New York. Instead, she had yoga pants, sweaters, and her favorite pair of worn jeans. The reason for this visit dictated that comfort would reign supreme.

Next week, Harold was scheduled for a hip replacement. He'd put off the procedure until his joints were worn down, making walking so painful he would grimace with every step. Ginny had tried to talk him into surgery the year before, after one of his rare visits to the city.

They had been walking arm-in-arm through Central Park when he'd spotted an open bench and begged her for a rest. Watching the pain in her father's features had been all she needed to know the time had come for the surgery. Since he refused to have it done outside Buckeye Falls, it had taken months for a spot to open with his local doctor. Ginny had complained, more than she probably should have, that there were hundreds of qualified doctors in New York. Harold could recover in the city and she could work from home. But as he usually does, Harold dragged his feet and insisted on waiting. It was his body, so she gave up the fight.

Ginny walked to the closet and opened the doors. She surveyed the contents and was about to hang up her clothes when she saw something in the corner. A glint of red sparkled in the fading daylight. "What in the world?" she asked, pulling the garment free. It was a full-length red dress, covered in sequins that sparkled red and gold. The frock looked slightly familiar, but Ginny wondered what it was doing in her childhood closet. The tags were still on, and it was from one of the local boutique shops. A distant memory nibbled at the corners of her brain, but she couldn't place where she knew the dress from.

Below her, Ginny heard her dad pottering in the kitchen. She would ask about the dress during dinner. She would also ask why his eggnog tasted different and why he insisted on placing her wedding picture back on display. The mere thought of her ex's name caused Ginny's heart rate to spike. It was a ludicrous reaction, one she blamed on being back in Ohio.

After hanging the last of her things in the closet, Ginny slid her suitcases under the bed and headed downstairs. Just as she reached the bottom of the stairs, she heard her father talking. "Yes, she got here an hour ago. Thanks for checking." Her father's back was to her, but she saw the landline phone in his hand. There was a pause while the other caller spoke. "I will, son. Talk to you soon."

Son? There was only one person her father called son. "Dad?" Ginny stepped into the kitchen, frowning at her father. "Who was that?"

Harold hung up the phone and turned back to the counter. "Just a friend checking in," he said casually, too casually for Ginny's liking. "Take a seat, it's time for dinner."

Ginny did as she was told and settled into her chair. While her father scooped up bowls of chili and covered them in cilantro and shredded cheese, Ginny took in the space. There were a few new items that caught her attention, one being the fancy set of utensils she spotted on the table. Gone were the old spoons she remembered eating chili with on her last visit, and in their place were shiny new ones.

"New utensils?" she asked when her father returned to the table with their meals. "Looks pretty fancy," she observed.

Harold shrugged and tucked into his chili with gusto, barely letting it cool. "Gift from a friend." Ginny nodded but waited for more. Together they sat in companionable silence and ate their dinner before Harold finally started talking. "They were a birthday gift. From Max."

Ginny was surprised she didn't choke to death when Max's name filled the space. "What? He's still giving you presents?" She was incredulous.

Their divorce had been finalized two years ago. As far as Ginny was concerned, Max had no reason to give her father gifts or remember his birthday. The notion that he remembered, that he still cared, did funny things to her belly, which had nothing to do with the spicy chili.

Harold sipped from his glass of water and finally met her gaze. "Max and I have dinner every Tuesday night. It's the night the diner is closed, and we've made it a habit. I know you won't like it, but I'm tired of keeping it from you. I'm sorry I did, Ginnybread."

Ginny let her spoon clatter to the table. "He asked you to lie to me?"

Raising his hands, her father shook his head. "No, he wanted me to be honest with you from the start. But I know you, and I didn't want to hurt your feelings or put you in an awkward position."

"My dad is having weekly dinner dates with my ex-husband. Forgive me if I feel put out." Ginny hated the tone of her voice, sounding like a haughty teenager. Her father was free to do what he liked, to see whom he liked, but it didn't mean *she* had to like it. Ginny balled up her napkin and tossed it onto the table. She had to focus on the trembling of her bottom lip, which was dangerously close to letting a sob out.

Harold wiped at his mouth and let Ginny have her moment. When she'd slowed her breathing, he rested his hand on hers. "Ginnybread, I'm sorry I kept our dinners a secret from you. Frankly, I didn't see the point in upsetting you long distance."

Ginny swiped at her eyes with the back of her hand. She hated that her eyes were misting over; she hated that, once again, Max was the source of her tears. "It's fine, Dad. I'm sorry I'm acting like a child about the whole thing." She leaned forward and wrapped an arm around his shoulder. "You're an adult who can make his own friends." When they pulled apart from their embrace, Ginny met his eye. "But please, don't invite him over while I'm here. I'm not back home for him—I'm here for you."

There was a flash on Harold's face, a look of panic that quickly dissipated. Ginny had so many questions, so many emotions churning through her. Had Max been stopping by since she'd left, or was this a recent thing? Why was he calling to check up on her? And what was the story with the red dress in her closet? Ginny knew something was up, and it pained her that she had no idea what.

*

Max stood in the walk-in fridge, his cell phone still pressed to his ear after Harold had hung up. Why on earth had Max called to check in on Ginny? Her plans didn't involve him anymore, and they hadn't for a while. But, dammit, there was a part of him that still worried about her driving all the way back from New York. Still worried that she wouldn't pay attention to the icy roads when she crested the hills of Pennsylvania. Ginny would get inside her own head, forgetting to concentrate on her surroundings. All bets were off if she were listening to a podcast.

Max told himself he was only calling for Harold's sake, just to make sure his friend's daughter arrived safely for her visit. But for all his denial, Max knew the real reason he'd called. He knew the real reason he was hiding away from his staff. Every time he fell down the Ginny rabbit hole, he turned into a shell of himself. If he had a nickel for each instance he'd obsessed about something he did or didn't do during the last year of their marriage, Max could build five more restaurants and still have money to buy a boat and sail around the world—twice.

Those last months together were bleak, to put it mildly. Max had dove head-first into getting the diner together for a grand reopening. He'd bought the place for way under asking price and was committed to getting it back to its former glory. Always a nameless local institution, the diner was the center of Buckeye Falls. It was the first place he and his family dined when they moved, and it was the first place Max remembered taking Ginny for proper dates. Making the diner his—and more importantly giving future Buckeyes a chance to make their own memories—had become an unhealthy obsession; an obsession he thought Ginny understood.

At the time, he liked that Ginny was busy with her own marketing career. Missed meals and phone calls added up while he was in the kitchen cooking and menu planning. The stolen moments he'd appreciated when they both came home from work had morphed into emotional land mines. What Max saw as working for a future together, Ginny had seen as moving forward *alone.*

"Snap out of it," Max chastised himself. No good could come from this type of soul-searching now, especially when he was at work.

Just as he reached for the handle, the door swung open and Evan let out a sigh of relief. "Found him!" he shouted over his shoulder to CeCe, who stood with her hands on her hips and a stern expression.

Max tucked his cell phone back into his pocket and brushed past Evan like he was on a mission. "Sorry, I'm looking for another bunch of parsley." Instantly, he realized his mistake when CeCe glanced at his empty hands.

"Top shelf on the right, next to the celery and carrots." She gave him a look that spoke volumes. That was the price for working with staff long term: they knew everything.

Fortunately for Max, Evan couldn't read the situation. "Hey, Max?" he asked, looking down at his feet. "I kind of screwed up and need your help."

Before he asked what happened, Max looked back to

CeCe and saw her expression shift. "What's up?"

Evan scuffed at the tiled floor with his sneaker and sighed. "I accidentally spilled a glass of iced tea on a customer." Crimson stained the young man's cheeks as a flush crept up his neck.

Max let out a sigh of relief. "That's all right, accidents happen. We'll pay for their meal and any dry cleaning. Do you need me to talk to them?"

Evan's shoulders slumped as the weight of his issue melted away, but CeCe wouldn't bury the story. "I think you're missing the headline here, Evan." She crossed her arms over her chest and stared down at her coworker. The poor guy didn't speak, but his cheeks looked like they wanted to burst into flames.

"Well, don't keep me in suspense," Max said, looking between his staff for answers. "What's going on?"

CeCe stepped forward and whispered, "He spilled it on Mayor Snyder."

Max felt his concerns over Ginny evaporate as CeCe's words sunk in. "Crap," he said, running his hand down his face. The situation warranted stronger language, but he didn't want to make Evan feel worse.

Mayor Anthony Snyder had been a thorn in Max's side for years. Nearly the same age, and former football teammates, Anthony and Max used to be friends. That was until there was a development bid to move the highway exit for Buckeye Falls, which would have killed the diner's business, as well as some other Main Street establishments. Max had led the call to stop the plan and stick with the current exit. Anthony's father was still the mayor at the time, but bad blood was bad blood. Keeping things the same had cost the mayor and his son a lot of money, a fact he was quick to throw in Max's face any chance he got. What the mayor didn't know was how much Max lost in the transaction. Not wanting to bother Ginny with the details, he'd kept his head down and focused on the end goal. All the time he'd spent working on the plan had come at a cost:

his marriage.

Frankly, Max was surprised Anthony even bothered coming to the diner at all. Then he remembered it was pot roast night and that brought out all the locals—including surly public servants. No one could resist his family's pot roast recipe, or the apple crumble CeCe made for dessert.

Max clapped a hand on Evan's back and sighed. "Go back behind the grill and make sure nothing is burning." He turned to face CeCe. "You help him. I'm going to go get a tongue-lashing from our favorite elected official."

Evan nearly sprinted toward the grill while CeCe rolled her eyes. "I'm sorry, Max."

Max shrugged, willing his heartbeat to stop racing. Between this turn of events and having Ginny back in town, he was not in his element. "S-stuff happens," he muttered as he stepped into the dining room.

As soon as Max was out on the floor, he was greeted with a sight that brought his blood to boiling. Mayor Snyder stood by his booth, widely gesturing to his gray suit. "It's probably ruined." He sighed at no one in particular. His wife, Natalie, a petite blonde—who spent more money on her hair color than Max did on clothes for a year—sat with her face shielded by her hand. The diamond of her wedding ring sparkled in the fluorescent lights. At least someone seemed embarrassed by the display.

Max walked past five tables before he made it to the mayor. The other diners hungrily followed Max's path to confrontation. Clearing his throat, Max planted his feet shoulder-width apart and waited for the mayor to notice his entrance. After another show of blotting the near-invisible stain on his pants, he turned and frowned at Max.

Striving to appear professional, Max extended his hand to the mayor. "Good evening, Mayor. So pleased to see you here tonight." His hand stayed empty as Anthony threw his napkin on the table. It landed with a soggy thud.

"Spare me the polite customer service routine, Max. What are you going to do about this disaster?" With a flick of his wrist, the mayor motioned toward the table. Their plates were cleaned, showing that while the wet lap was a nuisance, the food was clearly not the problem. A pile of soaked paper towels was stacked on the edge of the table, indicating Evan's attempts at cleaning up.

Max kept his voice loud enough so the onlookers could hear his side of the interaction. "I'll be happy to pay for the dry-cleaning costs, Mayor Snyder. And, of course, your meal is on the house. CeCe will box up a few slices of pie for you, Natalie, and the kids to enjoy at home."

The mayor gestured to his wife, who still looked like she wanted to be anywhere but there. "You think pie is going to make up for this ruined evening?"

Ignoring Anthony for a moment, Max eased into the opposite side of the booth to address the embarrassed woman. "Natalie, I'm very sorry if your evening was less than satisfactory. Is there anything else we can box up or prepare for you? If memory serves, you've always enjoyed our eggnog milkshakes."

Last year at the Christmas Jubilee, both Snyders indulged in CeCe's decadent creation. Rumor has it, it was the first time a carb had passed Natalie's lips in three years. "Thank you, but …" Her words were cut off when the mayor leaned over the table. Just as he opened his mouth to argue, Natalie finished her sentence. "I'm stuffed with pot roast and need to get my baby home." It was clear from her sarcasm that she didn't mean baby as a term of endearment. Looking at the mayor now, he did resemble a toddler who was told they couldn't have cookies for dinner.

CeCe joined the trio and handed over a bag filled with small to-go boxes. "Here we go," she said in a cheery voice that didn't fool Max. "I have two slices of apple pie, two of cherry, and half a dozen of our gingerbread cookies. We sure do appreciate your kindness about all of this." The two women were friends, and Max knew Natalie would be apologizing to CeCe for weeks about this.

Max had to bite the inside of his cheek to stop himself

from laughing. CeCe had managed the situation beautifully, and if the mayor wanted to get reelected next year, he needed to play it cool. Natalie reached out to take the bag, holding it protectively to her chest. "Thank you, CeCe. This is more than generous. I'll be sure to share with the kids when we get home." She winked, proving the kiddos would have to battle it out for the last piece of pie.

Next to him in the booth, Max found Natalie's coat. He held out the designer garment. "Let me help you get bundled up. It's barely forty degrees outside."

The mayor had no choice but to step aside as his wife stood. She placed the bag on the table, protecting it with her body. She clearly wanted those sweets. Max helped her shrug on her coat and smiled. "Thank you," she said. In a hushed tone, she continued. "I'm so sorry about this."

Unfortunately for everyone, the mayor had heard and stomped his foot. "Don't you dare apologize. We've done nothing wrong. I want that kid fired. If he can't handle the simple act of pouring liquid, he shouldn't have a job."

Now Max's hackles were up. "Thank you for the suggestion, Mayor Snyder. I will deal with my staff as I see fit. Frankly, I'm surprised you would want to separate a young local from his employment, and right before the holidays."

Once again, a hush fell over the dining room. The mayor finally lost some of his steam. He took Natalie's elbow and steered her toward the door. "You folks have a great evening," he greeted some of the tables on his way to the exit. The smile on his face looked as plastic as the bag Natalie held like precious cargo.

As they reached the door, Max shouted, "Be sure to send me the dry-cleaning bill." The mayor's face flashed red as he stomped out into the cold night. Before Max could finish damage control, CeCe was back with a tray of Christmas cookies. Stopping at each table, she gave free treats to everyone. He really needed to give her a raise.

When Max went back to the kitchen, Evan was zipping

up his coat. "Where do you think you're going?" CeCe asked, pushing past Max to get to her friend. "We still have five orders to finish."

Evan shook his head. "I'm leaving. You can consider this my notice, Max. I'm sorry to cause so much trouble." He stuffed his hands in his pockets and hunched his shoulders.

"Nope," both Max and CeCe said at the same time.

"Not gonna happen," Max continued as he strode to his employee. "I'm going to share a secret with you," he said. "That man is a pain in Buckeye Falls' ass." Max could tell it was working because the corner of Evan's lip quirked up. "Accidents happen, and you did everything you could to fix the situation. Mayor Snyder is miserable and likes to share his misfortune with anyone who doesn't do what he wants. I won't lose good employees because of that idiot."

CeCe nodded vehemently beside him, her expression stern. "You're not going to go anywhere, Ev. Now hang up your coat and help me deliver these orders."

The young man shot his gaze back and forth between the pair, finally nodding and peeling off his coat. "All right, but you have every right to fire me."

Max shook his head. "Not my style."

Evan followed CeCe back to the grill and served up a plate for table six. Max heard their banter as he walked back to his office. While he looked cool and collected, he knew this wouldn't be the last he heard from the mayor. He added it to his mental list of things to worry about.

Two hours later, the diner was empty, and he finally caught his breath. CeCe was turning the closed sign when Max heard her gasp. Mayor Snyder strode in with a plastic bag fisted in his hands. "Where's your boss?" he asked, still looking madder than he had a right to be.

"Right here," Max said, walking with purpose toward the man. "What can I do for you, Anthony?" Now that their audience was gone, Max was done pretending to respect the man. Too much history was caught up in their present, and he couldn't act as if he wasn't tired of the man's bullying. High school was done. Plus, Anthony was on Max's turf now. This needed to end.

Tossing the bag to Max, Anthony rolled his eyes. "Make sure to take it over to Theo's. I don't trust the Greens not to over-starch. I'd like it back by Friday."

Max smirked, knowing full well he was going to take the suit to the Greens. "Sure thing."

Anthony studied Max for a moment before sneering. "You think you have it all figured out, huh? Throw some free food our way and I'll forget that you screwed me and my dad over on the development deal. Well, I don't forget, and I certainly don't forgive." Max wasn't sure where the mayor was going with that, but he didn't have time to think before Anthony gave the final blow. "Make sure you say hello to that pretty ex-wife of yours. I heard she is back in town."

Max stepped forward, but CeCe linked her hand around his bicep. It was a steadying gesture that reminded Max things could get a lot worse if he acted on his impulse to pummel the mayor. "I shouldn't be surprised that you knew Ginny was back in town," he said through clenched teeth. "You always did have a thing for her."

Anger flashed in Anthony's eyes, but he didn't move. "It's a shame you screwed that up, but Ginny always was too good for you." Turning on his heel, he stomped out of the diner, letting the door slam behind him.

CeCe rushed to lock the door and turned back to find Max scrunching the bag in his hands. "Can you do me a favor?" she asked, taking the mangled bag from his hands.

"Only if it's not promising to clean the floor with that idiot," Max replied, trying hard not to run outside and kick the crap out of his former classmate.

"Go home and relax. There's a lot going on, and I need my boss to not murder the mayor. Okay?" She held the bag up between them. "I'll take care of bringing this to Greens tomorrow. I'm going to ask them to starch it so much it snaps in half when he tries to button the jacket."

Her snide remark helped Max relax, but he was still amped up. "Thanks," he muttered, walking back to the kitchen to gather his things. CeCe was right, he needed to go home and calm down.

Max also needed to not think about how much Anthony's words had cut him, how deep his insecurities really were. As much as Max hated change, right now he was looking for something to shift. He needed that pit in the bottom of his stomach to loosen. Otherwise he would never be able to really move on from Ginny.

CHAPTER 3

Ginny woke up to the unfamiliar sounds of breakfast being made. Rubbing the sleep from her eyes, she checked the time and gasped when she saw it was after eight. Normally, her mornings consisted of a six o'clock run on the treadmill, followed by a hurried cup of coffee on her way to catch a cab. She was usually in the middle of her workday by now. Fumbling for her cell phone on the nightstand, Ginny checked her work email to see what she was missing.

To say her boss was understanding of her time away would be generous—and a bald-faced lie. Ginny's boss, Lana, was no-nonsense to the core. She rarely took any time off, and the holidays meant nothing to her. Their office didn't have a Christmas party or tree in the break room. No one received a holiday card or gift, and God help the employee who asked for the day after Christmas off. The team used to tease that Lana gave Scrooge a run for his much-loved money.

Even a global pandemic hadn't stopped Lana's quest for employee domination. While most large firms had staff working from home indefinitely, her boss called staff back to the office as soon as the mandates allowed. A modular working environment was created that ensured all staff were present and working like the world was not currently burning. Ginny didn't usually mind, but thinking about it while nestled in her childhood room, it almost seemed barbaric. Work-life balance when she didn't have a life was one thing, but now it felt all wrong.

Flinging her feet off the edge of her bed, Ginny padded down the hall to get ready for the morning. A quick hair and tooth brushing made her feel human and ready to consume a pot of coffee. When she reached the bottom of the stairs, the heavenly scent of bacon and cinnamon beckoned her. "Good morning," she greeted her father, who shuffled around the kitchen in his pajamas.

Waving hello with his spatula, Harold turned back to the stove and flipped a pancake. "You're right on time. Breakfast is ready." Ginny helped herself to a mug of coffee and sat at the table, cradling the cup in her hands. She breathed in and enjoyed the moment.

If she didn't know any better, Ginny would think it was her childhood. Her father would get up before her every day to cook a hearty breakfast before he went to work and she left for school. The time of year didn't matter—what had mattered was spending a few minutes together before their days got away from them. The tradition continued every visit like clockwork, and right now she was grateful.

"Is there anything I can help with?" she asked, knowing he would wave her off.

Shaking his head, Harold said, "All set." He placed a plate in front of her stacked with silver dollar pancakes and four strips of bacon. Already on the table was a plate of cinnamon bread and the remaining cookies. This spread was better suited for a Christmas morning than a weekday.

Ginny slid the plate toward the middle of the table until she realized it was her plate. "We're not sharing?" She raised an eyebrow. Granted, they rarely shared meals, but this was so much more food than she usually ate in the morning.

Harold chuckled as he eased onto his chair. He slid a tub

of butter across to her and tucked into his own meal with gusto. "Ginnybread, when have we ever shared breakfast?" He dipped a strip of bacon into a puddle of syrup and groaned with happiness. "Besides, it's nice to make real breakfast. When it's just me, I usually have oatmeal."

"Something I'm sure your cardiologist prefers," she quipped. For all her hesitation, Ginny devoured her delicious meal. After her second cup of coffee, she leaned back and patted her belly. "So, what's on our schedule today?"

Harold topped off his own mug before responding. "This morning I was going to run some errands."

Ginny perked up. "I can do those; you're supposed to be resting. What do you need?"

Her father slurped from his mug and shrugged. "Nothing you can help with. I wanted to go to Main Street and get your Christmas gift. With the surgery, I won't be able to get out on my own before the holiday."

"Dad, you don't need to get me anything. I'm glad we're going to be here together." She patted his arm and smiled. "Seriously, don't trouble yourself."

Harold shook his head. "Well, I am going to trouble myself. It's Christmas, and my only daughter deserves a present. If you want to come along, you could go to a different shop or even stop by the diner."

Ginny froze, afraid to look up and meet her father's gaze. "Why would I want to do that?" she asked, now carefully trailing her fork through the remains of her syrup. Building a time machine to attend the Valentine's Day Massacre would be easier and less terrifying. Going to the diner—unannounced no less—seemed a fool's errand. *Hard pass.*

Harold stacked his dishes and stood, a little shaky on his feet. "You would want to do that because Max was a big part of your life. C'mon, Ginnybread. I raised you to have a heart." Her father's remark stung, as it brought back painful memories she wasn't prepared to revisit. Fights in the diner, ignoring each other at home—it all threatened to choke her.

Ginny sullenly gathered her dishes and walked to the sink. "I'll do the dishes," she muttered, not wanting to tell her father that the heart he raised her with felt broken and awkward in her own body. Seeing Max was the last thing she wanted to do, especially now, while she was busy with her father's surgery. *And very busy avoiding the past and anything connected to Max.*

Hoping for a distraction, Ginny looked out the window over the sink. "Oh, look," she exclaimed, "it's snowing!" She watched fat flakes flutter past the window, like they were living in a snow globe. Sure, it snowed in New York, and it was beautiful. But watching the snow in the country was something else entirely. The rolling hills in the distance were blanketed in white, the trees outside the window weighed down with two inches of fluff. Norman Rockwell himself couldn't have painted the scene better.

Her father came up behind her and rested his hand on her shoulder. "Think of how pretty this will be on Main Street," he surmised, squeezing her gently. "I'll go shower. We can leave in an hour." With that, he shuffled to the stairs.

Ginny finished the dishes in silence, occasionally looking outside to the wintery scene. It was calming, as most snowy days are. Without asking her permission, her brain brought back a memory of her and Max on a snowy day like this. He'd made his famous triple chocolate cookies, and they sat wrapped in blankets by the fire in their old house. They'd done other things in that blanket, but she wouldn't think about that now.

"Focus, Ginny," she scolded herself as she stacked the last dish on the drying rack. Ginny could deny that she thought about Max, but that would be a lie. There were lonely nights in the city when work ran late and she barely had time to eat takeout before falling asleep on the couch.

Those were the times she'd remember her and Max during the good years, during their time as a team. It was before they took each other, and everything they shared, for granted. The times before he became obsessed with recipe testing, redesigning the diner, and all things stainless steel. Granted, Ginny had a role in their demise. More times than she cared to admit had been filled with late-night phone calls, video conferences, and spreadsheets. Her career is what identified her, and she wouldn't apologize. Trouble was, other identifiers went to the wayside. Wife, daughter, and friend felt like foreign monikers when she was in the zone.

Max used to make midnight enchiladas on the days they both worked late. With a late-night talk show humming in the background, the pair sat on the couch devouring cheesy, spicy enchiladas. Max always gave her an extra one—the corner piece—which is why she used to be a lot curvier. Those were the good times; the times when they were in sync—the times they made time for each other. Ginny loved those days.

Now she couldn't reconcile the good times with how it all ended. And she definitely didn't have time to dissect it all now. When she turned, she saw her father dressed and ready to go. The creases at his mouth belied the pain he was still in, and Ginny was thankful his surgery date was mere days away.

Hitching his thumb over his shoulder, her father said, "I'm going to check the scores on TV. Let me know when you're ready."

Ginny looked down at her sweats and shrugged. "I could just go like this." She had nothing to prove to anyone in Buckeye Falls. Why bother getting dressed up for running errands?

Harold shook his head. "You haven't seen people in a while. Don't you want to …" His voice trailed off as he swirled his hand in front of his face.

"Dad, I'm not sure what this means"—she mimicked his hand movements—"but I think I'm offended."

"I'm saying that you can take your time—maybe put on

a little makeup." Before she could respond, he'd turned his back and headed toward his chair, his shoes scraping on the floor.

"I really am offended," she shouted after him. He ignored her and turned ESPN up to supersonic levels. Ginny gave up the fight and went upstairs to get ready. Twenty minutes later, she was dressed in skinny jeans, a turtleneck sweater, and enough makeup to make her look human. She wasn't breaking out the eyeliner today.

"Much better," her father approved when she walked into the living room. Ginny stopped herself from rolling her eyes. "If you want to move your car, I can drive us." Harold held up his set of keys, jingling them like he was taunting a toddler.

Ginny shook her head. "No, might as well get my money out of the rental. Plus, there are heated seats." She grabbed her purse from the hook by the door and shrugged on her coat. "Now, watch your step. I know you're about to have surgery, but let's not complicate matters."

Harold laughed but took slow steps to the car.

Once inside, Ginny blasted the heat and turned on the seat warmers. Harold laughed when his seat started warming up. "This is weird." He chuckled. "I either love this or hate it."

Ginny thought about the old pickup, which was still parked in the garage. Her father had driven that car for nearly two decades, but she knew teasing him about it would be fruitless. The Meyers didn't splurge if something was working.

Ginny shrugged. "It was part of the free upgrade. Not having my own car, I thought I'd splurge."

She took the very familiar roads toward Main Street, the center of Buckeye Falls. She kept telling herself not to worry, that the diner was at the end of the road, away from all the shops. Ginny was not going to see Max today. Yet her palms were so slick with sweat, she fumbled with the steering wheel.

When the car crested the hill and Main Street came into view, Harold pointed out his window. "They added a little parking lot over by the bank. It's free all day, so we can snag a spot."

Ginny raised an eyebrow. "Buckeye Falls charges for parking now?"

"Heated seats aren't the only things changing." He sighed. "Mayor Snyder added parking meters last year, claiming we needed the revenue. Frankly, I can't see how it brings in that much money, but what do I know?" Despite his casual tone, she knew her father had more opinions on town politics.

Ginny parked the car and swiveled to face her dad. "Mayor Snyder is still in office? Isn't he your age?"

As soon as the question left her lips, Ginny regretted it. Harold puffed out his chest and waggled a finger at her. "Young lady," he said, his tone dripping with sarcasm, "I'll have you know that I would be working now if it wasn't for this damned hip."

Struggling to hold back laughter, Ginny held up her hands in defeat. "You win. I'm sorry. It was a poor choice of words." She reached out and swatted her dad's arm. "So, who is in charge these days? Some young go-getter?"

Harold shook his head and grimaced. "You'll never believe it. It's Anthony, old man Snyder's son."

Ginny scoffed; she couldn't help herself. "You're kidding! That jack wagon is running the town? How did that happen?" She turned the car off and tossed her keys in her purse.

"No one else wanted the job, simple as that." Harold took his time getting out of the car. Ginny still wasn't sure it was a good idea for him to go out, but it was too late to argue.

"So, where to?" Ginny asked, looping her arm through his and ushering him to the sidewalk. Fortunately the new mayor had one thing on lock with this town; the sidewalks were salted and free of snow. "There's the boutique over there, and what about that place that Millie Wilson used to own?"

"Frick and Frack? Yep, it's still open. Just down by the park." He pointed to their left, and Ginny smiled. "I used to love her homemade jewelry when I was a teenager."

Harold smiled at the memory. "I remember. It was the only thing you asked for during high school."

Ginny thought about the bright beads and glittery necklaces she used to wear. Compared to her simple pearl earrings and silver chain, Frick and Frack's jewelry was darn near gaudy. Harold led the way down Main Street, pointing out what stores were new and which ones were renovated. Ginny recognized most of the faces they saw along the way, and almost everyone stopped to say hello and welcome her home.

Home. True, Buckeye Falls was her hometown, but Ginny wasn't sure she'd call it home anymore. "Where to next?" she asked as Harold steered her back to the street. They stopped in front of the tiny corner market, a favorite place for locals to get their groceries. In preparation for the holidays, the doors were weighed down with pine branches and red bows, giving a comforting Christmas vibe.

Instinctively, Ginny thought of Max. He'd run to the market countless times for ingredients over the years. They'd gone together so many times, simple routine errands she'd long forgotten, yet now seemed so important. They laughed over the size of the cabbages he needed for soup, or argued over how many types of cheese Ginny really needed for her grilled cheese sandwiches.

A smile tugged at Ginny's lips now as she stared at the familiar building. The last time she and Max had been inside, she'd leaned on him by the ice cream cooler. After a long week at work, they both agreed that sugar was needed, so they'd tumbled outside in their pajamas to get a pint of cookies and cream. Ginny still felt the warmth of Max's arm slung over her shoulder, the tickle of his breath on her neck when he'd lean down to kiss her.

Despite the cold nip in the air, Ginny suddenly felt parched and hot. She loosened her scarf from her neck and shook her head. It was best not to go down Memory Lane, especially in public with her father. She gave the market a parting glance and prepared to steer her father toward the boutiques when the door to the market opened.

A man stepped outside, clad in worn hiking boots and a bulky down coat. The red and black of a flannel shirt peaked out from behind the coat's collar. He held the door with his elbow for an older woman pushing a shopping cart. She thanked the man, and when he replied, Ginny's blood ran cold. She'd recognize that voice anywhere.

Blinking, Ginny begged her eyes to see someone else standing before her. It was as if her memories willed themselves back to life. Beside her, Harold perked up and lifted his free hand. "Max, over here." Max turned around, and Ginny felt the air leave her lungs. This was no trick of her mind. It was the real deal. *Well, hell …*

Time had been good to Max; there was no denying it. His dark hair was longer now, curling at the base of his neck. A few flecks of gray threatened to take over his temples, but he managed to look mature rather than haggard. Instead of the clean-shaven face she remembered, his chiseled jawline was now peppered with a few days of stubble. Suddenly, Ginny understood all the fuss with lumbersexuals.

Max's brown eyes darkened when he saw her, but his steps didn't falter. "Harold, good to see you." He moved one of his shopping bags to his other arm and shook her father's hand. When he turned to her, Ginny felt her breath hitch as he reached out his hand for a shake. *Really? They were in the hand-shaking phase of their relationship?*

Ginny reached out and took his hand, a shot of awareness coursing through her body as his fingers wrapped around hers. "Max," she said his name in greeting, hoping her tone was light, carefree.

"Gin." Max swallowed and squeezed her hand before letting it go. He didn't say anything at first, just studied her.

She was glad she had listened to her father about makeup. Bumping into her ex-husband with bedhead and sans mascara would have been mortifying.

Harold theatrically slapped his forehead. "You know what, I forgot that we're out of coffee beans. You kids catch up while I go inside and grab some." Miraculously, Harold didn't look like he needed a hip replacement. He practically sprinted into the store, leaving them alone on the sidewalk. Ginny half expected a cloud of cartoon smoke to come off his loafers.

Ginny was helpless for a moment, staring at Max like a fool. Perhaps she'd fallen into an alternate universe when she left the turnpike? Maybe her rental car was a time machine where she felt pulled to a man who bruised her heart? A man whose heart was certainly broken by her.

Either oblivious or uncaring of her current slack-jawed state, Max surprised her by stepping closer and giving her a genuine smile. "I'm glad you're back," he said. "It's really good to see you."

In that moment, staring into his warm gaze, Ginny couldn't disagree. She felt comfortable being so close to Max, so close to the worn paths of their past. This didn't feel like a foreign place; it felt like home.

*

Max's admission seemed to shock Ginny into utter silence. She stood there, staring at him, her mouth slightly open. He took the moment to shamelessly check her out, taking in her new darker hair color and thinner cheeks. Back when they were married, Ginny had curves. That's what happens when you're married to a chef: you get to try new recipes and savor the leftovers. Judging from her tired expression, he had a feeling she wasn't savoring much these days. It broke his heart.

Standing on the sidewalk staring at each other seemed foolish, so Max tried another tactic. "How are you?" he asked, shifting one of the grocery bags to his hip. CeCe had sent him out for extra herbs, fruit, and baking chocolate, and he always supported the local stores over the bigger chain grocers. Now he regretted not bringing his own canvas bags.

Ginny finally composed herself and said, “Fine. You?”

Max couldn’t help it; he barked out a laugh. “Wow, all those years together and I get a two-word greeting.” His laughter seemed to shake Ginny from her trance because she cracked a tiny smile. Max would give anything to see her smile on a regular basis.

“All things considered, I’m doing well. Nervous about Dad’s surgery but can’t complain otherwise. How are you? How’s the diner?” One of Ginny’s nervous ticks when they were together had been fidgeting with her fingers, either pulling on zippers or yanking on the edges of her sleeves. Max glanced down to see that some things never change. She was practically unraveling the scarf around her neck.

“I can’t complain either. Got a good team, and business has been good.” Max wanted to tell her everything, just like when they were together. He wanted to curl up on the sofa with a bottle of wine and Ginny wrapped in his arms. He wanted to tell her about the mayor and all the politics that were changing their hometown. He wanted to introduce her to CeCe and Evan, to have her be a part of his life. Right now he’d almost settle for one of their arguments or misunderstandings—anything to prove she was still in his life.

Instead Max settled for the chance to see her again, even if only for a moment on a busy sidewalk. He could tell by the number of people slowing their pace that they were becoming a spectacle. It’s not every day a divorced couple bumped into each other. Distracted, Max’s grip loosened on one of the paper bags, and it tipped over. Suddenly five oranges made their escape, cascading to the ground with comical thumps onto the sidewalk.

Ginny yelped and jogged after two that chose to bounce

toward traffic, while Max slid to his left and kicked two back onto the grass. The fifth orange bounced all the way back to the market's entrance, where a clerk pushed a row of shopping carts. The first cart's wheels rolled over the fruit, making a sad squishing sound as it was pulverized into the concrete.

Ginny stepped up to Max and dropped the two rogue citruses into his shopping bag. She leaned so close he could smell her vanilla perfume. "Well, that was certainly entertaining." She laughed. Her breath puffed into a cloud in front of her face, and her eyes danced with good cheer. She looked like his Ginny, like his wife.

"Th-th-" He hesitated, closing his eyes and willing his tongue to work. His pulse pounded in his ears, and Max cursed his blasted tongue for choosing this moment to fumble. "Thank you," he said, watching her eyes soften.

Ginny didn't look at him with pity, only with understanding. She knew his stutter loved to show up when he was nervous. "You're welcome." She stood there, looking up at him with an expression he couldn't read. Max wanted to toss the bags on the ground and pull her close to him. Pretend, if even for a minute, that they were together and he had the right to hold her again. His gaze faltered and landed on her lips—lips he was intimately acquainted with.

"There you kids are," Harold exclaimed, coming out of the market empty-handed. Since he was watching the pair, he missed the pile of orange mush and nearly slipped on his heel. The very last thing Max needed was to put Harold in the hospital a week early.

Ginny didn't miss a beat, gesturing to her father's empty hands. "Out of coffee?" she asked, raising an eyebrow.

Harold looked confused, then recovered and shrugged. "Yeah, only decaf. Can you believe it?" He turned to Max and winked.

Before he could think of what he was saying, Max offered, "You can come with me to the diner. We always have a pot of coffee at the ready. I was getting ready to start lunch. CeCe is making her death-by-chocolate mousse cake today, so you won't want to miss it."

Harold opened his mouth, but Ginny was quicker. "We really need to finish our shopping, but thanks for the invitation." The shutters were closed, and her expression was cold. This was post-divorce Ginny; this was the woman who walked away.

Max let out a sigh. "You're welcome anytime. You don't have to avoid—" But the argument died on his tongue.

Ginny shoved her hands in her pockets and looked to her father. "We should probably keep moving—it's not good for you to be on your feet this long." Pointing with her gloved hand, Ginny chuckled, albeit a little forced. "Especially with fruit salad all over Main Street."

Harold stepped closer to Max and patted his back. "Will we see you tomorrow night for dinner? I was going to try that chicken soup recipe you gave me."

Max almost blurted out his response, but he turned to watch Ginny's features. Her brow was furrowed in concern, though she didn't jump to say no either.

"If it's not an inconvenience, I'd love to." He met Ginny's gaze, hoping to see a hint of his wife in her eyes. She seemed so distant, and he damn near cried right here on Main Street.

"Of course it's not an inconvenience. You are family, and I'd like to see you before the surgery. Try to save some of that cake for dessert." Harold patted his belly and chuckled, the stocking cap on his head bobbing at the movement. If his hair was whiter, he could have been Saint Nick.

All Max got from Ginny was a mumbled farewell as she turned and walked away. Harold followed behind at a slower shuffle, and Max felt like the wind was knocked from his sails. How on earth had he let her go? And how could he possibly get her back?

Max's musing was interrupted by his cell phone chirping in his pocket. It was CeCe's ringtone, which meant he needed to get the ingredients to her before she had a fit. Hiking his bags higher, Max turned and trudged back to the diner.

"There you are!" CeCe groused when he kicked open the back door. "My butter is melted, and I was about to send out a search party." She greedily took one of the bags and dug until she found the bars of bittersweet chocolate. She walked to the cutting board, unwrapped the chocolate, then chopped it into chunks. "So, did you get lost or something?" CeCe gave Max side-eye while she finished decimating the chocolate.

Placing the remaining oranges on the counter, Max washed the fresh parsley in the prep sink. Careful to keep his tone neutral, he replied, "Sorry, bumped into some people and couldn't get away." If Ginny hadn't run away, he would still be there, staring and stuttering like a fool. Seeing her, mere feet away, had set his nerves on fire. He couldn't get enough of her, and he hated that she didn't want to see him.

Bless Harold for trying, but Max knew he wouldn't go to their home for dinner. Ginny left for a reason, and he had to respect her wishes to keep his distance. Although it did not mean he had to like it.

CeCe poured the melted butter into the chocolate, and suddenly the kitchen smelled like Wonka's factory. "That smells amazing." Evan groaned when he entered the kitchen. "Please tell me you're making enough for us."

Max smiled as the young man hung up his coat and shook a dusting of snow from his head. His blond hair stayed mused, giving him an aw-shucks quality. "Did it start snowing again?" Max craned his neck toward the tiny window by the exit and saw fat flakes falling.

Evan snuck a chocolate chunk when CeCe wasn't looking and washed his hands at the neighboring sink. "Yeah, just as I drove through town." Drying his hands, he turned to look at his boss. "Who was that pretty girl you were talking to?"

Max's hands froze over the colander. "Uh, when?" he asked. He felt his cheeks flush and wished he were by the stove to blame it on the heat.

CeCe smelled blood in the water and joined them. "So, there's a girl, huh? Who is she? Is she the reason I almost burned my butter?" She crossed her arms and waited for an answer. Max knew it was foolish to try to ignore his staff's questions, but he paused to collect his words.

"It's Ginny. She and Harold were out shopping. I saw them at the market." Evan, not knowing who Ginny was, seemed unsurprised. However, CeCe practically radiated with excitement.

"You saw her? What did she look like? Was she happy to see you? What did she say? What did you say?" Her hazel eyes had grown to the size of saucepans as she peppered Max with questions. "Why didn't you say something when you came in?" She swatted his arm with a tea towel. "I have so many questions."

Max laughed. He couldn't help himself. "I can see that."

Evan's blue gaze darted back and forth between the pair, trying to catch up. "Who's Ginny?"

CeCe didn't break eye contact with Max when she answered. "Max's ex-wife."

Evan nearly fell over. "You have an ex-wife?" he asked Max, a comical puzzled expression plastered on Evan's face. "How did I miss that?"

Max turned off the water with a sigh and left the herbs to drain. He wouldn't get any work done for a while now. Turning to Evan, Max said, "Yes, Ginny and I were married for a while. She lives in New York City."

"Why?" Evan asked, earning him a slap on the back of the head from CeCe. "Ouch! What was that for?" Rubbing the back of his head, Evan looked like a wounded puppy. His hair was officially a disaster zone.

CeCe rolled her eyes. "Kid, I love you, but you need to read the room. You don't ask someone why they got divorced; it's rude." To his credit, Evan looked embarrassed as he muttered an apology.

"Thanks, CeCe." Max appreciated her coming to his defense, but his celebration was short-lived.

"Although, I've wondered about that myself. Haven't seen a lot of women coming in here. Shouldn't you be, you know …" She wiggled her fingers and raised an eyebrow.

Max mimicked the gesture. "And what does that mean?"

Always helpful, Evan chimed in, "I think she means you're not getting any." This time Evan expected the head slap and braced himself. CeCe didn't hesitate before thwacking him with her tea towel.

"We'll talk about human interaction later," she warned.

Evan rubbed his head and took a step back from both of them. At least he was learning. "What I meant was," he continued, keeping his eyes on CeCe's hands. "Max is a cool guy, and I'm surprised there aren't a lot of chicks here." He shrugged, as if being a cool guy was all the help Max needed finding a date.

CeCe shrugged. "The kid's got a point. You still carrying a torch for Ginny? And more importantly, how did she look?"

"Hot," Evan said, now cowering from CeCe.

Max raised his arms to block her from Evan and sighed. "I'd like to make it through the year without a workman's comp injury claim."

CeCe relented, tucking the towel back into her apron strings.

Max couldn't argue that Ginny looked terrific. Her hair was shorter and a slightly different color, but she was still Ginny. Beneath the polish and shine of city living, there was a small-town girl who loved his hot chocolate at Christmas time and used to beg for mac and cheese on Fridays when they would watch movies. Not for the first time, Max wondered who was cooking for her and taking care of her. *Don't go there now …*

Even before he went to culinary school, Max loved to cook. His first gift to Ginny had been on their third date when he baked her a peach pie and brought it to Harold's house. She had seemed so touched that anyone would cook for her, and it started his fascination, and sometimes obsession, with cooking and trying new ways to make her smile. Over the years, he had learned cookies were her guilty pleasure, and she always preferred cheese and carbs to fruits and vegetables. Seeing her now, it didn't look like she was indulging like she used to, but that wasn't any of his business.

The sound of the oven timer brought him back to the present. Evan looked at the clock. "Oh, wow, it's almost time to open." He dashed to the wall for his apron and order pad and went to the dining room to finish opening the space.

CeCe pulled the first of her mousse cakes from the oven and seemed pleased with the result. "Can you save one of those for me, please? I promised one to Harold."

CeCe nodded but gave him a look that she knew something was up. "I'll save one, if you tell me what these oranges did to deserve this much abuse." She picked up a bruised fruit and frowned. "If these were the best the market had, I'd hate to see the worst."

"Long story." Max sighed as he put on an apron and got ready to cook.

Max promised himself not to interfere with Ginny if he wasn't invited, but that didn't mean he couldn't bring a little chocolate comfort to Harold before his surgery. Turning toward the stove, Max finished getting everything ready for the lunch rush. Ginny or no Ginny, he had a job to do. He could address the battling emotions later, because like it or not, Ginny still held a lot of real estate in his heart.

CHAPTER 4

Ginny didn't sleep a wink that night. Tossing and turning, she felt like she burned more calories than at the gym. Giving up on sleep at six o'clock, she threw the covers aside and went downstairs to start the coffee. While she waited for the pot to fill, she pulled out her laptop and checked her work emails. Lana would expect her to check in periodically. When the coffee pot was full, Ginny settled into work mode and scrolled through her inbox. There were a few small fires she could put out remotely, which gave her a sense of accomplishment after such a crummy night's sleep.

Of course, Ginny knew why she'd slept poorly. The reason was roughly six feet tall and clad in flannel. As it usually happens with men, Max was aging incredibly well. His wavy hair was flecked with a bit of silver, and the few wrinkles that creased his brow looked like they belonged there. It was truly unfair that Ginny spent hundreds of dollars a month to keep her hair in check and her face slathered in anti-aging creams, yet Max only had to get out of bed.

And then there was Max's stutter. When she heard his words falter on his lips, she wanted to hug him close. Back when they were in high school, Max's stutter was a popular target for bullies. In some ways, it was what brought them together. After a particularly cruel interaction with one of the football players, Max found a hiding place in the school's library. Ginny was studying for her English final when they bumped into each other in the literature section.

Max reached out to steady her, his hands lingering on her forearms. "S-s-sorry," he'd muttered, reluctantly stepping back and dropping his head. He'd worn his hair longer then, and it covered half of his face. "I n-n-need to watch where I'm g-g-going."

Her heart broke for the quiet boy in front of her. "No worries," Ginny had said, keeping her tone soft, like she was talking to a wounded animal. "I was about to snag that corner table, if you want a study partner." Turning, she waved in the general direction of the quietest spot in the library. It was a favorite hangout for Ginny, and never before had she offered to share it with anyone—not even her girlfriends. Even then, she knew Max was special.

Max's head had shot up so quickly, a tousle of dark curls fell over his left eye. Wordlessly, he swiped the hair away and nodded. Together they'd sat for an hour, not talking, just reading and enjoying the moment of peace. At the time, Ginny had been going through a rough patch at home. When she wasn't studying or hanging out with her friends, she was desperate for a place to hide away from the world. She was also desperate for someone who didn't want to pry into her personal life. Max had checked all those boxes—and then some.

Somehow, without ever planning it, they had met every day in the library for the rest of that school year. Whoever got to the corner table first would save the other chair. Max started bringing in little snacks to share when they'd gotten more comfortable with each other. First it was simple things like apples or a PB&J. Later it morphed into homemade snacks, like brownies or cookies.

On a particular quiet afternoon, the pair had been

wrapping up their study hour when the bell rang. Max shook his head and rummaged through his bag. "I f-f-forgot to give you this," he'd said, his gaze not quite meeting hers.

"What is it?" Ginny asked, even though she could already smell the cinnamon and vanilla.

"Ch-ch-ch-chocolate cake."

Peeling back the foil with her fingernail, Ginny had to stop herself from inhaling the wedge of cake whole. "You made this?"

Unable to find his words, Max simply nodded. Ginny had realized over the last months that his stutter had nearly disappeared in her company, but it was back with a vengeance. He'd been worried about her reaction to his gift, and her heart melted faster than a chocolate bar on a summer's day. "Thank you."

"You're welcome," Max had said with a smile. Ginny grew to love his smiles, and his company. As she tucked the cake carefully into her bag, she'd felt his hand on her arm. "Um," he'd muttered before clearing his throat. "If, um, you're f-f-free this weekend, I thought we could grab dinner or something?"

It had come out as a question, but Ginny knew Max meant the invitation as anything but casual. Since they'd met, she hadn't even glanced at another guy in school. Standing in front of her had been the sweetest man she'd ever known, and he wanted to take her out. More than that, he'd kept baking her little treats; kept asking her how she was doing. Max's interest in her had seemed to come from a place of good, not a curiosity of what had been happening with her home life. She'd appreciated that more than he could ever know.

"I'd love to grab dinner."

Max's shoulders slumped with relief. "You do?"

Ginny nodded, linking her arm through his. "Why don't you pick me up at my dad's place Saturday night?"

Without hesitating, he'd said, "It's a date."

And that was the beginning of it all—the beginning of

Max and Ginny.

Those were sweet memories Ginny hadn't allowed herself to revisit in years, and now they took over her muddled brain. Young Max and Ginny felt like strangers sometimes. Although suddenly the memories felt like the present, and she didn't know what to do with herself.

"Don't think about him," she chastised herself, pecking at her keyboard with a little too much gusto. She had too much work to do to fixate on her ex-husband. Even though his hair still flopped down in front of his eyes, and even though his smile still made her stomach clench.

"Who aren't we thinking about?" Harold asked as he joined her at the kitchen table. The sight of her sleep-rumpled father brought a smile to Ginny's face. His hair was mussed, a patch of gray standing straight up on top of his head. He looked like a retired Alfalfa. Harold wore the old blue terry cloth bathrobe she'd gotten him over ten years ago; the elbows were nearly worn through.

Ginny avoided the question. "Dad, didn't I get you that nice robe from Saks last year?" She stood to pour him a cup of coffee. After adding a splash of cream, she slid the caffeine toward him.

Harold leaned back in his chair and shrugged. "Yeah, but it's too nice. I feel like I should be sitting in a castle wearing it."

Ginny kissed the top of his head, smoothing down his bedhead in the process. "I'll remember that when I go shopping for next week." As she turned, her father stopped her by taking her hand.

"This is my Christmas gift this year. Having my Ginnybread home is all I need." Harold slurped from his cup and grinned. He looked more content than she'd seen in ages, especially for a man about to go under the knife. "What can I make for breakfast? Eggs okay?"

Ginny closed her laptop and cleared the table. Lana and the rest of work's little fires would have to wait. Ginny wanted to devote her attention to her dad. After a few minutes, they were settled back into their spots with steaming plates of eggs and toast. She felt herself relax as they ate and chatted about their plans for the day.

"I'm going to call the doctor this afternoon. I have a pre-surgery checklist to go over," Harold said as he ran the last piece of his toast through a puddle of egg yolk.

Ginny nodded and wiped her mouth with her napkin. "If you don't mind, I'll sit in on the call. I want to make sure I don't let you get away with anything." She winked as he laughed.

"Are you saying I might try something?" Harold asked, his tone mocking.

Ginny nodded, knowing her father would love to sneak a candy bar or have a beer before surgery. "I'll go shower and run to the store for some groceries. What do you need for dinner?"

Harold cleared his plate, taking a moment to respond. "I have a list on the fridge."

Pulling the list from the magnet, she saw a particular bottle of wine she knew her father wouldn't drink if it was the last beverage on earth. "What's the wine for?" she asked innocently, her pulse hammering.

"It's Max's favorite. You know, in case he makes an appearance tonight."

"Dad, I need you to respect my wishes here." Ginny hated the edge in her voice, but she felt the need to lay down the law. If seeing Max on the street for five minutes had made her this crazy, she knew an evening with him would make her certifiable.

To his credit, her father looked guilty. "He's a part of my life," her father said softly.

"I won't stand here and tell you I like that you're still in touch, but I'm not totally heartless. I need to know why you're pushing us together." Her father had never pushed the issue like this before, not even right after she'd moved to New York. Of course he'd slipped in little Max updates on their weekly phone calls, but it had never been this direct.

Maybe she got her direct marketing skills from her father?

For a moment, she feared she'd overstepped. Harold ducked his head and looked like he wanted to go to the hospital now—a routine hip replacement was likely more fun than getting the third-degree from his daughter. "I've been in his place," he said simply. "I've lost my other half, and I know it's brutal." He hesitated, as if unsure how much more to say. "I know it can be lonely."

Ginny splayed her hand over her heart, which was now doing the rumba inside her rib cage. "And I didn't?"

Finally her father looked up. "You did, Ginnybread. But you had the benefit of leaving town. Max is still here in the thick of it, and, frankly, I didn't want to leave him alone. I don't want to make you uncomfortable, but you can't pretend he doesn't exist."

Watch me, Ginny wanted to say. The look on her father's face told her it wasn't the time for snark. "Dad," she said, her voice sounding too tired for this early in the day.

Harold held his hands up, his own expression dull. "I didn't want to play this card, but I will." Ginny flinched, as if sensing she wasn't going to like what he had to say. "I want to see him before I go in for surgery." He watched his daughter's face fall and quickly amended "Which I know is ridiculous since this is routine surgery. But I'm nervous, and I want to see my people before I go to the chop shop."

There was no use arguing, so Ginny squared her shoulders and accepted her fate. "Fine, I'll get a bottle of wine." Just as she reached the top of the stairs, she heard her father call out from below.

"It's okay to let him in again. Time has a way of changing perspectives."

Ginny didn't respond, just walked into the bathroom and locked the door. She needed a moment alone to recover from the truth bomb her father detonated.

An hour later, Ginny roamed the aisles of the big chain grocery store outside town. Not that she was a coward or anything, but she wasn't going near the local market.

Realistically, she knew Max didn't live there, but she wasn't taking her chances.

When she pushed her cart into the frozen foods section, she bumped into another cart. "Oh, I'm so sorry," Ginny said. "I'm a distracted driver." She chuckled, hoping the other woman was all right.

The woman turned, and a flash of recognition ran across her pretty face. "Ginny Meyer? Is that you?"

Ginny blinked, trying to place the woman in front of her. She stared into the green eyes and the cluster of freckles on her cheeks. "Natalie Johnson?" Ginny stepped around her cart and pulled the woman into a hug. Natalie had been one of her best friends in high school and college, but then life happened.

Natalie giggled, returning the embrace. "It's Natalie Snyder now." She smiled and shrugged, her blonde hair bouncing with the movement.

Ginny gaped. "You married Anthony? My dad told me he's the mayor."

With another shrug, Natalie nodded. "Yeah, he was elected last year. It's still so weird to think about, you know?" She looked down at her cart, where Ginny saw a toddler strapped into the seat. The child's eyes were the same color as Natalie's, but the smirk on his face was definitely Anthony's.

"Madam First Lady of Buckeye Falls." Ginny laughed. "Who knew?" She stepped forward and cooed at the little boy, whose cheeks were as chubby and rosy as Santa Claus's. "And who is this little darling?" She wiggled her fingers in a wave.

"His name is Otis, and I'm Madeline. What's your name?" Ginny turned to see an adorable girl, no older than four, wearing a pink snow jacket and blonde pigtails. She was the spitting image of her mother.

Kneeling, Ginny got to eye level with Madeline and stuck out a gloved hand. "Nice to meet you, Miss Madeline, I'm Ginny. I went to school with your mom and dad." Madeline looked back and forth between the two adults, as if shocked they ever went to school.

Natalie sighed at her daughter's quizzical expression. "Yes, sweetheart, your mother used to be young."

Ginny laughed and shook her head. "We're still in our early thirties, doesn't that count as young?"

"Not to a four-year-old. We might as well be a million years old and roamed with the dinosaurs." Before Ginny could reply, Otis jabbered from his perch in the cart. He seemed to want some of the attention that was going around. Natalie pulled a toy from her coat pocket and handed it to Otis without breaking eye contact with Ginny. "So, what brings you back home?"

"Dad's having hip surgery later this week, so I wanted to be here to help."

Natalie frowned. "Right before Christmas? That's a shame."

Ginny shrugged. "It was the best time for my work schedule, plus at least I can keep him at home since it's the holiday."

Mention of Harold softened Natalie's features, and she smiled. "He's a sweetheart. I see him when I take the kids to the diner. He's always at the counter chatting with Max." When she realized what she'd said, Natalie's hand shot to her mouth and her eyes grew. "I'm sorry, is it okay that I …"

"Said my ex-husband's name? Yes, he's not Voldemort," Ginny teased Natalie, who still wore a worried look. "Seriously, it's fine. I know they're friends." Ginny was pleased with how quickly that admission slipped out—she almost believed it herself.

Now that the conversation had gone back to adult matters, both children got bored quickly. "Mom, I want to get another candy cane," Madeline whined. She tugged on the edge of Natalie's coat, bringing her attention to her daughter.

"In a moment, sweetheart. Mommy is talking to her

friend." Just as Natalie opened her mouth to talk to Ginny, a loud chirp came from her purse. Her face fell as she pulled out her phone. "It's Anthony." She sighed, turning the phone to silent and handing it to Otis, who promptly put it in his mouth.

"I'll let you go. I promised Dad I'd be home for his doctor's call anyway."

Natalie stepped forward and hugged Ginny again. "It was so nice to see you. You should come to the diner next week, after Harold's surgery. CeCe is doing a cookie decorating event, and I reserved a table. It'd be a great way to catch up."

Ginny raised an eyebrow. "CeCe?"

"She's the other chef at the diner, a total delight. She's basically Max's right hand."

Ginny schooled her features, but she didn't like how her body reacted to the mention of another woman being Max's anything. Which of course was crazy because he wasn't her husband anymore. She needed to get a grip. "Sure, that sounds like fun."

Natalie smiled and pulled the phone from Otis's drool-covered hands. "What's your number? I'll text you the details."

Ginny rattled off her number and said goodbye to Natalie and her kiddos. As she finished going through the grocery store, her mind wandered back to Max and this mysterious CeCe. Who was she, and more importantly, why did Ginny want to see her so badly? And why had she agreed to go to the diner? Was she insane? *At this rate, probably.*

Ginny was so distracted that when she pushed her cart toward the exit, she brushed past a pyramid display of oranges. The cart wheel nicked the display, causing a few oranges to break free and bound toward freedom. Ginny stared at a fallen orange at her feet and couldn't help but smile.

Could she look at another roaming citrus fruit and not think of Max? Probably not. Was that a good thing or a bad thing? She had no idea. What she did know was that it was a new memory of Max, and it made her smile. Ginny let these thoughts take over as she drove back home, where she promptly obsessed about a man who was no longer her concern.

Wasn't it nice to be home for the holidays?

*

The diner was closed, but Max worked on things for the week ahead. He cherished this quiet time in the diner, when it was just him and the food. Sure, there were the boring administrative tasks like ordering paper towels and doing payroll, but he lived for these peaceful moments where he could dice onions to the gentle hum of the kitchen appliances.

His moment of Zen was ruined when CeCe bounded in the back door, carrying two boxes. "Where can I put these?" she asked in greeting. Her hair was shoved under a stocking cap, and her cheeks were rosy from the cold.

Max quickly moved his cutting board, giving her the corner of the counter. "Here's fine. What is all that?" He watched CeCe plop the boxes—which had the logo of the local craft store on them—down with a grunt. He didn't consider CeCe crafty outside the kitchen.

CeCe opened the top box and pulled out a jar of red sprinkles. "These are my cookie decorating supplies. I know it's not until next week, but I wanted to get everything set up." She started pulling out jars and bags of edible glitter, sprinkles, and frosting, all the colors of Christmas. "What do you think?" she asked as she held up a candy-cane-shaped cookie cutter. "Isn't this too darn cute?"

Max agreed, his own holiday spirit growing as he watched CeCe. For a woman in her late twenties, CeCe often became childlike when the holidays came around. He'd hired her two years ago, fresh off a big job in Chicago. Between her time in culinary school and her impressive resume, Max knew he'd be a fool to pass up a chance at having her on his team. CeCe moved to Buckeye Falls to escape the city and enjoy small-town life. She'd fit in with him and the team from day one.

"So, when is this workshop again?" Max asked, going back to his chopping. He knew it was soon, but since Ginny had come back to town, he was pleased if he remembered what day it was, let alone any future happenings.

CeCe emptied the last box and surveyed her wares. "Next Tuesday. I'm hosting when we're closed, so it won't interfere with our normal customers."

Max nodded. "Are you expecting a big crowd?"

CeCe beamed. "Yes. I booked a whole table for Natalie and her friends. That's at least eight people, but the church ladies booked a table and so did the community center."

When CeCe came up with the idea two years ago, Max hadn't been sure what to picture. He'd thought it would be a few girlfriends gathered around a bowl of cookie dough. But when the mayor's wife was involved, it was truly an event. While CeCe was charging to cover supplies, a portion of the funds was going to the local food bank. Who could complain about that?

"So, what are you doing here? I thought after our busy week you'd actually take a day off."

Max laughed. "You're one to talk. You were here baking last night when I left."

CeCe shrugged, sorting her jars of sprinkles by color. Picking up a green jar, she shook it and listened to the rattling. "What can I say? I like my job." She winked at her boss before delving back to her sorting.

Two hours later, Max had his prep work done for the next day and had finished his produce orders with their vendor. He shrugged on his coat when CeCe joined him by the back door. "Here." She handed him a white cake box.

He took it and asked, "What's this?"

CeCe rolled her eyes. "You told me to save you some chocolate mousse cake for Harold. I literally had to hide it in the back of the walk-in so Evan wouldn't eat it." Max didn't move, just stared at the box like it was a ticking bomb. "What's the matter?" CeCe asked, noticing the shift in his mood.

Max struggled with how much to say, and not because CeCe was an employee. He was still sorting through his own thoughts about seeing Ginny again, and he didn't want to put that burden on CeCe. "It's nothing," he said, turning toward the door.

When his hand hit the knob, CeCe stopped him with her words. "If you're wondering if you should see your ex tonight, I think you should."

Without turning around, Max asked, "And why is that a good idea?"

CeCe didn't answer right away, and that made Max nervous. If she was choosing her words, they were going to be important. "Because it might do you some good to have a little closure. I know I'm not the relationship guru. Heck, I'm probably the last person who should give advice about love." Her laughter held no humor, and Max understood the pain in her statement.

"Yet I think I'm about to get some unsolicited advice."

Never deterred, CeCe plowed ahead. "Harold is important to you, and he's about to have surgery. You'll feel better seeing him. You've also been in a funk since your ex arrived back in town, so seeing her can only help."

"How do you figure that?" he scoffed.

"If you see her and it goes well, you'll feel better about things. If you see her and it's a disaster, then maybe you'll feel better about the divorce."

Max hated to admit it, but her logic made some sense. Not that he was going to give her too much credit. CeCe tended to let things go to her head.

"Thanks for the cake. I'll see you tomorrow."

CeCe waved and closed the door behind him. Max drove down the block to his cottage, which sat off Main Street. It was a cozy space with a surprisingly large kitchen. Back when he was house hunting after the divorce, Max knew he couldn't live in a big space alone. The trouble was, he also couldn't live in a place with a tiny kitchen. The cottage had been perfect as soon as he saw it, and he ended up offering over the asking price to secure his new oasis.

When he was inside, Max put the cake in the fridge and fixed himself a sandwich. He settled in front of the TV to watch a reality cooking show. Even though he spent every waking moment in a kitchen, he still found shows about food to be the ultimate way to relax. Plus, he often learned a thing or two. As he watched the sun lower in the sky, he knew he had to make a decision.

Max paced up to his bedroom, then washed his face and studied himself in the mirror. He'd let his beard grow out a bit, and his face seemed softened by the dark bristles. Idly, he wondered if Ginny liked the beard. Back when they were together, she'd said she preferred him clean-shaven. But a lot could change over the years. Max dried his face and walked to his bed, plopping down to gather his thoughts.

Of course, CeCe was right. Not seeing Harold before the surgery would be hard. While it was a routine operation, he thought of Harold as a father. If his own father was having surgery, he'd be there without a doubt. Then there was the Ginny factor. She seemed about as eager to have him for dinner as she was about getting a root canal. Could he put her through an uncomfortable interaction? He didn't think he could.

Max decided on a compromise. He would bring over the cake, wish Harold well with his surgery, and go back home. Harold would understand, Max was certain. After all, the only person who knew Ginny's moods as well as he did was Harold.

But that notion brought Max up short. Did he really know Ginny and her moods anymore? Was there someone in her life that was taking care of her in the city? Harold had never mentioned anyone serious, but then again Max wasn't sure that he would. Fathers don't usually talk about their daughters' dating lives.

Running a hand down his face, Max centered himself before changing into a button-down shirt and jeans. He wanted to look nice, just in case. There was no point in lying and saying it was for Harold. Gathering the cake and a six-pack, Max walked out to his car and made the short drive to Harold's house. His heart hammered in his chest the entire drive, but he kept telling himself he was doing the right thing.

When he pulled into the driveway, he saw the welcoming glow of the Christmas tree from the front window. He'd helped Harold decorate last week before Ginny arrived. Both men agreed she'd appreciate the gesture. Max hoped she did. He knew Christmas wasn't always easy for Ginny. It was the same time of year her mother left, so celebrating the season didn't necessarily go smoothly. While Harold seemed to sink into the holiday spirit, Ginny preferred to float around it. Sure she'd eat cookies and drink her share of eggnog, but she never volunteered to do anything overly festive.

Stepping up to the door, Max knocked twice and waited with his heart in his throat. A moment later, Harold opened the door and grinned. "Right on time, son." He ushered Max into the living room. "I was about to open a bottle of wine."

Max handed Harold the six-pack. "Brought your favorite IPA. I thought it would go well with the soup."

Harold took the cake box from Max, grinning like the cat that caught the canary. "Thanks, but this is what I've been waiting for."

Max laughed, knowing full well he couldn't compete with CeCe and her baking skills. "CeCe had to hide that from Evan. The kid has a bigger sweet tooth than you, if you can believe it."

"I can. I've seen that kid eat. He must have a hollow leg." Harold shuffled into the kitchen, Max following close behind him.

As he stepped into the cozy space, he saw a sight that caused his heart to drop to his shoes. Ginny stood at the sink, washing a bowl and humming to herself. She wore an old apron he'd seen Harold wear a thousand times, but it suited her at the moment. Her hair had fallen over her eyes, so only the curve of her jaw was visible. It was the loveliest sight Max had seen in ages.

"Now, you know me," Harold said, walking to the fridge. "If this cake doesn't go into a hiding place now, we'll have it instead of dinner."

Ginny turned around to see who Harold was talking to. She faltered when she saw Max. "Oh, hi," she breathed, studying Max for a second before averting her gaze.

It wasn't the reaction he wanted, but Max wasn't surprised. "I was dropping off a few things. CeCe would kill me if Harold didn't get her cake." The mention of CeCe made Ginny wince, but he had no idea why.

"That woman does amazing things with eggs, butter, and sugar." Harold patted his belly. "I think she's responsible for at least ten of these pounds." He laughed at his own joke before turning and retrieving a bottle of wine from the counter. "Sit, let me get you a glass."

Max stepped back and raised his hands like he was being robbed. "N-no. That's fine. I wanted to drop those off." He lowered his hands and gestured toward the fridge.

Harold shook his head. "You are staying for dinner. I need a real chef to tell me how I did with this soup."

Max looked at the table, noticing it had been set for three people. If he closed his eyes, he could pretend this was a few years ago and everything was normal. This was a normal family dinner, with the family that really mattered to him.

If they were back in time, he could walk to the sink and wrap his arms around Ginny, lean into her, and smell the skin at the nape of her neck. God, he missed those rights. The rights of a husband. At this moment, he would give his favorite spatula collection for one hour in the past. Swallowing the growing lump in his throat, Max said, "I d-d-don't want to impose."

Ginny surprised everyone by taking the wine from Harold and pouring a glass. She stepped forward and handed it to Max, her hand shaking slightly. A peace offering.

"Stay for dinner." It was an order, not a question.

Max might have been lying to himself, but he could have sworn the corner of her lip tipped up in a smile. Whether it was a trick of his eyes, her words seemed genuine. He took the wine and sipped, eager for something else to focus on. "Thanks."

Harold took Max's coat and patted him on the back. "Take a seat, son. Dinner's ready."

And with that, Max eased himself into his usual chair. He watched the love of his life serve bowls of soup and sit across from him in the warm kitchen. The air around him smelled like home, with garlic from the soup and a hint of mint from Ginny's shampoo. There was something comforting about knowing she used the same stuff even now. That meant there was a small part of her that was the same. Max took that kernel of truth and held it close to his chest. It might be foolish, but Max was allowing himself to hope that Ginny could be back in his life. A guy can dream, right? Maybe he'd get a Christmas miracle.

CHAPTER 5

Ginny nearly made a fool of herself at dinner. From her first taste of soup, she was in love. "Dad, this is amazing." She greedily slurped from her spoon and covered her mouth with her free hand. "I mean, what is this?" Glancing down at her bowl, Ginny would have thought she was at a five-star restaurant. This was not just her father's normal chicken soup; this was bliss in a bowl.

Harold beamed at his daughter, taking a moment to savor the first bite. "I can't take all the credit." He gestured at Max with his spoon. "Someone helped me with the recipe."

Max shrugged, tearing a piece of bread and dipping it into the broth. Ginny allowed a moment to study the movements of his hands, ones she was intimately familiar with. They were strong hands, with nimble fingers that could do anything from carve a turkey to bring her to the height of passion. Her spoon clattered back into her bowl. *Was it suddenly a little hot in here?*

Thankfully, no one seemed to notice her case of the vapors. "You did all the work, Harold. This really is terrific. Did you get the fresh cilantro?"

Nodding, Harold reached for a piece of bread. "I did.

Went by the market when Ginny was working."

Ginny's swooning was interrupted at her father's statement, and she asked, "When did you go to the market? I thought I got everything at the store for you."

Harold slathered butter on his bread and took a bite before answering. "When you were on a call with your boss. I knew you'd need privacy, so I went out for what I'd forgotten to put on the list."

Ginny frowned. She hadn't realized she was focusing so much on work that she'd missed her father leaving the house. "I'm sorry. Lana texted, and then I guess I lost track of time." Looking at Max, she saw him studying her. As soon as their eyes met, he looked down at the table and focused on his soup. He stared at the broth like it held the secrets of the universe. She could guess what he was thinking. Her long hours at work, the constant distractions; none of this was new to Max.

Finally, he looked up and snagged her gaze. The heat from his expression caused her skin to blaze. Taking her ice water, Ginny sipped until she felt her temperature lower. Maybe it wasn't Max. Maybe it was the heat of the soup. *There's got to be at least a dozen chili peppers in here, right?!*

"Are you still at the same marketing firm?" Max asked. It was an innocent enough question, but Ginny knew it took a lot out of Max to inquire. Her firm is the same firm that scooped her up and took her away from Ohio, away from him. It was one of the biggest marketing firms on the east coast, and she would have been a fool to pass it up. *But what about the person she passed up?*

Even now, there was a nagging question in the back of her head when she thought about getting the offer. She'd accepted without hesitation, never contemplated bringing Max along. He had his passion in the diner, and Ginny had assumed it was the sign she needed to move forward with her life. But now, eating a simple soup dinner in her childhood home, she felt a little callous for her choices. Not that she was backpedaling on her decision; she was merely being thoughtful. *It must be that wine.*

Before answering, she dabbed her lips with her napkin. "Yes, still at the same firm."

Max nodded once. "I'm glad you're doing so well there." The compliment seemed genuine, and Ginny didn't like how it caused her stomach to flip.

Harold leaned over and patted Ginny's hand. "Our girl got promoted last year, senior management now. Isn't that impressive?" The phrase "our girl" wasn't lost on Ginny. She couldn't tell if it was a slip of the tongue, or if her father was trying a last-ditch attempt at matchmaking. She hoped it was the former.

Max cleared his throat. "She certainly is. Congratulations, Gin." Ginny froze at the sound of his nickname for her. A simple thing, but Max was the only person who ever called her Gin. As if he noticed her flinch, Max changed the subject. "Did you add pre-ground cumin or the whole seeds?"

Harold looked wounded. "I tried to find the whole cumin seeds, but the market only had pre-ground. Do you think you or CeCe could hook me up?"

"Hook you up?" Ginny laughed. "Did you get my dad into an illegal spice trading ring?" Everyone chuckled, but Ginny was growing more curious about this mysterious CeCe. She wanted to know more about her but didn't know how to bring her up without looking obvious. Was this Max's girlfriend? It sounded crazy, even to Ginny, but she'd assumed Max was still single. What business was it of hers? She chastised herself, pulling her attention back to the delicious soup.

"Who else wants seconds?" Harold asked, pulling back his chair.

Max hopped to his feet and grabbed Harold's bowl. "I'll get it—you sit and relax." Max reached for Ginny's bowl but hesitated. "Can I get you seconds?" His eyes held hers this time, giving her a look that could peel the wallpaper off the kitchen walls. Ginny felt her toes curl in her shoes.

"Um, yes, please." Even though she was dying for more soup, Ginny knew she needed to pace herself. Without her morning runs, she was going to need to buy new pants if she kept eating like this.

As if he was reading her mind, Harold teased, "We need to keep you fed, Ginnybread. You've been in the city too long. You need some meat on your bones."

Ginny patted her stomach. "Dad, let's be careful, or I'm going to have more meat than I should."

Max placed her bowl in front of her and paused. "I think you look great." His voice was barely above a whisper, and Ginny wondered if the words were meant for her.

Ginny didn't have time to overanalyze, because there was a knock at the door. "Who on earth would come by at this hour?" Harold asked, pushing his chair back to answer the door.

Ginny rose and waved him off. "I'll check, Dad." She walked toward the front, feeling Max's gaze follow her. When she got there, she looked out the window to see an older woman with a shock of white hair. Ginny opened the door halfway and stuck her head out. "Can I help you?"

The woman looked surprised for a moment before collecting herself. She held up a platter covered in tin foil. "Is Harold home?" She waited a moment for Ginny to reply before adding, "You must be Ginny. I've heard so much about you." The woman moved the platter to her elbow and stuck out her hand. "I'm Mona Fynn."

Not wanting to be rude, Ginny took the woman's hand. The shake was firmer than she'd expected, but Mona's eyes were kind and eager. "Nice to meet you, Mona."

From behind her, Ginny heard her father's familiar shuffled footsteps as he joined them at the entrance. "Mona! Don't just stand there, come on in." He placed his hand on Ginny's shoulder and gestured for Mona to join them.

Mona stepped inside the living room, bringing along a puff of snow from her coat. "I wanted to drop these off with you now, since you won't be back at the community center before your surgery." The look of concern on Mona's face made Ginny weary. It was the expression of someone who was more concerned than a neighbor would be. There was a spark in those eyes, and judging from her father's expression, he was enjoying the moment.

"So how did you two meet?" Ginny asked, taking the platter from Mona's hands. It had to weigh at least five pounds. "Oof," Ginny grunted as she carried it to the kitchen table.

Max had joined them, handing Mona a glass of wine. "Mona is the director of the community center. She's also the head of the Christmas Jubilee planning committee this year."

Mona flushed at Max's praise. "I want to help. Max and CeCe are doing all the heavy lifting this year."

There was that name again, CeCe. Ginny didn't want to bristle, but she was feeling like an outsider in her own home. Well, in her father's home. "You are?" she asked Max.

Max shoved his hands in his pockets. "Yeah, it's the least we can do. CeCe has a cookie party set up for next week, and we're catering the Jubilee Ball."

The Jubilee Ball. Just the name of the event flooded Ginny with memories of happier times. Well, mostly happier times. Max used to take Ginny every year, twirling her around the dance floor and kissing her under the mistletoe. The Jubilee Ball was the social event of the year in Buckeye Falls, and Ginny had been silly enough to forget about it. Of course the event was still happening. The world didn't stop because she wasn't here to witness it.

Ginny hadn't been to the Jubilee in three years. The last one she was in town for was right before she left for New York. Max was distracted and she assumed they weren't even going to make it, but now she wasn't so sure. If he was involved now, did that mean he was always interested?

Then that red dress up in her closet flashed before Ginny's eyes. Where had that come from? It was on the tip of her tongue to ask, but Mona kept talking. "I hope you'll be able to join us, Harold. I'm saving you a dance."

Harold winked at Mona, and Ginny suddenly felt like she was totally clueless. "The doctor said I should be out of bed within a few days of surgery. The Jubilee Ball might have to go on without me, I hate to say. Maybe Max can throw me over his shoulder and carry me to the dance floor."

Ginny opened her mouth to ask what was going on when Max took her elbow and guided her into the kitchen. "You two catch up. Ginny and I will clean up dinner." Max didn't let anyone argue, and her father seemed pleased with the change of company.

When they were in the kitchen, Ginny lowered her voice to a whisper. "Who is that woman, and what is going on? Is she … is she my dad's girlfriend?" Ginny didn't know why the idea was so foreign. She knew her dad was a nice man. Any woman would be lucky to have him in her life—she just didn't think anyone did besides her.

Max hoisted the soup pot to the counter, opening a cabinet for a bowl to store leftovers in. Ginny watched him for a moment, yet again caught off guard by how familiar Max was with the layout of the kitchen. "How often do you come over here to see Dad?" she asked.

Max shrugged. "Do you want to know about that, or Mona? I'm happy to tell you anything you want to know, but you seem all over the place right now."

Ginny crossed her arms over her chest and jutted out her chin. "I am not. I'm fine." She hated how petulant she sounded, especially with Max.

Reaching out, Max brushed his thumb over her chin. The trail of his touch curled her toes. Apparently her body needed to get the memo that his touch shouldn't affect her that way.

"You're in defense mode."

"I am not," she complained, even though he was reading her like a book. Damn him. "I'm confused as to what is going on here. Why are you teaching my dad how to cook Thai chicken soup? How do you know where the bowls are, yet I can't seem to find anything? And who is this woman bringing food and making googly eyes at Dad?" Against her better judgment, she jutted her chin out even further. At this rate she was going to get a crick in her neck from all the pouting.

Max covered a bowl with plastic wrap and tried to school his features. Ginny could tell he wanted to laugh. "Mona is a sweet lady. Your dad could do a lot worse." His tone was casual.

Ginny absolutely hated being this far out of the loop. Sure, she was living her life in New York, but she foolishly assumed her father was like Max, kept in a bubble where nothing changed without her. Frankly, she hated how it felt.

Filling the sink with soapy water, Max started scrubbing the soup pot. Without having to ask, Ginny took a dish towel and stood beside him. Within minutes, they were silently doing the dishes in their old, familiar rhythm. When Ginny faltered with where to put the can opener, Max reached out to the drawer by the fridge. "It goes over here," he said.

"I knew that," Ginny whined as she shoved the can opener into the wrong drawer. Max bit his lip but didn't say anything, taking a moment to watch her. It was making her squirm, and not in a good way. "Why are you staring at me?" she asked, hanging the towel on the stove handle.

"Because you're here," Max said simply. "I haven't seen you in years, and I'm getting my fill." He drained the sink and wiped down the table before reaching for his coat on the back of his chair. "I should get going, but let me know if you need any help with Harold when you're back from the hospital. I've got the diner covered, and I can help with anything at all."

There were a few snide remarks Ginny could spew, but she kept quiet and merely nodded. She knew there would be things coming up in the next few days that she'd need help with. It never occurred to her to call Max, but it should have. She knew that even after all this time, Max would pick up the phone when she called. Truly, he was a good man.

Wait, what was all this? One quiet night at home with her ex-husband was driving Ginny crazy. "I'll walk you out," she offered. Perhaps the cold night air would clear her mind of these racing thoughts.

Max put on his coat and stepped back to the living room where Harold and Mona were animatedly discussing something in hushed tones. Her father seemed agitated, and Ginny asked, "What's going on?"

"Nothing," Harold said, leaning forward while Mona fluffed the pillow at his back. He grimaced a little but didn't complain. "We were just talking about the Jubilee."

Mona patted Harold's leg and beamed. "Your dad is one of the best planners we've ever had. He's giving Santa's elves a run for their money."

Ginny knew her father liked to stay active in Buckeye Falls, but she had no idea he was into party planning. "You are?"

Harold shrugged. "It's a fun group, and I always liked the Christmas Jubilee. I kind of fell into it when Mona took over the planning committee."

Max motioned toward the couch and smirked. "Mona did more than take over the committee. She brought us into the twenty-first century. The Jubilee actually has a social media presence now."

Whipping her gaze back and forth, Ginny felt like a defective bobblehead doll. "Wow. I had no idea the Jubilee was getting so big."

Mona frowned. "It might be getting too big. Even with Max and Harold helping, it is a lot to take on. Plus, my grandson told me our last Instagram post was"—she held her hands up and did air quotes—"totally lame."

Max covered his mouth to hide his smile. "It wasn't bad."

"It certainly wasn't inspired," Mona countered, waving off his praise.

Ginny pulled her cell phone from her pocket, scrolling

through Instagram. "What's the name of the account?"

"Buckeye Falls Christmas Jubilee," Max said, so close she felt the warmth of him seeping through her sweater. *It really was getting too hot in here.*

Holding back judgment, Ginny scrolled through the event's page. It wasn't as bleak as she was expecting, but there was a lot of room for improvement. "Who else is helping on the committee?" she asked, not liking where her mind was going. Once a marketer, always a marketer.

Counting off on her fingers, Mona said, "Well, the three of us, Natalie, a few of the church ladies, and CeCe."

"Who is in charge of social media and promotions?"

Mona glanced around, as if the answer were right in front of her.

Ginny had the sinking feeling it was. "Um, no one? We all sort of"—she trailed off and flapped her hand in the air—"chip in when we can."

This wouldn't do. Every professional bone in Ginny's body vibrated with the need to fix this page—to fix this whole situation. While her mind spiraled with all the things wrong with the marketing, Mona reached into her purse and dug out a brochure. "These are the mock-ups for this year's fliers." She thrust it into Ginny's hand, and Ginny fought against rolling her eyes. Clashing color schemes and '90s clip art covered the mint green paper. They were possibly the ugliest brochures she'd ever seen.

"Wow," was all she could say as she stared down at a brochure better suited for a time capsule. Reason and all common sense flew up the chimney like a puff of smoke as she looked around at three sets of curious eyes. "I'm not making any promises," she said, knowing what she was about to do was a big deal. "But I can look at the social accounts. You know, see what I can do."

Mona beamed. "Really? Harold said you're a wonder with marketing, but I never thought you'd be able to help."

Beside her, Ginny felt Max. He was warm, steady. A few hours ago, his closeness would have irked her, but now it felt comforting. "Are you sure you have the time for this?" he asked, his brow creased in concern. "I mean, you have your job and prepping for Harold's surgery."

Either not sensing her hesitation, or not caring, Mona plowed ahead. "I'll tell the committee you'll join us on Thursday night for the meeting. If you think you'll have something to show us?" She held up her hands, every available finger was crossed, her expression that of a child on Christmas morning.

Suddenly fearing she'd overstepped, Ginny looked to her father. "And you're sure I'm not stepping on any other elves' toes? The last thing I want to do is make waves."

"Nonsense," he assured her. "It's not every day a big city hotshot offers to do your marketing." She couldn't deny the pride on her father's face made her feel ten feet tall. Her career had always been important to her, but Ginny didn't worry about what others thought about it—even her family.

"Where is the meeting?"

"The community center," Mona said as she shrugged her coat back on. "Maybe Max can pick you up so you know where to go?" Mona nodded at her own suggestion before hugging Harold and heading toward the door.

Max was hot on her heels and jogged to open the door. "Drive careful, Mona." Turning back to Ginny he said, "Can I talk to you for a second?"

From his perch on the couch, Harold said, "You kids do what you need to. I've got ESPN for company." Before either of them could take a step outside, the TV blared with a basketball game. Ginny had to ball her fists at her sides to keep from plugging her ears.

"What's the matter?" she asked after Max steered her to the porch. Mona had already made her exit, the sound of her car's tires crunching as she backed onto the road.

Max cupped the back of his neck and sighed. Suddenly he looked exhausted. "You don't need to do this."

"The marketing thing?"

"Any of it," he surmised. "I know it's a lot, and you're

going to be busy with Harold, and—" He stopped his rambling and made eye contact, his gaze searching. "We can handle it."

Ginny knew he was right, that a local holiday event was hardly worth her energy, but she really wanted to help. "I don't mind." And since she was in the business of surprising people tonight, she added, "And if you don't mind picking me up on Thursday, I'd appreciate it."

Max swallowed, his Adam's apple bobbing with the motion. In the dim porchlight, Ginny observed the five o'clock shadow from earlier in the week was becoming a full beard. It suited him. And the fact that she noticed that annoyed the hell out of her.

"S-s-sure. I'll pick you up at six." With that, he turned and bounded down the porch steps to his car. She assumed he ran away before she could change her mind.

For a moment, Ginny stood in the quiet evening breathing in the clean country air. The only sounds were from the TV and a few dogs barking in the distance. Gone were the familiar horns and sirens of New York, and she was surprised to discover she didn't miss it. Walking back inside, she curled up on the couch next to her father. When he wasn't looking, she turned the volume down to a level that wouldn't wake the dead. She dozed, her head listing to the side. As her eyes grew heavy, she thought about ideas for the Jubilee and found herself growing excited to create something new. Though she also couldn't help but wonder what had she just gotten herself into?

*

The entire drive home, Max replayed the last two hours on a loop in his brain. Seeing Ginny, spending time with her and Harold had felt like a balm to his soul. When Mona suggested he drive Ginny to the committee meeting, he nearly kissed her—Harold's reaction be damned.

Once things got hectic with the Jubilee planning, Max

had seen the social media and marketing sliding. Granted he was no expert, but he knew enough to know it was bad. Like, a middle school group project bad. Max hoped there was a part of her, regardless of how small, that looked forward to spending time with him. No matter how long the ink was dry on their divorce papers, Max loved Ginny and wanted the best for her. Working herself to exhaustion would not do.

When you build a life with someone, around someone, it's hard to flip a switch and pretend that everything is fine. The one saving grace for Max was the diner, which ironically had been the nail in the coffin of their marriage. Ginny had wanted bigger things from life, and Max wanted a small-town life with Ginny.

Early in their marriage, they'd discussed what they wanted to do after college, when their new degrees seemed to open the world at their feet. Max had always wanted to be a chef. From his childhood days of helping his parents in the kitchen, to hiding there with his late grandmother when things were rough, food was his happy place. He'd started working at the diner, the biggest restaurant in Buckeye Falls, just to get his feet wet in the restaurant world.

One day the owner approached him to say he was retiring and moving to Arizona to escape the Ohio winters. Max knew it was a great opportunity for him and Ginny to set up real roots in their hometown and make their way. But Ginny had been making her own plans.

Where Max always knew he wanted to cook, Ginny struggled to find her place in the professional world. Throughout college, she'd had half a dozen internships to find what would make her happy. She'd also bounced around jobs outside town, seeing if she could fit anywhere. She'd tried finance, hospitality, and even waited tables at the diner for a few months. Finally she'd taken a job in Columbus at a marketing firm. Her commute had been long, but Max thought it was worth it to see the look of satisfaction on her face every night when she came home.

Then it all fell apart. Ginny had impressed the bosses at their New York headquarters, and a job offer quickly followed. While Max was planning their small-town life, Ginny had decided she wanted to try big-city living—alone. To say he was completely blindsided would be a lie. Max had seen the tiny shifts in their relationship. But at the end of the day, he knew Ginny, and he knew what they had was special.

Now, standing in the diner's kitchen at dawn, Max shook himself back to reality. He had a lot of things to prep before opening. Going down Memory Lane could wait. His win for the week was knowing Ginny would be spending time with him. Max practically radiated excitement from his head to his toes.

"Someone's in a good mood," CeCe greeted him from the back door. She had a bag of rice tossed over her shoulder, and she kicked the door closed behind her. "I was driving past the restaurant supply store last night and thought I'd get rice to make risotto for the weekend. What do you think?"

There were few things CeCe made that Max didn't love, but risotto was not one of those. It was one of the best. "Um, I think you need to get cooking. Are you making the lemon parmesan or the mushroom and Swiss?"

CeCe tucked a lock of hair behind her ear and stared at the ten-pound bag of rice. "Honestly, I was thinking of trying that bacon and blue cheese recipe. Do you think that's too much?"

"I think it's just right," Evan said, joining them and shrugging his coat off. "Is that for tonight?" His eyes sparkled with anticipation.

Max loved Evan, but he worried about the kid. At twenty-three, he was still figuring out what he wanted to do in life. There was an obvious attraction to CeCe, and Max worried he'd get his heart broken. CeCe was older, wiser, and had a strict no-dating-coworkers rule. Evan didn't stand a chance.

CeCe shook her head. "Probably not until the weekend. Here, take the other end and help me carry this to the shelf." Together they lugged the bag of rice off the counter. Max grabbed a towel and disinfected the counters. For some reason, the ritual of cleaning put him in the right frame of mind.

Evan returned and put on his apron, grabbing a box of sugar packets. "I'll start my prep work," he said, walking out to the dining room. CeCe returned and retrieved a box of flour and a bag of sugar.

Max watched her studying the ingredients. "What are you thinking today?" he asked.

CeCe rolled her shoulders and sighed. "I can't decide. Should I do something chocolatey or something fruity?"

Max gestured to their whiteboard on the back wall, which displayed the day's specials. "Pick something that goes with chicken pot pie and Greek lemon soup."

"Fruity," CeCe confirmed, getting herself into work mode. Max had noticed CeCe's shifts from her first day at the diner. In a matter of seconds, she went from joking about something to expertly melting chocolate for a cake. When it was time to work, CeCe was there to work.

Their doors opened an hour later. Max had fallen into his familiar rhythm of cooking the diner's popular brunch items when Evan came back to the grill with a goofy look on his face. "Hey, boss, you got a second?"

Using his wrist, Max pushed a lock of hair from his face. He had just placed eggs on the griddle and had to watch them. "Not really, what's up?" Max asked, his eyes never leaving the eggs. He knew these were for the town's poker club, and those guys would never let him hear the end of it if their eggs were dry.

Evan shuffled his feet back and forth and waited while Max buttered toast and slid thick slices of bacon onto waiting plates. "Well, there's a lady out front."

Max had to bite his tongue at Evan's vague way of describing seemingly important situations. "We serve a lot of female customers, Evan. You're going to have to throw me a bone here."

"Well, she asked for you specifically. If that makes a difference." Evan shrugged, as if that answered all of Max's questions.

"Is she unhappy with her meal?" Max asked, filling the last of the poker club's plates and sliding the tray across to Evan. "Bring this out to table five. I'll come out in a second. What table has the unhappy customer?"

Evan looked confused. "She's not at a table. She walked in and asked to see you."

Max pulled his hand through his hair and stifled a groan. "Evan, I'm going to take a moment to brew a fresh pot of coffee. Get these meals to table five, find out what she wants and come back. Okay?"

Evan balanced the tray on his shoulder, careful to keep the plates from bumping into each other. "You got it, boss." Evan walked out of the kitchen, giving Max a moment to collect himself before the next rush of orders.

CeCe burst through the doors with a grin on her face. "There's a pretty hot woman asking for you out there. A bunch of people seem to recognize her, but she won't take a seat. She's standing by the door, as if she'll burst into flames if she steps inside." CeCe put down a bin of dirty dishes by the dishwasher.

Now Max really did groan. "I'm guessing it's Ginny."

CeCe chuckled. "Either your ex, or a vampire." She smiled at her own joke before continuing, "Damn, Max. I can see why you still pine after her. She's certainly a looker." She craned her neck to look through the window in the door. Max took a moment to walk to his tiny office and run a comb through his hair. He'd hoped the next time they saw each other he'd be prepared. Now he was covered in food and smelled like a combination of sweat and bacon.

"CeCe, cover the grill for a second. I'll be right back."

Smirking, CeCe took her place and grabbed a spatula. "You realize you're going to have to give me the dirt on this, right? I can't be the only person living an interesting life in this town."

Max was offended. "My life is interesting."

Lifting a shoulder, CeCe focused on the stack of uncracked eggs in front of her. "Your life here is interesting. I can't say what it looks like when you're not inside these walls." There was no time to unpack that statement, so Max threw his arms in the air and walked into the dining room.

It took all of two seconds for Max to find Ginny standing ramrod straight by the door, her purse clutched against her chest. She was talking to the hostess, Helen. "It's no trouble at all, dear," Helen assured Ginny. "We have spots at the counter, and I could get you a cup of coffee while you wait."

Ginny shook her head and smiled. When she saw Max approach, she managed to look both more relaxed and terrified. "Hi." Her voice came out in a squeak. She cleared her throat and tried again. "Erm, good morning."

Max patted Helen's arm. "We've got this covered. Thank you for your help, Helen." Helen grabbed a stack of menus and walked around them toward the customers entering the diner. Without thinking, Max reached out and took Ginny's elbow, steering her toward the kitchen.

"Where are we going?" Ginny asked, looking like she wanted to bolt for the door.

Max kicked open the door to the kitchen and gestured toward the office in the back corner. He knew Ginny knew where his office was, but still, he directed her. "Let's go to my office." Max felt Evan and CeCe's eyes on them as he guided Ginny and closed the door behind them.

The space was small, barely holding a desk and two chairs. Max moved a stack of invoices off the spare chair and tilted it toward Ginny in invitation. "Thanks," she muttered, lowering herself onto the edge of the seat. It was like she was trying to be as uncomfortable as possible in his presence, and Max wasn't too proud to admit that it stung.

"So, what's up?" Max asked, leaning back in his chair

and surveying his ex-wife in his own space. Like the night before, she was dressed for the city. Her jeans were tight and her boots were better suited for a runway than an icy rural sidewalk. Not that he was complaining about how Ginny looked. He'd seen her at her best and worst, and he'd never not been attracted to her.

Ginny had a confidence Max always admired. No matter the situation, she was poised and in her element. He assumed it was what made her so good at her job. Now she didn't seem as confident as she stared down at her purse, still clutched in her hands. "I wanted to talk about the Christmas committee."

Max figured that was why she was here. He didn't blame her, especially after Mona pulled a fast one on her. Bless her heart, when Mona sensed Ginny's willingness she'd pounced. "You want to get out of it," he surmised. To say he was disappointed would be the understatement of the century. "I understand. I can see if CeCe can help me out with the marketing." Max couldn't be sure, but the mention of CeCe seemed to bring a small flinch from Ginny. He didn't know what to think about that.

Ginny swallowed, still not looking up from her lap. "I don't know how I can do a new project while I'm taking care of Dad."

Max leaned closer, keeping his tone even. "You know that Mona and I would never suggest anything that would take you away from Harold during his recovery. If you can't make the meetings, I could follow up with what the committee needs from you. Plus, you know I can help with anything for Harold. I want to be there for him, and for you."

His last words hung in the air between them as the silence stretched out. Back in the day, the air hadn't been so heavy in this tiny office. When he'd first reopened the diner, he and Ginny spent a lot of good times in this space. From getting the menus printed and folded to a few stolen kisses, Max loved the memories Ginny brought back.

"I want to help because I can tell it's important to Dad," she rushed to add. "But I will take you up on your offer." Finally she looked up and met his gaze. "About tomorrow night, before the meeting," she said, glancing down to watch her fingers toy with the hem of her sweater. "Dad's invited you to dinner, if you're free."

Max was the opposite of free on Thursday night before the meeting, but he knew he could make it work with his team. "Yes, is five o'clock all right?" He'd shut down the diner if it came to that because nothing would stop him from another meal with two of his favorite people.

Ginny nodded, looking as if she were about to stand. Suddenly she stopped, falling back against her seat. Her face was drawn, and she looked exhausted. "Thanks, Max. I knew I could count on you."

Before he could stop himself, Max closed the distance between them, kneeling to meet Ginny eye to eye. "Yes, you can. And you can tell me what else you need for Harold. I'm here, okay?" Without asking permission, he reached out and took her hands in his. They were smooth yet cold from the winter chill. He squeezed them and waited for her to pull back, but she returned the squeeze and sighed.

"I'm really scared," she whispered. "I know it's a routine surgery, but what if he …" Her words were lost on a sob. Ginny pulled her hands free and covered her face. Her shoulders shook from the effort of holding back her tears.

Max sprang into action, cradling her close and rubbing her back while she cried. "Shhh, let it out, Gin." He knew she was hurting, but Max savored this moment of closeness. Ginny hadn't been vulnerable in front of him in years, and it did funny things inside his rib cage. He liked, no loved, being the person she turned to.

Finally Ginny pulled back far enough to catch Max's eye. "Thanks, I didn't mean to come here and cry in your office when you're busy."

"You're welcome to cry in my office anytime," Max said, instantly grimacing. "Damn, that came out all wrong."

Ginny giggled, her smile lighting up her face and sending Max's pulse skyrocketing. "I know what you mean, and I appreciate it." Ginny pulled a tissue from her coat pocket and dabbed at her eyes.

A lump formed in his throat, and he felt his words falter on his tongue. "S-s-sure. Happy to help."

Ginny reached out and rested her hand on his cheek. Despite his beard, he felt the heat of her touch on his skin. "Max." The name came out in a breath that tickled his nose. She leaned closer until he could count the freckles on her cheeks. Max knew every freckle—twenty-seven on her right cheek alone—every pore on her face. His favorite Ginny constellation looked like Orion's Belt.

Knowing he wouldn't get the chance again, he put his hand on her shoulder, drawing her even closer. The crisp scent of her mint shampoo washed over him in invitation. When their lips were nearly touching, fate intervened in the name of Evan.

"Hey, boss, there's a line out the door. Can you help with—oh crap!" he exclaimed, stepping back and letting the door slam shut. Through the door Max heard hurried footfalls as Evan ran away.

Max cursed under his breath as Ginny shot to her feet. They both knew the moment was gone. He only hoped it wasn't gone forever.

"See you tomorrow," she said, tossing her purse over her shoulder and stumbling to the door.

Before Max could follow her, he heard the kitchen door close and realized the chance to catch her was over. But at least he would see her tomorrow, and Max was holding on to hope. Fate had brought Ginny back to Buckeye Falls for more than Harold. In his heart, Max knew this was their second chance.

CHAPTER 6

Ginny changed her outfit for the third time in five minutes. She suddenly had nothing to wear. She heard her father downstairs on the phone. Since she met Mona, her father didn't see the point in pretending the woman wasn't an important part of his life. Ginny could not begrudge him that, especially after everything that happened with her mother.

"We're not going there now," Ginny chastised herself while she pulled on her fourth sweater and shrugged at her reflection in the mirror. "This will have to do." She sighed. She was trying to look effortlessly put together, not like she was trying too hard.

Ginny wasn't sure what had happened between her and Max at the diner, but she was putting it way back in her mind. Like buried behind thirty-two years of life buried. Like the last scene in *Raiders of the Lost Ark* buried.

There was no point thinking about it. They were exes, and they shared years of history, of baggage. It only made sense that they'd touched and comforted each other. And even if that waiter hadn't interrupted, Ginny was sure nothing would have happened. *Yeah, right.*

What she was afraid to even consider admitting how

close she'd been to kissing Max. He was right there, all sweet and supportive. And she'd be the world's biggest liar if she denied how good he looked in his apron. That damn piece of white cotton made him look good enough to eat; good enough to savor.

"Ginnybread, it's almost dinnertime!" Harold bellowed from the base of the steps.

Ginny grabbed her purse and headed downstairs. When she reached for the railing, her steps faltered. Now she heard two voices, and one of them was definitely not Mona. The tightness in Ginny's belly was all the warning she needed to know that Max was already here. When she reached the bottom of the stairs, her father stepped toward her and gave her a pat on the cheek. "I thought we'd eat with the game tonight. Cleveland's up by ten going into the last quarter."

Surveying the living room, Ginny saw her father had the TV stands set up and the basketball game on. "Sure, let me go get dinner. Have a seat." As Ginny spun on her heels, she walked right into a wall. The wall smelled like pine and was covered in a cable-knit sweater the color of undecorated Christmas trees.

"Max, I didn't see you there," she offered lamely, enjoying the feel of his hands on her arms as he steadied her. She knew she should move, but her feet were cemented in place.

Psyching herself up, Ginny let her gaze roam all the way from Max's broad chest to the beard that was starting to fill out. His caramel eyes sparkled down at her. "It's good to see you again, Gin."

Gin, her nickname sounded like a song on his lips. Lips she shouldn't be thinking about. Was it suddenly hot in the living room? Ginny reluctantly stepped back, breaking Max's hold on her. She pulled at the neck of her sweater and headed toward the kitchen. She needed a glass of ice water and a moment alone. If she and Max were going to be working together, she needed to get used to being around him again. Acting like a schoolgirl in his presence would get really old, really fast.

The heavenly aroma of melted cheese and spices wafted toward Ginny when she walked to the stove. The kitchen was spotless, and there was a covered dish resting on a trivet. "I made enchiladas," Max said as he joined her. He opened the fridge and grabbed three bottles of water and a jar of salsa. "I hope you still like them. Harold loves them, so I thought it would be fun."

Ginny lifted the foil on the pan and groaned. "Three cheese enchiladas with avocado crema, oh my goodness." Over her shoulder, she winked at Max. "It's a shame you didn't bring enough for everyone else."

Max chuckled. "I'll get this plated up. You join Harold." Ginny reached out and took her water bottle, their fingers grazing. The awareness that zinged through her caused her skin to flush. If she stood with him in this kitchen much longer, her face would match her crimson sweater.

"Thanks," she muttered, backing away from him. Ginny's mouth was watering for more reasons than one as she watched Max plate their dinners. It was a familiar sight that shouldn't curl her toes, but here she was acting like a fool. When she joined her father, she chugged half her water in an attempt to cool off.

"Oh, c'mon, guys!" her father shouted as his team missed a free throw. "I'm telling you, you'd think these guys don't have any athletic ability." Shaking his head, he took the proffered water bottle and sighed. "Even I could have sunk that shot, and I'm old and about to have hip surgery. These guys can't even dribble."

At the mention of dribbling, Ginny nearly poured her water onto her lap at the sight of Max entering the cramped room. He came in with three plates balanced in his hands, his gaze intent on not dropping them. His face was slightly scrunched in concentration, and Ginny couldn't deny how adorable he looked. He was still the quiet boy she'd met in the library.

"We're still in early season. Give them time to find their

new rhythm." Max placed their plates in front of them before settling into his spot next to Ginny.

Ginny felt like she was sitting in a time capsule. This was what their weekly dinners at the house were like—basketball on TV, the men talking sports, and Ginny simply enjoying being with her two favorite people. The differences were minute, and only a trained eye could spot them. Instead of sharing a TV stand, she and Max were about a foot apart. When the meal was over, they wouldn't be washing the dishes together and stealing kisses. Most importantly, they wouldn't be leaving together and going home together.

For all the differences, there was one similarity that caused Ginny's eyes to mist. "You gave me the corner piece," she whispered, looking down at her plate. She'd always loved the edge pieces of anything from the oven, but especially Max's enchiladas. The tortillas were nearly burnt, the edges curling into the red sauce.

Max looked at her and gave her a look she couldn't decipher. It seemed sad but also hopeful. "I'll never forget what you like, Gin. Especially when it's one of your favorite foods." Not knowing what to say, Ginny took another swig from her water bottle, cursing her decision to wear such a warm sweater.

Beside them, Harold watched and smiled. Ginny nearly said something, not wanting to break her father's heart when she left again and things went back to normal. Normal, a notion that suddenly seemed so foreign. She'd only been back in Buckeye Falls for a few days, but she was feeling like New York was lightyears away.

Her father's question broke her revelry. "Is the mayor going to be at your planning meeting tonight?"

Max smirked. "Oh yeah. I'm sure he wouldn't miss the chance to take charge of something he has no business being involved in. The good thing is I can return his suit."

Harold barked with laughter, nearly choking on his enchiladas. "Did you take it to Greens?" he asked while he blotted sauce from his face.

Max laughed and nodded. "Oh yeah. CeCe had them add so much starch he won't be able to move his legs for fear the fabric will snap in half." Harold kept laughing as Max wiped a tear from his eye.

Clearly she was missing an inside joke. "What did I miss?"

"Our favorite mayor threw his power around when no one asked for it. One of my waiters spilled iced tea on him this week, and we're obliging his request for free dry cleaning."

Ginny scraped the last bite from her plate and settled back into the couch, enjoying the feeling of a full belly. "I bumped into Natalie at the grocery store the other day. I didn't realize they had married."

Max's face turned serious. "How did she look?"

Ginny raised an eyebrow. "Uh, fine I guess. I met her kids too. They seem sweet."

"We're worried about her," her father said, muting the TV during a commercial break.

This was news to Ginny. "You are?"

Max nodded. "Yeah. Ever since Anthony got elected, he's not quite himself. I mean, obviously things are different since high school. But there's something different about him. It's like all he cares about is how everything looks."

"He thinks he's JFK and she's Jackie. I hate seeing it, but at least it should hurt his chances for re-election in the spring. Everyone in town is fed up with his attitude, if nothing else." Her father grimaced and turned the TV volume back up. "That guy needs a reality check."

Max rolled his eyes. "He needs a firm kick on his backside."

Ginny decided to break the tension. "Natalie invited me to the diner, actually. She said she booked a table for a cookie decorating party?"

Max grinned. "Yes. CeCe decided to add some holiday activities to the diner during Jubilee week. We already sold out, so it's good you got a spot."

Ginny nodded but felt herself deflate. "CeCe sure sounds like a miracle worker," she said under her breath.

Her father chimed in immediately. "That girl is a lifesaver. Best damn baker this town has ever seen, and what a sweetheart."

Max sputtered with laughter. "Sweetheart? If I told CeCe you said that, she'd spit in your lemon meringue pie."

Harold's chest shook with laughter. "She would, wouldn't she? Oh, well, it'd probably still be incredible. When you snatched her up, this town got a lot sweeter. You're a lucky man," her father concluded.

Ginny had to bite her lip to keep from frowning. "I'll get this cleaned up. We should probably go." She stood up too fast and her empty water bottle tipped onto the floor. Max stood and chased it around. He followed her into the kitchen a moment later and loaded the dishwasher.

"Are you okay?" he asked, hanging up the dish towel.

Ginny nodded and smiled. "Fine," she lied. "Let me grab my purse—we don't want to be late." She walked over to her father and kissed his cheek. "See you after the meeting."

"Take your time," he ordered, waving goodbye to Max from his post by the door. "No curfew, you kids have a good night."

Max saluted. "Yes, sir."

Ginny burst through the door, nearly slipping on a patch of ice on the porch. Max was right there, reaching out again to steady her. This time, he let go as soon as she was on her feet. The lack of his touch made her feel naked, and not in a good way.

Gesturing to his car, Max said, "I'll drive." Ginny slid into the passenger's seat. It was the same old car from their marriage. It struck Ginny then how certain relics from the past are forgotten. Not having been in this car for years, now she was bombarded with random memories. Mundane trips to the grocery store, or their road trip down to Florida to visit Max's parents—the memories washed over her in a wave.

"The car's still looking good," she mused, running her hand over the dashboard. Like his kitchen, Max always kept the car spotless.

"It's easy when I don't drive too much. I walk to work most days, and I haven't left Buckeye Falls in months. And when I do, CeCe usually drives." He was silent for the rest of the drive, allowing Ginny to stew in her own frustrations.

Suddenly, she was beyond jealous of the other woman in Max's life. She didn't know what it meant, but she knew it was crippling her. Though sitting with him on the way to a town meeting was not the time to unpack her jumbled thoughts. Ginny would save it for when she was back at the house with a full glass of wine.

*

Max gripped the steering wheel so hard he thought it would crack under his fingers. Having Ginny this close was torture of the highest order. At least when they were at Harold's house, he had enough distractions. But sitting here, sharing the same air and listening to Christmas carols, was too much. Eartha Kit needed to do a better job distracting him.

His mind was a jumble of questions for Ginny. What was she thinking? Did she remember the last time they were in the car together? Does she realize he still kept her hair ties in the glove box, just in case? But Max kept his mouth shut. It wasn't that he thought he'd stutter. It was the opposite; he feared he'd never be able to stop talking. He wouldn't be able to stop himself from begging her for more time, for more of anything.

Fortunately for his sanity, the community center was only a ten-minute drive. He parked his car next to a familiar BMW. Either the mayor or Natalie was in attendance. Max said a silent prayer it was the latter and climbed from the car. Sprinting, he rushed to open Ginny's passenger door.

"Thanks," she said as she stretched next to him. He got

a whiff of her perfume and had to stifle a groan. He was acting like a horny teenager, and he hated it. Ginny took the lead and walked up the snowy path.

As soon as she opened the door, they were accosted by half of the town's gossips. "My stars, it's Ginny and Max Sanchez," Mrs. Sanders proclaimed from her spot at the snack table. A woman in her late seventies, she was known for her peanut butter cookies, her poor memory, and her sharp tongue. She lived for gossip, and her hungry eyes made Max squirm.

Beside him, Max felt Ginny bristle, but she didn't correct the old woman on her name change. Max was grateful for that, as he hardly needed a reminder. "Mrs. Sanders, you're looking lovely," Ginny crooned as she walked over to hug the woman. "Why, you haven't changed a bit."

Mrs. Sanders waved off the compliment. "Oh please, you're one to talk. You look as young and fit as ever." Holding up Ginny's arms, she stepped back to appraise her. Max didn't know how Ginny wasn't rolling her eyes, but she kept smiling. "I can tell you aren't eating your ex-husband's cooking anymore. You're too skinny." To remedy the situation, Mrs. Sanders handed Ginny a fistful of cookies. "Here."

Ginny took them and laughed. "I already had dinner, but I'll snack on these later."

Mrs. Sanders seemed satisfied and turned her attention to Max. "So, what are you planning on doing to keep your ex-wife in town?" she asked, crossing her arms over her ample bosom. Her gaze assessed him behind her smudged glasses.

Max felt his cheeks bloom crimson, but he wasn't rising to the bait. "I think I see a couple seats over there." He gestured with one hand and guided Ginny by the small of her back with his other. His fingers flexed at the feel of her beneath his touch. Max's senses were in overdrive. After years of a Ginny drought, he was suddenly drowning around her. Judging from her carefree demeanor, he was the only one affected by their closeness.

Ginny slid into her seat and took off her coat. The stack of cookies sat on her knees, wobbling with the movement. "You have to eat at least two of these," she whispered. "Between your meals and Dad's farmhouse breakfasts, my pants barely fit."

Before he could stop himself, Max said the first thing on his mind, "You look great to me, Gin." Ginny's head shot up and her eyes grew. "Sorry, I mean." Max held up his hands as if to ward off her wrath. Just as he was back peddling, he shook his head. "No, actually, I'm not sorry. You look wonderful. I hate when you beat yourself up over a few pounds."

Ginny's face softened and she smiled. "You always say the nicest things, Max," she said.

Max chuckled. "Clearly not always, but thanks for taking the compliment." He reached over and snatched two cookies from her lap, popping one in his mouth, whole.

Because timing was everything, Natalie chose that exact moment to squeal and run over to Ginny. "You're here! I heard Mona hooked you into the Jubilee planning, but I'm so glad you're here." Max felt himself relax when he saw how happy Natalie looked. Glancing around the room confirmed her overbearing husband was nowhere in sight.

"Natalie, hey!" Ginny exclaimed while hugging her with one arm. Her cookies were clutched in her free hand, crumbs falling to the floor. "You want to join us?" she asked, pointing to the open seat on the other side of Max.

Natalie nodded, lifting her enormous purse over her head while she shimmied past Ginny. Max didn't want to give up his spot next to Ginny, but he knew the two friends would want to talk. "I'll slide over here," he offered.

"I wouldn't hear of it," Natalie said. She stopped walking and waited for Ginny to move over next to Max. At that moment, Natalie was Max's favorite person. Judging from the expression she wore, she read his mind. Once Ginny was up next to him, their knees knocking in the cramped row, Natalie winked at him. "Nice and cozy," she mused, plopping her purse onto the floor and landing on a pile of cookie crumbs.

Ginny looked over at Max and shrugged. "Nice and cozy."

Muscle memory took over, and before Max could stop himself, he'd draped his arm around the back of Ginny's chair and leaned toward her. It was an action he'd done countless times over the years, so he hadn't thought about what it would look like or mean.

"All right, Buckeyes," Mona greeted from a tiny podium at the front of the room. She wore one of the ugliest Christmas sweaters Max had ever seen, blood red with a sequined Rudolph on the front. When he stared at it too long, it made his eyes water. "Let's call the meeting to order." Mona banged her fist on the podium, causing it to wobble.

A hush fell over the room as Mona got the group's attention. From behind him, Max heard Mrs. Sanders mumble something to the women in her party, but he couldn't make out what she said.

"We have an hour before the cleaning crew arrives, so I'll be brief," Mona said, looking down at a stack of papers perched on the podium.

"That'll be a first," muttered someone in the crowd.

Mona's head snapped up and she sighed. "Yes, Lucy. I'll try to keep it short this month." The room tittered as Lucy Jones was put in her place. Max felt bad for the older woman, as she wasn't the only townie that hated long meetings. There had been more than one occasion when Max had to sit on his hands so he didn't fidget and play with his phone.

For the first ten minutes, Mona went over the recap of their last meeting when they assigned who was doing what for the Jubilee festivities. Max tuned most of it out, since his job was pretty simple. Bring food, that was that. What had captured his attention now was the heat radiating off Ginny.

She'd settled into the crook of his arm like it was nothing. When he knew she wasn't looking, Max would study her face, counting the lines of freckles from her cheeks to her jaw.

"If you keep staring at me, I'm going to think I have enchilada sauce on my face," she said between clenched teeth. "What's wrong?"

As if he was burned, Max pulled back and put his hands in his lap. "S-s-sorry. I guess I z-zoned out." Fidgeting, Max studied the floor until he was certain his brain had caught up with his mouth.

Ginny reached out and put her hand on his and squeezed hard. "Shh, don't worry. I'm only teasing you." Her smile was warm, and it reminded Max of the first time they met at school.

It had been a similar situation, Max staring at her in wonder as he settled into his first week at school. His father had been in the Army, so Max never stayed in one place for very long. By the time high school started, his parents were ready to stay put. They'd settled on Buckeye Falls and never looked back. Well, Max never looked back. As soon as they retired, his parents moved to the sunny shores of the Gulf Coast.

Moving to Buckeye Falls for Max meant finding a permanent home. He adored the small town and all its quirks. That first week in school, kids had either ignored him or made fun of his stutter. After fumbling over his words in algebra, Max had decided it was better to be quiet and appear stupid than embarrass himself further. With his head in a book in the library, Max tried to blend into the walls.

"You know, I read that last semester for Mrs. Bricker's class. I probably still have my notes if you want them." Ginny had pulled out a chair and sat across from him like it was the most natural thing to do. "She's famous for asking about parallels to Greek mythology, so you'll want to be ready for that."

She'd met his gaze and her eyes lit up as she smiled at him. Max had never been so drawn to a woman in his life, and he'd felt intensely awkward and nervous. Licking his lips, he'd sounded out the words in his mind, hoping his body would catch up. "Th-thanks. That's nice of you." Striving to look casual, Max shrugged and smiled back.

Ginny reached across the table, her hand open toward him. "I'm Ginny, by the way. Welcome to Buckeye Falls."

Max took her hand, savoring the soft feel of her skin. "Max," had been all he could handle. Their skin touching had short-circuited his already muddled brain.

"Nice to meet you, Max. Mind if I study with you this hour? I need to prep for my chemistry exam."

Max shook his head and looked back down at his novel, which had been long forgotten. When the bell rang an hour later, he'd assumed he'd never see Ginny again. She'd done her good deed with the new kid and would evaporate into the ether. Fortunately for Max, he'd misjudged her kindness. They met up again a week later in the library, starting a routine he was all too happy to follow. They'd sit together every day, and the fact that she'd save him a seat melted his heart. It had proved to Max that there was sweetness in the world, and in Buckeye Falls her name was Ginny.

"A group of us are going to the new drive-in movie theater this weekend. Do you want to join us? You could meet some more people."

Despite the fact it was a group outing, Max had felt like he'd won the lottery. He nodded several times, willing his tongue to cooperate. "Yeah, that s-s—" He hesitated as the letters faltered on his lips. "Sounds nice," he'd finished with more effort than he wanted to admit.

Ginny pulled a sheet of paper from her notebook and jotted down her phone number. "Awesome. This is my number. Give me a call tonight, and I'll give you the details." She'd tucked the paper into the front pocket of his jacket and smiled. "If my dad answers, don't worry about him. He's a teddy bear." She spun on her heels and started back down the hall. Over her shoulder, she'd said, "Just be yourself, Max."

Max never forgot her kindness, and he fell in love with Ginny that afternoon. It took him months to get the courage to ask her out on a proper date, because he was too nervous. Yes, she was gorgeous, with a head of wild wavy hair and a smattering of freckles, but her heart made her special. It was the same heart that was beating next to him now, giving him the same patient looks she had all those years ago.

Natalie stood, shaking Max back to the present. "I just have a few things to add on behalf of the mayor," she said, a smile plastered to her face. Natalie scooted out of the row and headed toward the podium. While Mona's outfit was a holiday horror show, Natalie was dressed like a First Lady in a fitted skirt and blouse. "On behalf of my husband, thank you all for your help in getting this year's Jubilee together."

Ginny leaned close and whispered, "You know, it looks like Natalie should be the one running the town. She's really good." Max had to fight the shiver that raced up his spine at the feel of Ginny's breath on his ear. Unable to slow his heart rate, he leaned back and tried thinking about baseball or all of the invoices he had to pay. Anything to get out of his head and stop drooling over Ginny.

"Any questions?" Natalie asked from the podium, her megawatt smile lighting up half the community center. Max blinked, realizing he'd missed half her presentation.

A woman in the back raised her hand. Max recognized her from the diner, chicken salad with extra grapes. "What about marketing? Last year's Jubilee attendance dipped for the first time in ten years. How are we going to make a profit if no one knows what we're doing?"

Before Natalie could answer, Mona jumped back up to the podium and waved. "I can answer that question, Agnes. We have our very own marketing guru here to help, Ginny Sanchez." Gesturing toward Ginny, Mona looked as proud as a peacock. "Of course, we have Ginny's skills Sonny Bono," she declared.

Ginny bit her lip to keep from laughing. "I think she means pro bono," she said under her breath. Max felt a ripple of laughter escape him, which he tried to cover with a cough.

"Sonny Bono's dead," Agnes lamented from the back row. "I hope we have better entertainment than a dead man."

Mrs. Sanders interjected with her own thoughts on the late crooner. "He wouldn't be worth the expense if Cher wasn't with him."

Ginny cleared her throat, standing to address the room. "Good evening," she said in what Max assumed was her business voice. It was a matter-of-fact tone that cut to the far corners of the crowded space. Everyone stopped talking, their attention entirely on her. "I'm Ginny Meyer," she carefully corrected, "and as Mona said, I'll be helping with the marketing."

Agnes, finally understanding no one was coming back from the dead, raised her hand. "I'm not looking a gift horse in the mouth, but what's your experience?"

Before Ginny could rattle off her credentials, Mona interjected. "Agnes, this is Harold's daughter. You remember."

Agnes slapped her hand to her forehead and guffawed. "Of course, Max's ex-wife." Despite the fact that Max didn't mind the reference, he knew it bothered Ginny.

Getting to his feet, he jumped to Ginny's defense. "Well, Ginny is her own woman and an absolute dynamo. And I can say with the utmost confidence that we'll have the best Jubilee in years with her at the helm." A small round of applause filtered around them as everyone drew their attention back to Mona.

"I share in Max's confidence about Ginny's skills. We will send an update on the marketing plan in the weekend's e-newsletter. Until then, please enjoy some cookies and refreshments. Good night, everyone." Mona waved and gathered her papers.

From Natalie's chair next to Ginny, Natalie grasped her arm. "I'm so glad you're here. I know it's exactly what we need to breathe new life into our marketing. The days of hanging up fliers at the grocery store are over; we need to do social media, email blasts, the whole nine yards." Leaning over to Max, Natalie continued. "And when you have a minute, let's talk about the menu."

Max nodded. "You know where to find me."

Natalie's phone chimed, and she retrieved it from her bag. "It's Anthony. The kids are ready for bath time. I should go." She stood, hoisting her purse up on her shoulder. "How about I swing by the diner tomorrow before the lunch rush, does that work for both of you? I can kill two birds with one stone."

Without thinking to ask Ginny, Max agreed and asked Natalie to stop by at 11:30. "That should give me time to get the menu draft from CeCe. We'll see you then."

Natalie placed a manicured hand over her heart and sighed. "That girl is a freaking miracle worker. Don't ever let her go."

Max grinned. "I don't intend to."

Giving a final wave, Natalie disappeared into the crowd. Max looked at Ginny and saw her face had fallen. "Oh geez, I'm such an idiot. I didn't ask if you'd be free tomorrow. I know there's a lot going on with Harold's surgery prep, and I just …"

Ginny leaned down and scooped up her purse. "Where's the exit?" she asked, not bothering to look up and make eye contact. Max gestured toward the rear of the room, where fortunately no one was standing. Ginny didn't wait to see if he would follow. She tucked her coat under her arm and plowed ahead.

When they reached the parking lot, Max took in a gulp of cold air. The community center had gotten stuffy, and being so close to Ginny had brought his temperature up a few degrees. Ginny's eyes flashed with fire. "Why didn't you correct people? You're going to make it that much harder for me to leave. And don't you dare set my schedule. You're not my boss." She whirled her arms about, slicing the air into cross sections. An angry blush colored her cheeks, and her chin wobbled from holding in tears. "You don't know what it's like, Max. You don't."

Max stepped forward, unable to hold back his own mounting frustrations. "I don't know, Gin, because you n-never tell me." His voice was hoarse, but he kept the tone low, willing his mouth to cooperate. "You l-l-left—you didn't say a word. I don't know how to act around you when you've been a g-ghost for the last two years." He raised his hand, waggling two fingers to punctuate his point. He prayed to any god or deity that existed that she had missed his last stammer. It was bad enough sounding tongue-tied, but Max certainly didn't want to sound like a character on *Scooby-Doo.*

Ginny stomped forward three paces and jabbed Max in the chest with her index finger. "I've been a ghost these last two years? That's rich. What about you? Huh, Max? I don't recall seeing your face or hearing your voice. Two can play the ignoring game, you know." Crossing her arms over her chest, Ginny let out a tired breath, her speech having exhausted her.

Max ran a hand through his hair and chewed on his bottom lip. Everything Ginny said was news to him. The notion that she expected him to find her, to reach out to her, was such a shock he almost laughed. Not only had Max driven up to New York, he'd picked up the phone so often it was comical. Every time something bad happened, he wanted to share it with Ginny. Every time something good happened, he wanted to share it with Ginny. If a customer said something funny, or Evan cracked a new joke, he wanted to tell Ginny. He wanted her to know every facet of his life, and he never dreamed she still felt the same way. Honestly, it baffled him.

"What was I supposed to t-think? You left me on Christmas Eve and sent divorce papers before champagne on New Year's. Gin, you b-b-blindsided me. I thought I was doing what you wanted, leaving you alone." Max slumped on the hood of his car, taking a moment to clear his thoughts and slow his racing heart. Being stuck inside a defective washing machine on the spin cycle would be more relaxing.

Ginny tugged at the bottom of her sweater, worrying a piece of fabric between her fingers. "We felt like strangers. You were always at the diner, and I was always working on proposals. I thought I was doing the right thing. I thought I was avoiding the trap of my …" Her mouth clamped shut and she didn't pick up her argument. Instead, she threw her head back and looked up at the clear, cool December sky. In the fading light of the community center's lights, Ginny looked like an angel. She was aglow in the dark space, her sweater casting her in a red haze. She looked ethereal.

Max stood, leaning away from his car. "You didn't finish your thought," he said carefully, stepping toward her. His steps were measured, as if he were trying not to scare away a frightened animal. In that second, Ginny looked nearly feral.

"It's not worth finishing," she whispered. The temperature had dropped, and her words puffed out in a hint of steam before disappearing into the night.

Max balled his fists at his side, forcing himself not to shake Ginny by the shoulders. When they'd had arguments in the past, they usually ended like this. Ginny was on the cusp of telling a truth she was always too afraid to verbalize. It shouldn't surprise Max that she petered out again tonight, but it still hurt. He wanted Ginny to have enough fight in her to put forth the effort to save their relationship—at the very least to attempt civility.

Behind them, the doors to the community center opened and people poured out. Ginny blinked before stomping toward Max's car. She yanked on the door handle twice before he could fumble with the keyring to unlock the doors. Ducking her head, she slid into her seat and slammed the door. The bang echoed throughout the parking lot.

Max glanced over his shoulder and saw that no one was too close to have seen their fight. Buckeye Falls was known for their gossip train, and he didn't want to board. Gently opening the driver's door, Max got behind the wheel and turned on the car. The chorus of a familiar tune blasted through the speakers, but Ginny reached out to turn off the radio before he could. Their fingers grazed for a second before she snatched back her hand and started fumbling with her sweater again.

Driving back to Harold's, Max kept his eyes on the road. He didn't talk about the Jubilee or their fight or how being with Ginny made him feel alive for the first time in years. Max never felt whole if she wasn't by his side. Regardless of their spat, she owned his heart and his soul. He needed her back, but if their time together this season continued like tonight, he knew it was a losing battle. He needed to figure out if getting her back was even possible.

CHAPTER 7

"I never finish an argument," Ginny muttered, tossing her purse onto the kitchen table and rummaging for the rest of Max's wine. "I'll show *you* never finish an argument." She pulled a glass from the cabinet and hesitated, instead grabbing the bottle and wrenching the cork out with her teeth. Taking a healthy slug, she slumped back on the counter and coughed when the alcohol hit her throat.

"I see the planning meeting went well." Harold chuckled from the doorway, wearing his pajamas.

Placing the bottle on the counter, Ginny stepped forward and shook her head. "I'm so sorry. Did I wake you?"

Harold waved her off and padded to the fridge, where he retrieved a beer and gestured for the kitchen table. "Not only is it barely nine o'clock, but it looks like we're drinking tonight." Not waiting for his daughter to answer, he pulled out his chair and eased onto the cushion with a grimace. While he didn't complain, it was clear that his surgery couldn't come soon enough.

Ginny grabbed the wine and joined her father, snagging a juice glass on her way past. Drinking alone with the bottle was one thing, but having her father as an audience took some of the wind from her sails. "So, what are we talking about? The Cavs? The Browns? The current state of U.S. politics?"

Harold popped the top of his beer and took a sip. "Wow, you really do want to depress me, Ginnybread." The records of her father's favorite teams were almost as depressing as her love life. "You're the one coming home and stomping around like a toddler having a temper tantrum. What gives?"

Suddenly the label on the wine seemed fascinating. Ginny picked at it with her fingernail until Harold cleared his throat. "I literally have all night. I'm retired now, you know."

Ginny poured wine into the glass and sipped before talking. "I'm a little wound up after the meeting. Nothing to get worried about." She patted her father's hand in a placating gesture he didn't buy.

Harold frowned. "Mona texted to say you were a hit. What happened?"

Bless Mona for her optimism, but Ginny was still raw. She felt undermined by Max, and yet she felt in the wrong for putting him in such an uncomfortable position. After the holidays, she got to return to her life in the city, but Max was stuck here with the gossips. Why did that bother her?

"I sort of had a fight with Max." She sighed. "I don't want to talk about it. Can we leave it alone?" Ginny finished her glass and topped herself off before Harold slid the bottle out of reach. He didn't say anything, just sat and drank his beer while she battled her internal monologue. The kitchen clock ticked away, keeping time with the humming refrigerator.

Finally, Ginny couldn't stand it. She jumped to her feet and paced the kitchen, trying to burn off restless energy. "Why didn't Max stop me when I left?" The question hung in the air for a moment, surprising Ginny that she voiced the thought at all.

Harold rubbed at his chin and took a moment to collect his thoughts. His eyes were downcast, his posture was rigid. "I think you need to ask Max that question."

Ginny plopped back down into her chair and placed her head in her hands. "I tried to tonight," she said into her elbows. Perhaps if she stayed hidden, Max would leave her be and she could pretend her marriage wasn't a painful subject.

"You and Max don't really fight, but you sometimes don't talk either," Harold observed.

"Tell me something I don't already know." Ginny groaned, remembering she'd promised Natalie she'd see them tomorrow. "And I need to go to the diner tomorrow to meet with Natalie. I never should have promised to help with the Jubilee. I never should have agreed to see him. What is he even thinking?"

"From firsthand experience, I can safely say that what happened between you and Max is between you and Max. No one knows what happens between a husband and wife, except for the husband and wife."

Ginny scoffed. "Unless even they don't know."

Raising a finger in the air, Harold straightened his shoulders. "Then I think we found the problem. Were you two fighting or just poorly communicating?" Ginny raised an eyebrow, but Harold continued. "Again, I speak from experience. It's easy to blame the other party, to assume they didn't care enough. But have you actually spoken to Max? Have you had a real conversation since you've been back in Buckeye Falls?"

"Geez, Dr. Phil. I had no idea I'd have both of the men in my life put me in my place." Her tone held no anger, only the fading edge of sarcasm. "I need to talk to Max, don't I?"

"Yes."

"And I need to help with the Jubilee, don't I?"

Harold finished his beer and walked to the sink. Rinsing the can, he studied his daughter in the reflection of the kitchen window. "You promised to help because you're a professional. Your skills can help a lot of people right now, people who care about you and this town. I won't have my daughter beating herself up for a misunderstanding with her ex-husband and doubting her abilities." He paused, tossing the can into the recycling bin. "But then again, I don't want you to stress out over the Jubilee. Between my hips and the holidays, I know you'll be busy while you're here. You staying sane and happy is all I want. I mean it."

Ginny felt a sudden wave of emotion as her father's words hit her. She knew he only wanted what was best for her, but that didn't mean she felt less overwhelmed. Right now, the only thing she doubted was her ability to keep her heart away from Max. So many emotions were coming to life, no longer satisfied with being buried behind a twelve-hour workday. "I don't know if I can go over there."

Harold shuffled to the doorway and dimmed the lights. He waited until Ginny rose and joined him in the hallway. He linked his arm through hers, and they walked up the stairs together. When he reached his door, he turned and met her gaze. "You can always call Natalie and reschedule. Invite her and the kids over to the house—it could be fun."

Ginny would be lying to herself if she said she wasn't tempted. But she knew Natalie would ask questions, and they were questions Ginny didn't have answers to. "No, I'll be a big girl and go over to the diner. I'll leave after the call with the doctors."

Flinching, Harold turned and walked into his bedroom. "I was hoping you'd forgotten about that."

"I'm not going to forget the main reason I'm back in Buckeye Falls, but nice try." She stuck her tongue out, much like she had as a bratty teenager. She heard her father's rumbling laugh through the door.

As Ginny tucked herself into bed, she stared up at the ceiling in her childhood room. There were holes from when she'd hung fairy lights in high school, a few scraps of tape from old boy band posters. Even after years away, Ginny could trace the familiar cracks in the ceiling from memory. So much had happened with her and Max over the years, but deep down, she knew they weren't finished with each other. She didn't know what that meant or looked like, but as she faded to sleep, it was Max's face that entered all her dreams.

The loud clattering of pots and pans woke Ginny. Muffled profanities followed by more clattering got her out of bed and downstairs. Her father leaned over the floor where a pile of coffee grounds was scattered. "C'mon," Harold muttered as he chased the pile around with a damp tea towel.

"Good morning," Ginny greeted with a hand on his arm as she dragged him to the table. "You sit, I'll get the vacuum. Are you trying to completely blow out your hips before surgery?"

Harold leaned back and frowned. He looked worn out, like making coffee took all his energy. "Damn surgery can't come soon enough. I used to be a little worried, but now I think it'll be worth it to move around again. I feel old, Ginnybread."

Ginny placed a fresh mug of coffee in front of her father and kissed his cheek. "You're not old, you're older. There's a difference. You looked pretty young last night," Ginny offered. She dropped two pieces of bread in the toaster and went in search of the good jam.

"Last night?"

"Yeah, when you were texting with Mona." She winked at her father, who flushed and bit back a smile. "You're allowed to have friends, Dad. Maybe even a girlfriend?"

Harold waved her off. "If a man my age has a girlfriend, chances are she'd be younger than you. Mona is my …" He trailed off in search of the right word. "Lady friend? No, that somehow sounds worse."

Ginny pulled two unevenly toasted slices from the toaster and carried them to the table. "I'm adding a new toaster to your Christmas list," she mused.

Harold slathered his bread with butter and jam, clearly not bothered by the ugly toast he was about to eat. "So, are you going to the diner this morning?"

"Talk about a Mona subject change. I'm getting

whiplash."

"Mona isn't going anywhere; you're going to be late." Harold sipped from his coffee and smiled. "I'm glad you're going over there. You and Natalie are quite the dynamic duo. Remember those science fair displays you girls did in high school? Plus, CeCe could use the help. She works miracles, but she's only one woman."

Going down Memory Lane wouldn't distract Ginny from more praise for CeCe. Despite all her mixed emotions with Max, Ginny's pulse skyrocketed to think of him with another woman. It was all Ginny could do not to throw her mug against the wall. "I'm sure she's very busy," she muttered. "Considering how perfect she is, how does she find the time for anything? Is she up for sainthood, too?"

Harold chuckled from his perch at the table. "Uh-oh," he teased, "do I sense some jealousy?" He watched Ginny shove two slices of bread into the toaster before stabbing a stick of butter with a knife.

"I'm not jealous," she insisted.

"Then maybe stop taking out your frustrations on my butter. That's my last stick." Harold raised an eyebrow as Ginny surveyed the damage her knife had inflicted.

"Sorry," she mumbled.

"There is no reason to be jealous of CeCe. She's been the best right hand to Max, but you're still his girl. Always will be, if you want my opinion."

This statement brought Ginny's blood pressure rising, but for completely different reasons. A tiny grain of hope bloomed in her chest. "I'm not his girl, Dad. I probably broke his heart when I left."

"No probably about it," he concluded.

"Well, I won't start that conversation now. Especially since Max has moved on and found someone so freaking wonderful." Ginny collected their plates and put them in the dishwasher. "I'm getting dressed, be down in a minute."

An hour later, Ginny was behind the wheel of her rental car and pulling into the diner's parking lot. When she stepped onto the concrete, her feet slid on a patch of ice. She reached out for something to steady herself, instead sliding headfirst into the young waiter she met earlier.

"Hey there," he said, reaching out and steadying Ginny as she found her footing. The heels of her boots slid under her. "Careful. I was just coming out to salt the parking lot again."

Ginny caught her breath as she pulled free. "Thanks, that was a close one."

"No worries, I'm glad I was here. Max would never forgive me if you fell." He stuck his hand out and grinned. "I'm Evan, by the way. Nice to meet you, Ginny."

Ginny took his hand and gave it a quick shake. "Nice to meet you, Evan. And thanks for …" Her words died on her lips when Max strode toward her, a look of concern creasing his features.

"You all right?" he asked when he reached them. "I looked out the window and saw Evan save the day."

Ginny flushed, her cheeks combusting in the morning sun. "Yep, I'm fine. Your guy Evan here has lightning-fast reflexes."

Evan offered a crooked grin, and Ginny decided she liked the kid. "I better get to salting the rest of the lot. Who knew a little snow would cause this much trouble?"

When Evan was a few paces away, Max took Ginny's hand and laid it on the crook of his elbow. "Come on. My insurance won't cover my ex-wife suing me." He winked and led the way into the warmth of the diner.

As they reached the door, Ginny's steps faltered. "Max, we should talk about last night."

Max's jaw tensed. "We do need to talk, but not now. Natalie's waiting." He kept his gaze ahead of him and dropped Ginny's arm when they stepped inside. She felt the chill of his absence immediately.

Delicious smells assaulted her senses when she walked inside. Her stomach growled, reminding her she'd only eaten three bites of terrible toast that morning. Whether

Max heard her stomach or not, he pointed to a corner booth where Natalie waited. "Take a seat, I was about to bring out a sampler of what we want to serve at the Jubilee."

Ginny patted her stomach. "Good, because I'm starving."

Max reached out and traced the lines of her jaw with his thumb. The intimate gesture curled her toes in her boots. "You need to remember to eat, Gin. You're going to waste away in front of me." Dropping his hand, he retreated to the kitchen. She could have stood there staring after him like a lovesick fool, but her musings were interrupted.

"Over here!" Natalie waved. "I snagged the best seat in the house." She moved her purse and patted the booth cushion. "Max went to grab some samples, but I thought we could talk social media while he plates everything."

Ginny was grateful for the distraction because all she wanted to do was replay that moment with Max a million times. Simple moments like that had often been taken for granted during their marriage. Thinking back, she wondered how many times Max had casually touched her and she didn't even register the action, didn't pay attention to those careful caresses when they really mattered. A thousand? A million?

"Sounds good," she agreed as she sat next to Natalie.

Natalie slid a manilla envelope toward Ginny and shrugged. "I already have a few things mapped out, but I want your professional opinion." Despite her nonchalant attitude, Ginny could tell Natalie was nervous.

A part of Ginny was nervous too. If she really was there to be the marketing wizard, she didn't need the mayor's wife coming up with her own ideas. But all of Ginny's concerns evaporated as soon as she looked at the first mock-up for social media posts. Everything was planned and scheduled, including possible images. Granted, it wasn't the same caliber as what Ginny was used to seeing in New York, but Natalie definitely knew what she was doing.

"Natalie, these are really good ideas." Ginny retrieved a

pen from her purse and started circling the portions that were ready to use.

Natalie sipped from her glass, clearly embarrassed. "You don't have to humor me, Ginny. If this is trash, I want you to tell me."

Ginny finished making notes and slid the pages back to Natalie. "I wouldn't lie to you, trust me. Since my name is attached to this, I won't let you push something bad. This plan makes sense, I just added a few notes to streamline things. See?" Ginny pointed to her changes in the margins, and Natalie visibly relaxed.

"That makes a lot of sense. I can see why you're such a big shot in New York." Natalie's words were genuine, and they made Ginny feel ten feet tall. Sure, she'd received promotions and praise from Lana over the years, but there was something special about having a friend notice her abilities.

"Thanks, that means a lot."

Natalie turned in the booth and smiled. "Now that the pesky work is out of the way, you can tell me what is going on with you and Max. Don't think I didn't see how you two looked at each other. Is something going on there?" It was like they were back in high school, and Ginny didn't know if she wanted to laugh or cry.

"Here we go," Max said as he placed two platters in front of them. Each platter was filled to the edges with different treats. The first tray had savory food, from sandwiches and sliced vegetables to a pastry that looked like it was stuffed with cheese. The other tray had sweets, from chocolates and brownies to various cookies.

Natalie wasted no time, grabbing one of the cheesy pastries and eating it in one bite. "Needless to say," she said around the mouthful, "CeCe has to make at least a thousand of these." Natalie swallowed and wiped her mouth before eating a second piece just as quickly. "Ginny, you need to try these. They are now famous in Buckeye Falls."

Max smiled, clearly pleased with Natalie's reaction.

"CeCe has been working on these for years, and we can never keep them around for more than a couple of hours. I don't even bother putting them on the menu anymore because they're gone before word gets out."

Ginny reluctantly picked up a piece, hoping it would taste like garbage. No such luck. As soon as the savory filling hit her taste buds, Ginny knew the hype was justified. "Oh my gosh," she said, wiping at crumbs as they landed on her lap. "This is sinful."

Max pulled a pen from behind his ear and made a note on the clipboard he was holding. "All right, so that's a firm yes on the cheesy bites."

Natalie grabbed a third one and popped it into her mouth. "Frankly, we could serve only these and no one would complain."

There was no doubt that Natalie was right, and it made Ginny hate CeCe a little bit more. "Where is the chef, anyway?" she asked, striving to appear casual. If Ginny had seen the wonder woman on her last visit, it hadn't registered.

Max wrote something else before looking up to meet her gaze. "Oh, she's off this morning. I have her covering the dinner rush so I can bring Harold his dinner."

"That's so thoughtful," Natalie cooed, taking the words right from Ginny's mouth.

But that was Max, wasn't it? Always putting others' needs first. It's a notion that should have made Ginny feel warm inside, but instead the cheesy bite curdled in her stomach. At one time, Max thought she hung the moon. Ginny had been so career-focused, she'd missed what was right in front of her. Now he was someone else's, and she needed to remember that.

Right on cue to deliver that reminder was Lana, in the form of a string of text messages that buzzed in her coat pocket. "Sorry." Ginny sighed and groaned at the laundry list of tasks Lana threw at her. These requests were the work of at least two people, and that's only if both were in the office and hopped up on espresso.

Max turned all his attention to Ginny. "Everything all right? It's not Harold, is it?" His concern for her father was the only thing that penetrated through her frustration. Natalie looked up from the now-empty plate of cheesy bites with a look of concern. To be fair, it could have been because the savory little morsels were gone, but Ginny knew Natalie was concerned for her.

Striving to keep her tone light, Ginny shrugged. "Work stuff."

Natalie nodded, seeming to understand all the meaning in those two words. Max was less forgiving.

"I thought you had this time off to take care of Harold. They didn't give you leave?" There was a lot of weight in his words, based on years of watching Ginny work herself into a stupor. She nibbled on her lip, stalling for time because she didn't have a good answer. And she certainly didn't have the answer that Max wanted to hear. "Tell them you need the time, Gin." His voice was lower, so only Ginny could hear.

Standing to her feet, Ginny slid from the booth with her phone clutched in her hand. "I'll be right back." She raised her index finger and smiled at Natalie. "Think you can hold down the fort for a few?"

Natalie nodded, gesturing to her own stack of papers next to Max's clipboard. "We've got enough to keep us busy, but don't think we're finished with our discussion." Ginny knew enough about Natalie to know their conversation was far from over.

Max caught up to her, gently reaching for her hand. "Why don't you use my office? The last thing I want is you slipping on the ice again." Without waiting for her response, he guided her back through the kitchen and opened his office door. "Take all the time you need," he said. Before he left, he stood in the doorway and studied her for a long moment.

Afraid to breathe, Ginny kept hold of his intense gaze and felt her insides churn for a much more pleasant reason.

"Max, I …" but her words were cut off by a new string of buzzing coming from her phone.

Max shrugged and closed the door behind him. There were far too many memories just like this moment. A pending work emergency pulling her from time with Max. He never put up a fight, and that somehow made it so much worse.

Suddenly the door swung open and Max strode in, closing the door behind him. "You know what," he said as he plucked the phone from her hand. "Do you really need to take this?" he asked, dangling the phone in front of her. "I don't want to jeopardize your career, but I also can't stand to see you so stressed."

Max held the phone until it stopped buzzing, and Ginny let out a sigh. "I don't really need to take it, but she'll keep calling if I don't answer." Right on cue, Lana started calling again. Max's knuckles turned white from clutching the phone. Ginny reached out and turned it off, placing it on the desk between them. Without the clanging from that darn device, the tiny office was silent as a tomb.

"I want to ask you something," Max said, his voice barely a whisper. Ginny nodded, too afraid to speak. "Can I take you to the hospital with Harold? I don't think you should be alone when he's in surgery."

Ginny rose to her feet and smoothed down her sweater. She didn't have to see a mirror to know that her eyes were likely as red as the fabric. She needed to get a grip, and fast. "That's really sweet, Max. But you don't have to go to the trouble."

Max rested his hands on her shoulders. "Gin, no matter what happened between us, I'm always going to be here for you. And for Harold. I don't care what a piece of paper at the courthouse says, you're s-s-still family."

Ginny watched a pained expression flit across his face and disappear.

Now the dam broke. Tears slid down her cheeks, and her chin wobbled as Ginny dove headfirst into a sobbing fit.

Max pulled her to his chest. She shook as the tears fell, enjoying the support of his arms around her waist. "I'd like that." She coughed, striving to not completely break down. "I'm still scared."

"Then I'm there," Max replied, hugging her tighter. "I'm here, Gin."

Ginny allowed herself this moment. An opportunity to cry without worrying about her father, to enjoy being close to Max again, to let out pent-up tears she didn't know she was holding. It felt so natural and right, and Ginny worried about the defenses that Max had already steamrolled. She'd only been back in town a week, and she knew she was falling for Max again. She knew she couldn't. She shouldn't. He was too sweet and kind, and he deserved better than her and her baggage. There were reasons she left in the first place, and Ginny had to remember that. The trouble was, she was starting to forget why they were important in the first place.

*

Max helped Ginny clear the kitchen table after dinner. He'd brought over a pot of soup he made at the diner. Much to Evan's chagrin, Max took the whole pot with him. "That's the perks of being the boss," he teased a deflated Evan.

From his spot at the table, Harold rubbed his belly and chuckled. "Good thing I can't eat after eight o'clock—you stuffed me to the gills, Max."

Ginny smiled at her father, handing a dried plate to Max to put away. He took the plate, being sure to reach out and run his fingers across Ginny's. He collected these stolen touches, burying them deep in his heart to revisit later. Little things gave him hope, like when she didn't pull back when he reached for her. Certainly, it could be because of the stress of the moment, but Max was glad he could be there for her.

"Remember what the doctor said, you need to stop

drinking at eight p.m. too." Ginny raised an eyebrow at her father, who had just popped the top of his favorite beer. The clock hanging over the table read 7:50. "You planning on chugging that? If we're turning this place into a frat house, I'll pull out the red solo cups."

Before Harold could argue, there was a knock at the door. "I'll get it," Max offered as he strode from the kitchen. On his way past Harold, he snagged the beer and took a pull. "Thanks for getting this ready for me," he teased.

Harold shrugged. "Can't blame a man for trying."

"Trying what?" A female voice asked from the doorway. Max watched Ginny turn to see Mona, wearing another festive, if slightly ugly, holiday ensemble.

Max could tell the notion of Harold dating shook Ginny, but she did her best to conceal her discomfort.

"Hi, Mona, what a nice surprise. If I had known you were coming by, we would have waited for dinner," Ginny said.

Mona shook her head and waved off Ginny's belated invitation. "Oh, no, thanks, dear. I was coming home from my book club and wanted to check on Harold before tomorrow." She pulled her gloves off and settled herself across from Harold at the table. He reached out and squeezed one of her hands, causing Mona to flush.

Max sipped from the beer and grimaced at the bitterness. He was a wine man through and through, but he knew Harold would hate the thought of a beer going to waste. Ginny watched him from the sink, her eyes dancing with mischief. "How about we go to the living room? You need to fill me in on the menu courses for the social media posts." Not waiting for his response, Ginny pulled a bottle of wine from the counter and took two glasses from the drying rack.

As soon as they were in the living room, Ginny took the half-drunk beer and downed it in three gulps. "Now who's ready for a frat party?" Max laughed.

Ginny covered her mouth to hide her belch, then placed the bottle on the coffee table and uncorked the wine. "Here, you look like you need to wash your mouth out." Max took the wine and sipped, enjoying the fruity flavor. "Thanks for taking one for the team back there." She nodded toward the kitchen. "Alcohol is a big no-no this close to …" Her voice caught and she busied herself with pouring more wine into both glasses.

Max watched her hand shake, causing a few drops of wine to splash onto the coffee table. "Let me help," he offered, grabbing a crumpled napkin to blot the growing puddle. Ginny took a moment to center herself. He listened to her lengthening breaths. Her fingers were tangled together on her lap, and he wanted to pry them apart to help her calm herself.

But that wasn't why Max was there. He was going to support Ginny. This time, he was playing his cards differently. A chorus of laughter erupted from the kitchen as Harold said something to Mona. After a moment, their voices hushed, and Max couldn't hear what they were saying.

Ginny looked longingly into the kitchen. "They seem good together." The admission didn't appear to cause as much pain as Max had expected, and he felt a surge of pride for Ginny's attitude.

"I won't disagree with you." Max picked up his glass and settled back on his side of the couch. He was careful to keep a whole cushion of space between them. Ginny was opening up to him, and he didn't want to spook her. "Mona's a good person. You met her before, but I know it's been a while."

Ginny studied her hands for a moment, not looking up from her lap while she spoke. "Yeah, I might remember her. Truth be told, I didn't give a lot of thought to the residents of Buckeye Falls when I left."

Although not a surprise, Ginny's admission stung. To avoid the growing lump in his throat that would surely affect his speech, Max merely nodded. Ginny looked up for the first time since they sat down, her eyes taking in his likely sour expression. "I shouldn't have said that. I'm sorry."

"Y-y—" Max licked his lips, which had suddenly gone as dry as sandpaper. "You're only being honest."

Ginny leaned forward to place her glass on the table. She reached out and took one of Max's hands, tugging him a bit closer to her. He didn't hesitate and followed her lead. "Well, I'm not being totally honest."

Max raised an eyebrow in confusion. "You're not?"

"No," she replied. "The truth is, when I left Buckeye Falls, I was petrified. Within my first week in New York, I had gotten lost every time I tried to find my apartment, nearly got mugged on the subway, had a fight with my neighbor over the placement of my doormat, and cried every day during my lunch hour."

Forgetting his promise not to crowd Ginny, Max slid over until their legs touched. The heat from her seeped through his jeans, and he had to focus on his words. "Why didn't you call me? I could have been there in a heartbeat."

Ginny shrugged, the motion sending her hair off her shoulder and down her back. He loved seeing her hair down, literally and figuratively. She always looked more relaxed and natural when she let her messy hair do what it wanted. With a scoff, she gave him the answer he expected. "I knew you would, which is why I lied."

Max remembered that first week all too well. After helping Ginny pack up the rest of her belongings and store them in her rented truck, he'd waited for the reality of the moment to crush him. He was losing the love of his life, and instead of trying to keep her, he helped her pack. He'd regretted that decision every day since she'd left town.

The last time he'd heard from Ginny was when she texted to say she'd arrived in New York. *I'm home* was all the text read. Reading those pixilated words confirmed that Ginny considered New York her home, not the little cottage they shared in Buckeye Falls.

Not knowing the truth, Max had pictured glamorous nights on the town, with Ginny decked out in all her favorite clothes. His nightmares had been filled with visions of men in sharp, tailored suits, wining and dining, and, heaven forbid, worse, with his wife.

Three months after Ginny left, Max took a weekend off and closed the diner. He'd lied and said his parents needed him in Florida, but in truth, Max just needed to see Ginny. Harold said she was fine, but Max felt like he wouldn't believe it until they were face-to-face. Until he could see her thriving, Max couldn't relax.

In an act Max certainly wasn't proud of, he'd stolen a peek at Harold's notebook to get her address. Hopping in his car, Max took to the highway to find his girl. Despite the horrible nightmares, he was not sure what he would find when he arrived in the Big Apple. Pulling his car up to the curb in front of her building, he'd idled for a moment, trying to decide how to play his visit. Casually bumping into her wouldn't have made any sense, but neither would cornering her outside her place.

Just as Max had talked himself out of finding her, he saw a familiar form walking down the sidewalk. Since she'd left Buckeye Falls, Ginny had changed. Her hair had been cut above her shoulders, her face had been a little leaner, and her clothes a lot tighter. She'd been carrying a takeout bag in one arm and her oversized handbag in the other. It was a familiar bag, one he'd bought her years before. Seeing it with her then had made his heart melt a little. Despite her city-slicker lifestyle, she'd kept this one gift from him.

When she reached the front stairs to her building, Ginny fumbled with her keys. A woman stepping outside recognized Ginny and smiled, holding the door open. Max watched the pair exchange pleasantries before Ginny stepped inside and out of view. He knew in that instant he wouldn't follow her in. She seemed at home, like she'd finally found her place in the world.

Hazarding a glance at Ginny now, he saw more of the girl he fell in love with than the polished woman he'd seen in New York. The natural hair, the fuller cheeks, the fact that she hadn't worn heels since that first day he saw her.

This was the Ginny he knew, curled up on the couch on a cold winter evening with a glass of wine and a story to tell. Lord, how he missed these nights together. When the dinner dishes were put away and the house was quiet, they used to sit and talk for hours.

"Penny for your thoughts?" Ginny asked, pulling him back to the present.

Max cleared his throat, focusing on getting his mouth working. His stammer had shown itself enough lately. "Just thinking about social media." Downing the last of his wine, Max pushed the glass away. He was driving home, and he wouldn't have more than two drinks in one sitting.

Ginny chuckled. "Liar. I know that expression, and you're not thinking about Facebook or Instagram right now."

The words were on the tip of his tongue, begging to be released. Max wanted to tell her how happy he'd been since she'd been back in town, how much brighter his life was when she was in it. Instead, he chickened out and pulled his phone from his jeans pocket. "I was thinking that Natalie will kill me if we don't come to an agreement on what the cover photo looks like for the Jubilee."

Only hesitating a moment, Ginny stood and retrieved her laptop from her tote. "All right then, let's talk about cover photos and menu courses."

Max was both relieved and disappointed that Ginny didn't push the issue, but he knew she had a lot on her mind. Twenty minutes later, they'd agreed on several pictures and had them uploaded to all social media platforms.

"See how that green matches the font of the fliers better?" he asked, reaching across to point at the laptop.

"You're right, how did I miss that?" Ginny stared at the screen and nodded. "You're good at this."

Max shrugged. "I blame CeCe. Since I hired her, we've gotten a new menu and have painted the place. She said I needed to learn about color groupings or something like that." CeCe had been a force to be reckoned with since the moment she signed her hiring papers. At first it had caught Max off guard, having someone as his right hand who wasn't Ginny. But after a few months, they found their rhythm and Max couldn't imagine his life without CeCe, or her nagging.

"Those pictures are wonderful," Mona mused. She walked into the living room, her nose buried in her phone. "I got the alert that the Jubilee page was updated, but this is better than I hoped for."

Ginny's face lit up at the compliment, and Max was so proud of her skills. No matter how things ended, Max would always be proud that Ginny had gone after what she wanted, even though it wasn't him.

"You think so? I almost bumbled the colors, but Max saved the day."

They watched Harold shuffle into the living room. His gait was slow and his teeth were clenched. "How about I help get you upstairs for bed?" Max suggested, getting to his feet and taking Harold's arm. He tried to let the man keep his dignity, but Max couldn't stand to see Harold in so much pain.

"Actually, I was hoping I could help Harold get settled in." Mona's tone was light, but it was clear the woman wanted a few minutes alone with her man.

Looking to his friend, Max could see this suggestion wasn't unwelcome. "That would be nice." The smile crossing the older man's face was undeniable. "Besides," he said, reaching out and taking Mona's hand, "I think you two could help Mona with something."

Mona perked up, reluctantly dropping Harold's hand as she scurried to where her handbag hung. "Do you have a few minutes, Max? I really could use a favor."

Granted, he wanted to stay with Ginny a little longer, but Max was not about to turn down the offer to help Mona. "Sure, what's up?"

By now, Ginny had joined their little trio, her brow arched in curiosity. Mirroring his own question, she repeated, "What's up?"

Max watched Ginny glance to her father, whose arm was now slung lovingly over Mona's shoulder. She didn't seem bothered by their affection, and he was proud of her. Ginny could get protective over her father—and rightly so. It had been just the two of them for a while, so naturally she would want the best for her father.

"Here's the thing," Mona said, drawing Max's attention back to the matter at hand. "I left some of the promotional fliers and decorations at my friend's house." Everyone paused to see where this was going. "It's my friend Elsie, you see."

"Okay?" Ginny asked, looking more than a little confused.

"She's going out of town tomorrow morning, and I won't have a chance to swing by her place tonight." Mona frowned, reaching up and tapping her temple. "I don't like to drive too late at night."

Max shoved his hands in his pockets and leaned back on his heels. "Where does Elsie live?"

Harold extended his free hand and slapped Max on the back. "Atta boy. I knew we could count on you."

Mona grimaced. "You can say no, Max. Elsie lives in Elm River."

Biting back a groan, Max kept his expression neutral. "What side of Elm River?"

Now Mona looked like she'd sucked a lemon. "The, um, southside."

Elm River was the neighboring town to Buckeye Falls. It was just as small and was connected by a winding back road. During the right time of day, the drive was gorgeous. With the sun nearly set, it would be a long and boring drive. But he couldn't let Mona down. And judging from the look on Harold's face, he wanted a few minutes alone with Mona. Max could relate, so he did the right thing and nodded.

"I'll head out now."

Mona beamed, rummaging in her handbag for a scrap of

paper. "Here's Elsie's address. I'll text her so she knows to expect you."

Max tucked the paper in his pocket and leaned over toward Harold. "I'll see you bright and early tomorrow. Rest up."

"Thanks, son," Harold said, his eyes looking tired but content.

Ginny strode past Max and yanked on her coat. "I'm coming with you."

Max couldn't deny her offer made his chest expand. "You are?"

"Yes. I remember that drive. I'll feel better if you're not alone." Whether or not she knew, her offer made Max feel like he'd won the lottery. Being in the car alone with Ginny sounded better than an all-inclusive resort in the Caribbean.

Not missing a beat, Harold waved as he slowly turned for the stairs. "You kids have fun. I won't wait up." He winked at Max, a gesture Ginny had missed while she buttoned her coat.

Ginny stepped over and patted Mona's arm before leaning in to kiss her father's cheek. "I'll check in on you later." Turning to Mona, she added, "And don't let him eat or drink anything. He's being a little too sneaky."

"Pfft, I'm not a child," Harold insisted, although his expression said otherwise.

"You heard Dr. Ginny. Let's get you ready for bed." Mona linked her arm through his and led Harold upstairs. Their paces were steady and slow, their shoulders touching as she guided him up each step. It was a sweet sight that made Max jealous for reasons he didn't want to delve into at the moment.

When Max and Ginny stepped out into the cool air, his steps faltered. "You don't need to trouble yourself. I'm sure this is the last thing you want to do tonight."

Ginny laughed, a puff of her breath escaping in a cloud. "No, you're wrong. The last thing I want to do is be the third wheel to my father's date." Pointing toward his car, she said, "Let's roll."

Without hesitating, Max bounded down the porch steps and opened the passenger's door. He wasn't going to ignore this gift of Ginny's time. He planned to savor every moment in her company. He couldn't explain it, but there was a subtle shift between them. It was precarious at best, but Max was going to handle Ginny, and the situation, with kid gloves. She was too important to lose a second time.

CHAPTER 8

Ginny eased back in the passenger's seat, her legs stretched out in front of her. For a moment, Max was quiet. From the corner of her eye, she watched him turn onto the backroad that would take them toward Elm River and this farce of an excursion. She was not fooled for an instant. This was all about her father and Mona wanting a moment alone.

Despite not knowing about their relationship before coming back to town, Ginny had quickly discovered she was cramping her father's style. "I'm trying really hard not to imagine them doing anything untoward back there," she said with a shudder.

Max barked with laughter, the motion causing the steering wheel to jerk. "Sorry." He huffed out another laugh before dabbing his eyes with his sleeve. "That's literally the last image I need." He flashed a wide smile before returning his attention to the road.

"I don't know what's gotten into me," Ginny admitted, her finger mindlessly tracing the stitching on the car's seat. There was a buoyant sensation keeping her light, carefree. "You know what this reminds me of?"

"Hmm?" The wordless question reverberated through

the car, drawing her gaze back to Max.

She watched his arms shift as he turned the car again. The flannel shirts were not new, but the way Max filled them out was. He had always had a fairly athletic build, albeit with a little extra padding from so many hours in the kitchen, but since she'd returned, she'd seen little changes to his appearance that were hard to ignore. The stubble that peppered his jawline, the extra creases by his eyes, these were evidence of their lost years. He was certainly looking good. Not that she noticed. *Yeah right…*

When he'd held her in his office, it felt like she was protected from the world—like she could burrow away in his arms and ignore her problems. But wasn't that a funny notion, considering a couple weeks ago she'd thought of Max as one of her problems?

"You were saying?" Max asked, yanking her from her musings.

"Oh," Ginny said on a sigh. "I was thinking about when we'd drive to Elm River in high school."

Max's smile widened, the skin around his eyes crinkling. "I remember." His voice sounded a little raspier than normal. "I don't think we ever went to Elm River with pure intentions."

"Ain't that the truth." She had no idea why she was taking them down this particular path of conversation, but here she was, throwing the doors wide open and exposing her thoughts to Max. "Those were good times." The truth escaped her lips in a whisper.

Silent for a moment, she wondered if Max had heard her. Before she could change the subject, Max replied, "No, Gin. They were the *best* times." His fingers flexed on the steering wheel as he maneuvered them around a bend in the road.

"When was the last time we were back here?" Ginny couldn't keep the question inside; it practically crawled out of her.

"Probably three years at least."

She didn't doubt him, as Max always remembered. While

some of her girlfriends would lament their partners forgetting their anniversaries and birthdays, Ginny always knew Max would surprise her. It wasn't that she didn't think about the good times now, but she couldn't pinpoint certain details like Max could. He was practically the librarian in their relationship, cataloging every moment and filing it away for safekeeping.

As the car stopped at a red light, Ginny looked outside. This was a quieter part of town, with a row of houses on either side of the street. Each house was decorated for the holidays, with lights twinkling all around them. It was hard not to feel the holiday spirit when it surrounded them.

Before Max could accelerate when the light turned green, Ginny saw the old ice cream shop on the corner. "Pull over!" she shouted, leaning forward and slapping her hand on the dashboard.

Max jumped beside her but did as he was told. "Jesus, Gin. What is it?" He put the car in park and turned to face her. His eyes shone with concern, his hand instinctively reaching out to touch her arm. "You s-s-scared the hell out of me."

Shaking her head, Ginny felt guilty for startling him. "I'm sorry, but look." She hitched her thumb over her shoulder at the small shop and smiled. "Remember?"

At her words, Max's face morphed into an expression of pure joy. "Of course, I do." He turned the car off and pocketed his keys. "Looks like they're still open."

Ginny hadn't meant for Max to stop for ice cream, especially in forty-degree temperatures, but she wasn't going to argue. Clambering from the car, her feet slid on a patch of ice. Max was by her side in an instant, steadying her and holding her firm. "Thanks," she said, her gaze locking on his. Despite her brain telling her it was a bad idea, Ginny felt herself leaning into Max's embrace. This was becoming too familiar, too comfortable. The feel of Max's hands shouldn't still have this effect on her. Yet here she stood, with oatmeal in her skull and a jackhammer in her chest.

The ice cream shop was lit up like it was the middle of summer. Oversized plastic ice cream cones flanked the entrance, and the air smelled like waffles and hot fudge. Ginny's mouth watered as she stepped inside, Max hot on her heels. She was delighted to discover the same older woman behind the cash register, a paper hat on her graying head. She and her husband owned the shop and were staples in the community.

"Good evening," she said with a wave. When she registered who they were, she clapped her hands and squealed. "I haven't seen you two in ages. How have you been? Come on in!"

Ginny flushed at the owner's reaction, but could not fight the smile on her own face. "We're good," she said, not bothering to step out of Max's grip. Since he'd steadied her by the car, his hand hadn't left her arm. Now she leaned into him as she glanced into the glass display cases. A rainbow of confections glinted back at them, all tempting her with more calories than she needed in a lifetime.

"We *are* good," Max said beside her, his grasp tightening slightly.

This felt so pleasant, perusing ice cream flavors like it was the most important task of their day. It was the perfect distraction from her father's impending surgery. Not to mention, it felt good being with Max in easy company. There was no fighting, no tension. They were two people out for a little treat. *Be careful,* her heart screamed. *You don't want to hurt him again.*

"Let me guess," the woman said with a mischievous grin. "I know it's been a while, but I think I remember." She tapped the side of her head and stared, looking like a fortune teller about to drop a truth bomb from the great beyond. Ginny doubted the woman could remember their orders, but it was fun to play along.

"I'll be impressed if you remember, Gloria." Max stepped up, pulling Ginny closer. She wasn't surprised he remembered the owner's name, but then again that was Max for you. Thoughtful, always thoughtful. It's funny how she'd forgotten that.

Gloria snapped and pointed to Ginny first. "Mint chocolate chip in a cone, whipped cream and two cherries." Before Ginny could confirm her order, the woman turned to Max and said, "Rocky road in a dish with caramel sauce."

Max chuckled. "All right, I'm officially impressed."

Ginny scoffed. "I couldn't even remember my order."

"Coming right up," Gloria said and went to work making their desserts. Despite her age, she was nimble and operated the spring-loaded scoop with the accuracy of a marksman on a shooting range. She was the Annie Oakley of ice cream.

Leading the way toward the front window, Max pulled out a chair for Ginny and they settled in for their treats. "This place looks exactly the same." She noticed as she looked around. Despite the holiday season and near-freezing temperatures, the ice cream shop remained open all year round. Back in the day, she and Max would drive out for ice cream and a break from their routine. It was a simple outing, one that usually ended with cherry-flavored kisses.

Wordlessly, Gloria delivered their sundaes. Max pressed a twenty-dollar bill into her hand and winked. "Thanks, Gloria."

She flushed and pocketed the money in her pink apron. "You kids have a good night."

"We will," Ginny and Max said in unison.

She couldn't help herself, she actually giggled. Sitting here and now, Ginny felt like her old self for the first time in a while. Her mind might be racing with a million competing thoughts on her relationship with Max, but she could not—and would not—deny she was having fun.

Max dug his spoon into his ice cream, a string of caramel trailing behind. As he took a bite, the sticky sauce clung to his growing beard. Without thinking, Ginny leaned across the table and swiped at the spot with her thumb. "You have a little …" Her words faltered as Max's tongue darted out of his mouth. How had she forgotten what an inviting mouth he had? His lips were plump and fit perfectly against her own. *Woah, girl! Slow down.*

Clearing his throat, Max's gaze slid to her lips. *Did he want to kiss her too?* Suddenly Ginny longed for their high school days, when all they had to do was glance at the other to know what they were thinking. Now it was all too raw, too muddled. History and the time apart made things too complicated. Idly she wondered if it were possible to even try again. Was that old adage about not going home again true? Ginny feared it might be.

"Thanks," he breathed, his throat bobbing as he swallowed.

God, even his throat looked erotic in the fluorescent lighting of the ice cream parlor. She turned and hoped to find a distraction outside the window. Unfortunately, with the bright lighting of the shop and the night sky outside, the image of the pair reflected back. The scene was cozy, intimate. Bending toward each other, their knees knocking under the table, they looked like they belonged together.

No, that was wishful thinking—lustful even. Ginny was drooling over her ex-husband like a horny teenager, and it had to stop. Yet for all her chastising, she knew it wasn't that simple, because things with Max had never been simple. The thing now was, she knew he would be worth the effort. She just had to decide what to do about that.

*

Max thought he was having an out-of-body experience. Maybe he'd died and was stuck in limbo, hovering over his body like a ghost in an old movie. It was the only thing that could explain what was currently happening. Ginny stared at him with an expression that he knew, fondly and intimately. She was into him, and he had no idea what to do.

Nearly choking on a hunk of nuts and marshmallows, he asked, "How's your ice cream?"

Ginny slurped a blob of whipped cream from her cone. "Sinful," she mused.

Yeah, sinful just about covered it. Max took a moment to studiously examine his own dessert as he struggled to catch his breath. Things with Ginny over the last week had yoyoed in every conceivable direction. One minute they were fighting, the next they were ignoring each other, and now apparently, they were provocatively eating ice cream in the middle of nowhere Ohio.

A buzz in his coat alerted Max to a text, and he debated checking his phone. Before he could decide, Ginny's phone beeped from her purse. They looked at each other and froze. "That can't be good." She huffed as she retrieved her phone.

Max beat her to it, opening a text from Harold. *don't worry, kids. Elsie dropped the decorations off at the center. have fun!*

"Yeah, we've totally been had," Ginny said on a chuckle.

Max froze, waiting for her reaction to morph into something less amused, something more hurtful. But to his pleasant surprise, she simply turned back to her ice cream and hummed as she ate.

As Max ate the last of his ice cream, he heard the squeaks of Gloria's sneakers on the tiled floor. "I hate to say it," she said as she joined them at the table. "But I might have to lock up early. It's been a long day, and I'm knackered."

"Not a problem, Gloria." Balling his napkin up, Max tossed it into his empty bowl and gathered Ginny's trash. He walked to a trashcan before helping Ginny with her coat and scarf, his hands resting on her shoulders longer than was necessary. He savored the extra moment of closeness.

"Seriously, thanks for staying open. This has truly been delightful," Ginny said.

He believed Ginny as she allowed him to help her with her things.

The older woman's lips quirked. "I saw you two in the parking lot, and I had to see you. It's been a rough year, you know." With her hand, she waved to the space around her.

"I lost Fred, so the shop doesn't feel quite the same."

Ginny splayed a hand over her heart and gasped. "Oh no, I'm so sorry."

Max remembered the older man. He was roughly the same height as Gloria, and together they ran the shop. Having lost Ginny to divorce had been painful enough. Knowing she could be gone forever like Fred brought a knot to his chest that he tried to avoid.

Repeating Ginny's condolences, Max added, "Is there anything we can do?"

Gloria shook her head, her eyes still smiling. "You are both darlings to ask, but I'll be fine. Our kids come up on the weekends, and to be honest, I am not ready to move on. This was our place, and when I'm here, I feel like Fred is still with me."

Ginny offered a watery smile. Turning to Max, she caught his eye, but he couldn't read her expression. There were a lot of emotions in that gaze.

"It was good to see you." Ginny reached out and clasped the woman's hands in hers. "Thank you for staying open a little longer for us."

"Anything for love, dear. Fred and I adored watching couples come in. I know we sell ice cream, but love is sweeter than anything else." She winked as she stepped back and opened the door. Max put his hand at the small of Ginny's back and guided her into the cold night air.

He'd be full of sprinkles if he said the other woman's words didn't hit their mark. Love did make everything sweeter. That was especially true when the person you love felt the same way. Max wasn't naïve enough to think one ice-cream cone would patch up his relationship with Ginny, but it felt like a damn good place to start.

When they got into the car, Ginny buckled up. "I guess we should head back, if that's okay."

"Sure," Max said as he turned on the car and fidgeted with the knobs for the heat. He was distracted, his thoughts ping-ponging between Fred and Gloria's love story and theirs. It killed him not to know what Ginny was thinking, but he still wasn't ready to poke the bear. This evening had felt like heaven, and he wanted to stay in the land of make-believe.

Ginny turned on the radio, and Max was surprised when she chose a Christmas station. She leaned back and hummed along to a song about miracles and wishes, her head tilted toward the side. Lost in the moment, he nearly missed the sight of a deer crossing the road in front of them.

At the last second, he slammed on the brakes and threw his arm across Ginny to protect her from the potential impact. He felt her frame lurch forward against his arm, and he nearly lost the contents of his stomach all over the steering wheel. Fortunately for them—and the deer—the car stopped just in time. After swallowing past the bile in his throat, Max found a few words—or at least syllables.

"G-G-Gin." Max felt his tongue sticking to the roof of his mouth. His brain felt too foggy to articulate anything.

"Holy shit!" Ginny gasped, frantically looking through the windshield. The deer stared at the car, the beams of the headlights reflecting off its glassy eyes. After a moment, it turned and galloped into the woods and out of sight. The last thing Max could make out was its cotton tail bobbing away.

Maybe it was the adrenaline of the moment, maybe it was the belly of sugar and the smell of Ginny's perfume, but Max couldn't hold back his reaction. He pulled over to the shoulder and turned on the four-way flashers. His hands shaking, he reached out and took one of Ginny's hands and squeezed before bringing it to his lips and kissing the inside of her palm. The sensation of her warm skin calmed him slightly, but the moment still shook him.

"Are you o-k-k-kay?" he asked, his eyes scanning her for injuries.

Shaking her head, Ginny scoffed. "That was insane."

"I'd s-s-say."

Ginny's eyes turned soft as she took in his haggard

expression. "Are you okay? Those were some lightning-fast reflexes."

"Yeah, I'm f-f-fine," he lied. While it could have been worse, Max knew he was uneasy. The notion of something happening to Ginny, especially after learning of poor Fred's demise, shook him to his core.

"You don't look fine," Ginny helpfully added. "In fact, you look like you actually killed Rudolph." She tilted her head and snag his gaze and cracked a smile. "We're all okay, Max. I promise." Her hands patted her chest in confirmation.

Finally, he felt himself exhale and sag against the seat. "That was nuts."

"Yep." She snorted, reaching out and resting her hand on his thigh. "But everyone survived. You didn't kill Santa's right-hand man." When he didn't react right away, she added, "Or us. We'll live to tell the tale of our trip to nowhere and the deer who tried to kill us."

Max chuckled, slowly at first until he couldn't hold back his laughter. Ginny joined in, and soon they were doubled over in a fit of giggles. Damn, it felt good to laugh. It felt darn near orgasmic to laugh like this with Ginny. They used to be best friends. They used to laugh every day.

When they'd caught their breath, Max put the car in drive and headed back to Harold's house. He was exhausted and knew Ginny felt the same. They were hours away from surgery, but he hoped the night proved to be the entertaining distraction she needed. It certainly had been for him.

Pulling into the driveway, Max wasn't surprised to still see Mona's car. He parked beside her. Turning to Ginny, he said, "Potential holiday homicide aside, this was really nice."

He held his breath and waited for Ginny's reaction. She offered a genuine smile as she leaned down to gather her purse. "It was perfect. Really, Max. I had a good time."

"Let me walk you to the door."

"Worried about that Buckeye Falls crime?" She winked,

proving she was still in a playful mood.

Max shrugged, not caring how corny it was to walk his woman to the door. "Nah, just wanted to make sure you don't slip in those silly boots."

Ginny glanced down at her feet and frowned. "I love these shoes. I got them at a trunk sale at Saks last year."

"And I'm sure they're great when it's not an ice-skating rink outside."

"Haha. If it will make you happy, I'll let you walk me to the door."

"If this was high school, you know I would."

Ginny smirked. "If this was high school, you'd be doing more than walking me to the door."

In the close confines of the car, Max didn't miss the flush creep up her cheeks at the mention of their former dates. There were very few nights out that didn't end in passionate kisses and stolen moments. What Max wouldn't give for one of those now.

Whether sensing where his mind had gone, or merely leaning into the moment, Ginny didn't move to get out of the car. She was close enough that he could count the freckles on her neck, and he wanted to trace the path with his tongue. *I really need to get a grip.*

Ginny licked her lips. "Max, I …"

But she didn't have the chance to finish her thought, because Mona was there knocking on the car window. Both jumped at the intrusion, and for the first time he wished Mona was anywhere but in Buckeye Falls.

Ginny blinked and pulled back, opening the car door and stepping out to join Mona. "How's Dad?" Ginny asked, not bothering to hide her concern.

"Oh, he's fine. Just fell asleep."

Max couldn't tell if Mona was embarrassed about interrupting them or lying about getting them out of the house, but she groaned. "Thanks for giving us a few moments. But please know, I really did need those decorations."

Ginny hiked her purse up her shoulder and shook her head. "Do not worry about it, Mona. We had a nice time."

"I won't keep you," Mona said as she backed toward her car. "I know tomorrow is a big day."

Max saw Ginny's shoulders sag and her expression shift to something he couldn't decipher. It was clear she was kicking them both out, and he wouldn't delay the inevitable. The night had been a pleasant surprise in more ways than one. "I'll be here by eight tomorrow to help you get Harold downstairs. He'll be grumpy from lack of caffeine and food."

Ginny's mouth opened, but she snapped it shut. "Sounds great, thanks."

Before she could escape, Mona pulled Ginny against her in a powerful bear hug. "Thank you for coming home to help Harold. And for all your work with the Jubilee. I hope you know how much we all appreciate it." The older woman's voice hitched.

Ginny looked uncomfortable, but Max couldn't tell if it was the hug or the general situation. "Can I walk you out, Mona?" He extended his elbow for her to take. "Harold would never forgive me if you slipped on the driveway."

Mona released her death grip on Ginny and flushed. "Good night, dear. You will keep me posted tomorrow, won't you?"

"Of course. Thank you both for your help," she said in parting as Max closed Mona's car door. Standing on the porch with only the light of Mona's headlights, Ginny looked so small and fragile. The red of her sweater practically bled into the night sky.

"You're sure you're okay?" he asked, standing next to his car. Ginny nodded, wrapping her arms around her torso. "Get inside and back by the fire. You'll be no good to Harold if you're a popsicle." Ginny's teeth peeked out from behind her lips—exactly the reaction he had wanted. "I'll be here by eight, I promise."

Ginny backed toward the door, never letting her gaze

drop from his. "I trust you," she said quietly. If the street wasn't deserted, Max would have assumed he misheard her. But her words rang clear, and they bolstered his resolve.

"Good night." Getting behind the wheel, Max drove home in a fog. Part of him worried about Harold, even though it was a routine operation. What he really couldn't stop obsessing about was Ginny. From their work on the Jubilee to helping with Harold, Max promised himself he would be her rock. No matter how hard she tried to push him away, he was standing firm this time. Tonight the woman by his side felt like the Ginny of yesteryear, and it was like an early Christmas miracle. A kernel of hope bloomed in his chest, and Max savored it. Things might be different this time around.

CHAPTER 9

Ginny paced through the house that night. Sleep was not an option, as she had too many competing thoughts vying for space in her muddled brain. She did laundry, triple-checked that her father's overnight bag was packed, scoured the stovetop, and gathered more firewood from the shed. She did anything to keep busy, anything to stop thinking about her father's surgery … and how excited she was to see Max in a few hours.

She was also pretending that she wasn't thinking about his lips, or the fact that she desperately wanted to taste them. God, why had she fangirled over her ex-husband like that? And why couldn't she stop thinking about how soft his flannel shirt felt on her fingers, or how safe and protected she felt in his embrace? *Get a grip, Ginny!*

During times like these, stressful times when uncertainty clouded around her, Ginny gravitated toward the kitchen. Whether over a cup of coffee or a meal, she liked to center herself in the warm space. There was something about being surrounded by happy memories and familiar scents that slowed her racing heart.

But for all the happy memories in this kitchen, there were a couple that tore her up inside. One of these memories Ginny kept hidden away because it was too much to even speak about. On a morning like this one, when no one was awake and the house was still, Ginny had watched her mother leave.

It had been in early high school, and Ginny had gotten up early to make hot cocoa since she knew she wasn't allowed to have it with breakfast. This act of quiet defiance had been about as rebellious as she'd gotten back then. And if she were honest with herself, it was as rebellious as she got now. She didn't like to cause scenes, period.

That morning she heard a quiet thud at the base of the stairs and a few muffled profanities. Thinking her mother was bringing down the laundry, Ginny got up to help, carefully covering her mug with a tea towel. "Good morning," she'd said, turning the corner and coming face-to-face with a reality she hadn't been prepared to see.

Her mother stood there, dressed in her favorite jeans and sweater, graying hair pulled back at the nape of her neck. A cloud of perfume had wafted up to greet Ginny, who'd raised an eyebrow at her mother. There'd been two suitcases splayed on the floor between them, her purse hung over the railing. "Oh," her mother said, lowering her gaze. "I thought you'd still be in bed."

Ginny shrugged, not sure why she was feeling so guilty. Even at fourteen she knew she was seeing something that was about to rip her world in half. "What's going on?"

Her mother sighed and stepped past her daughter, pulling the suitcases back to standing and grabbing her coat from a hook by the door. For a moment, she didn't say anything, just quietly buttoned her jacket up to her neck. "I'm going away for a while," she'd said to the floor, her familiar gaze not reaching up to meet Ginny's.

The month before, Ginny's grandparents had been in a slow-speed auto accident. While she hadn't heard much since then, she'd assumed her mother was off to take care of her ailing parents. "Is it Gran and Gramps?" Ginny stepped closer, instinctively reaching for her mother's hand.

A look crossed her mother's face at the question, like the excuse had never occurred to her. Licking her lips, her mother looked around the house in front of her. Carefully cataloging each nook and cranny like it was the last time she'd see it. Ginny hadn't been sure what to say, so she followed her mother's gaze from the Christmas tree in the corner to the spot on the ceiling where the heater leaked.

Finally, her mother spoke, "I'm leaving." Her sharp gaze finally met her daughter's, and Ginny shuddered at the lack of emotion in her eyes. Her father was the sweet one, the one to pull someone in for a hug while listening to their problems. He was steady and friendly, the type of man you'd want as a friend, as a father. Her mother had always been more reserved, sometimes looking down her nose at Buckeye Falls and its residents. At the time, Ginny didn't understand how anyone could feel that way, but now it brought a chill to her skin that a pot of tea couldn't warm.

That was all the explanation Ginny had gotten from her mother. She'd turned on her heel, wheeled the pair of suitcases into the dawn, and never looked back. Ginny never got a letter, call, or email. The only thing her father got was a divorce petition sent a few weeks later from California. They'd been sitting on the porch swing, wrapped in blankets, watching the trees shake in the February chill.

A black town car had pulled up to their garage, and Ginny felt both of them hold their breath. Was this bizarre nightmare over? Was her mother going to emerge from the car and everything would go back to normal? But it hadn't been her mother. It had been a man in a suit who'd approached them without a smile. "Harold Meyer?" he'd asked, not even trying to soften the news.

"Yes, I'm Harold." From underneath the blanket, her father squeezed her knee in silent support.

"You've been served," the man said, thrusting a manilla envelope at her father before taking the stairs two at a time back to his car. In less than a minute, he'd left a gaping hole in their tiny corner of the world.

Ginny waited for her father to react. To stand and scream, rip the papers to shreds. Why wasn't he fighting for her mother? Why wasn't he railing against what she'd done? But her father didn't do any of those things. He'd tucked the envelope into the side of the porch swing and wrapped his arm around his daughter. "We're going to be fine, Ginnybread. We're going to be fine," he'd assured her through his closing throat. Ginny didn't miss the hitch in his voice, and the sound gutted her.

Ginny swiped at a tear that had fallen down her cheek. All these years later, those memories still burned her. Just as she stood to get another cup of tea, her phone rang. Hurrying to answer it, she was dismayed to see it was Lana.

"Hello?" she asked, hoping it was a butt dial.

"Good, you're up. I need you to run a few reports for me. No one is answering their phones, and I need these numbers by eight."

Ginny scoffed. "Lana, I can't do that. My father is having surgery in a few hours." Ginny waited for her boss to apologize and suddenly grow a soul, but no such luck. Apparently, Scrooge hadn't been visited by the three ghosts of Christmas yet.

"What, are you performing the surgery? You'll have time to run the numbers. I need you to do this for me, then you can go back on vacation."

The vein in Ginny's temple throbbed. Not only wasn't this a vacation, but Ginny had never taken a vacation in the two years she'd worked for Lana. Sure, she'd taken an occasional three-day weekend to see her father, but never more than that. Not to mention, this wasn't a fun trip. Calming herself with a deep breath, Ginny replied, "No, you'll have to find someone else."

Lana was relentless. "No one else is answering. I need these numbers."

Ginny pulled her phone back to see it was barely six o'clock. "That's because they're probably still asleep. The office doesn't open for another two hours. Please, Lana, I need to be with my family." Her family. When Ginny said those words, she was thinking about more than her father. Max's kind face popped into her mind, and she felt herself calm at the thought of seeing him again so soon. "I have to go."

Then Ginny did something she'd never done before; she hung up on Lana. Turning her phone off, Ginny cleared up her teapot and mug and went to take a shower. She needed to be ready when her father was up.

By the time she was dressed and walking downstairs, she heard her father's voice. "I don't think a cup of black coffee is going to make a difference."

She halted halfway down the stairs at the sound of Max's chuckle. "All right, Harold, let's look at it this way. Not only will the doctors have to postpone your surgery, but you're going to have a very upset Ginny on your hands. Do you really want to disappoint her?"

Ginny smiled at Max's tone. He'd always been so patient with her father, which clearly hadn't stopped since she'd left town.

"Fine." Harold sighed. Ginny heard the clattering of the coffee pot being put away. "I'm going to watch Sports Center," he pouted.

"You know, you always said pouting doesn't look good on anyone," she teased as she entered the kitchen. Fortunately her father was dressed and ready to go. Max looked ready too, in jeans and another flannel shirt, resembling someone prepared for a Marlboro ad more than a hospital waiting room. But Ginny wasn't complaining. Flannel was quickly becoming her favorite thing.

"Good morning," he greeted her with a small paper-wrapped package. "I brought this for you." He placed it on the table.

Harold frowned. "Don't I get something?"

"Yes, a new hip in about"—Max made a show of looking at his watch—"two hours." Ginny ducked her head to hide her smile. Harold mumbled something and shuffled into the living room as fast as he could.

"You didn't have to bring me anything," she chided as she picked up the package. It was warm and smelled like butter and cheese.

"Wait until you see what's inside before you say anything." Max winked.

Ginny unwrapped the most perfect-looking breakfast sandwich she'd ever seen. Nestled between two buttery biscuits were an egg, cheddar, and bacon. "Oh my gosh, this looks amazing." She leaned over to make sure her father wasn't watching. "Didn't you bring one for yourself?"

Max shook his head and pulled out a chair for her. "Nah, I ate mine already. I was going to wait and be a gentleman, but I was starving."

Of course he'd made her breakfast. Max had always been up when they were married, trying out new recipes and making sure she had her coffee and a full breakfast in her before the long drive to Columbus. Now, sitting with him at the table and enjoying the meal he made, brought a lot of mixed emotions. "Thank you," she whispered, "this is really nice."

Max took his chair opposite her and rested his hand on hers. "You need to eat, and you need to take care of yourself. I'm not saying ice cream isn't the meal of champions, but you need protein." His lips quirked before he added, "Harold needs you to be strong. Now, dig in so he can finally get some relief from that damn hip."

Ginny did as she was told, inhaling the sandwich faster than she thought possible. It was warm and comforting, just like Max. In a lot of ways, the two men in her life were very much alike. They were supportive and kind, always there with a smile or joke when she needed it. Ginny wondered how she'd taken them both for granted over the last few years.

Once she was finished, Max ushered Harold to his car. "Get in the front seat, you'll have more legroom," he ordered.

"Don't need too much comfort today, son. They're about to slice and dice me like a Christmas ham," Harold grumbled.

Max laughed. "Don't go ruining ham for me, Harold. That image is going to stick with me all morning." He closed the door and turned to see Ginny watching their interaction. She hadn't meant to stare, but she couldn't seem to stop herself. "Ready?" he asked, jogging back to the porch to take Harold's overnight bag from her.

Ginny let her fingers trace his as he took the bag. Her eyes stung when she remembered where they were going—she couldn't reconcile their current reality. Her dad was about to go to the hospital.

"Uh-huh," she sniffed.

Max dropped the bag and pulled her into his arms. It was a fierce hug that took the air from her lungs, but it was also exactly what she needed. "He's going to be fine. In a few hours we'll watch him scold the nurses for not turning on the right basketball game. He's a tough cookie, Gin. It's going to be all right." His grip on her was vicelike, but she wasn't complaining.

Ginny rested her head on his chest and felt the rumble of Max's supportive words. He smelled piney and familiar, and she wanted to stay like that forever, leaning into his weight. Shaking herself, she stepped back and gave him a watery smile. "You're right. I'm being a bit melodramatic."

Max scooped up the bag and took Ginny's hand. "Nah, you just love him."

Ginny let Max lead the way to the car. Much like someone would treat a child, he waited until she buckled into the back seat before sliding behind the wheel and taking them to the hospital.

In a moment of weakness, she let herself pretend she still had a sweet husband who took the lead when she needed him. A husband who would take a day off work to be there for her father, who would cook and help with home projects just because he didn't want Harold to overdo it. But here was the problem—Ginny *had* had that life.

Now Ginny's eyes were tearing for a different reason. Perhaps it was the stress of the day, maybe it was Lana's pushy phone call, but Ginny felt like she wasn't where she needed to be. There was a small seed of doubt growing roots in her belly, taking hold. Was it too late for her and Max? Could she really be happy back in Buckeye Falls?

Despite the myriad of questions flitting through her brain, Ginny knew she felt more at home in that moment than she had in years. It terrified her, but it also excited her. For the first time in a long time, she saw potential for a happily ever after with Max.

*

Max had trouble keeping his eyes on the road. It was a short drive to the hospital, but every few seconds he looked in the rearview mirror to see Ginny. She was fidgeting a lot, way more than usual. Her hands kept balling and then ringing themselves, and her brow was knit in deep concentration. No matter how long they'd been apart, he could read his ex like a book.

Speaking of predictable, Harold chimed in when they drove past a McDonald's. "Oh, we could get a quick coffee there. We're so close to the hospital, I'm sure it wouldn't even get into my system." Max watched the man's expression in the window's reflection. He looked as excited as a kid on Christmas until Max kept driving.

"Honestly, Dad. I'm impressed by your dedication to caffeine. Even I didn't know you had it that bad." Ginny laughed from the back seat. Whether it was Harold's intention, his daughter relaxed a bit at his caffeine hijinks.

Max was relieved to see Ginny unwind a bit. The mood in the car shifted as soon as Max pulled up to the unloading lot at the hospital. Since this wasn't an emergency, it was a less crowded entrance. Harold sighed when Max put the car in park and got out. Jogging around the front of the car, he opened both Harold and Ginny's doors. Harold shook away Max's hand, pulling himself to stand.

"Let me do it, son. Soon enough I'll be doped up and drooling." He ran a hand through his thinning hair, squared his shoulders, and stared down the hospital like a general preparing for battle.

Ginny, on the other hand, let Max hold the door and took his hand when he offered it. He squeezed it quickly before releasing and tucking it into the crook of his elbow. He led the trio through the doors and faltered when there were two reception desks. "Do you know which one we want?" he asked Ginny.

"Short term," she said. "Fortunately, Dad's considered short term." Ginny leaned closer to Max when the receptionist popped her head up and greeted them.

She was a pleasant enough woman, with a ready smile and bright eyes. Max knew she'd frequented the diner more than once, but he couldn't place her name. "Max, how are you?" she asked, waving a hello.

"I can't really complain. Just need to get my buddy Harold checked in for surgery."

At the mention of his name, Harold eased forward and nodded. "Nice to see you, Janis. Haven't seen you since the Fourth of July parade."

Janis had lived in Buckeye Falls longer than anyone, except maybe Harold. She was a few years older than Ginny and Max, and she and her kids were very active with the town's activities. "Well, I've been busy. Jaxon got into varsity soccer. Can you believe that at barely fifteen? Then Chelsea got into chess and has tournaments all over Ohio. It's a wonder I have time to work and breathe."

Despite Janis's friendly banter, Max felt Ginny tense more and more the longer the conversation continued. When Harold asked how Janis's husband was, Max cleared his throat to interrupt. "Sorry, Janis, but do you know where we need to take Harold? I think his surgery is scheduled for the next hour."

Janis nodded and turned to her computer. "Let's see here," she muttered as she typed away on her keyboard. "Looks like you're here for a hip replacement, right, Harold?" The older man shrugged, like he didn't care what they did with him. Janis started going through a checklist of things, checking him in and verifying he hadn't eaten in at least twelve hours.

"Unfortunately, I'm thirsty and hungry as a man on a deserted island," Harold grumbled.

Janis giggled and handed him a clipboard. "I know. It must be rough with a chef like Max in the family." She winked at Max and slid a pen across the counter to Harold. "Take a seat on those blue chairs. One of the nurses will be with you in a moment."

Max guided Harold and Ginny to the waiting area, pleased that Janis considered him part of the Meyer family. It shouldn't give his heart such a lurch, but it did. Truth be told, Max never stopped feeling part of the Meyer clan. His own parents rarely visited Ohio, and he had little to no desire to spend his limited days off in the swamps of Florida. Of course, he loved his parents, but he never had much of a deep relationship.

When he'd married Ginny, Harold was there to fish and cook and talk sports anytime. Even after she left, Max was relieved when that part of his life continued. He'd never admit this to Ginny, but he thought Harold and he saved each other when she left for New York. Neither one had seen her move coming, so they mourned her together.

Before Ginny could start fidgeting, a nurse came out with a wheelchair. "Harold Meyer?" she asked the empty waiting room.

Harold made a show of looking around and finally pointed to himself. "I guess you're looking for me." The nurse smiled and walked closer, helping him into the chair.

Ginny jumped to her feet, practically stepping on Max's shoes. "Can I come back too?" She rushed forward, resting her hand on her father's shoulder. Max could see her fingers trembling, and he wished there was something he could do to distract her.

The nurse shook her head and took control of the wheelchair, easing it a foot closer to the doorway. "I'm sorry, but the family cannot come back to the surgery prep rooms. If you leave your contact information with Janis, she can call you when the procedure is done. He should be out of surgery by early afternoon."

Ginny took a step closer, her eyes growing two sizes in panic. "But I want to—" Before she could continue, Harold turned in the chair and patted her hand.

In a low voice he said, "Ginnybread, it's okay. I'll be out and doing cartwheels before you miss me." Ginny shook her head. Harold glanced up at Max and smirked. "I told Max to keep you company and distract you. You follow his lead, and you won't even notice I'm gone. Buckeye Falls has the best doctors in Ohio, and I know it'll be all right."

Ginny's face crumpled as she let the tears fall. She fell to her knees and threw her arms around Harold's shoulders. "Dad." She hiccupped into his neck as her body shook with sobs. "I just …" She coughed and kept sobbing, a series of unintelligible words slipping from her mouth.

Harold cooed and rubbed her back, letting his daughter get her tears out. To her credit, the nurse was patient and let them have their moment. Finally, she looked at Max and apologized. "I'm sorry, but I need to get Mr. Meyer prepped for surgery."

Max nodded, stepping forward to peel Ginny off Harold. "Gin, we need to let them go. It's going to be fine; you'll see."

Harold reached up and patted Max's arm, and Max thought he might break down too. Harold was like a father to him, but he was going to be strong for Ginny.

An hour after Harold left, Janis came out to tell them he'd been taken into surgery. Ginny had been pretty quiet, alternating between staring at the floor and picking at her nail polish and pacing the small waiting room. When Janis went back to her desk, Max knew he needed to take action. The thought of sitting in that cramped room with an anxious Ginny for hours seemed daunting.

Rising to his feet, he rubbed his hands on his jeans and sighed. "How about we go home and regroup?"

Ginny looked like he'd slapped her. "Excuse me? Dad's still in surgery," she accused him. "I can't leave."

Max leaned down on his haunches and met Ginny's watery gaze. "You heard Janis, so far, so good. There's nothing we can do here, other than wear a hole in the cheap vinyl flooring. Let me make you some lunch and we'll get some air. Come on, Gin."

Ginny shook her head, but she didn't say no. Max reached out and took both her hands in his. Tracing his fingers over her knuckles, he leaned closer and lowered his voice. "Do you know how ticked Harold would be, knowing you could have had a grilled cheese sandwich right now? I think you owe it to him to have a cheesy lunch in his honor."

When they were married, Max had made countless grilled cheese sandwiches for Ginny. They were comfort food, celebration food, and depression food. No matter her mood, it always brought a smile to her face, and that was a sight he needed now more than ever.

Ginny nibbled on her bottom lip, glancing toward the exit. Max knew he had her. "We'll be back in an hour?" she asked skeptically.

"Whenever you want. I promise." He released one of his hands and splayed it on his chest. "I will have you back here before he's out of surgery, and with a belly full of carbs and cheese."

Finally Ginny cracked a smile. "A girl can't really argue with that," she mused.

Max pulled Ginny to her feet and drew her close for another hug before they left. On their way out, he gave Janis his cell phone in case anything happened. Once they were in the car, he thought it would be easier to take Ginny back to his place instead of Harold's. When he got onto Main

Street, he kept driving.

Ginny looked out the window, confusion creasing her forehead. "This isn't the way back to Dad's place."

"Perceptive as ever." Max laughed. "I'm taking you back to my place. It's closer, plus I know I have plenty of bread and cheese."

Ginny turned to him. "Your place?" Her expression suggested he was taking her to Buffalo Bill's basement from *Silence of the Lambs*. He was a little disappointed, as he felt like last night they'd made headway in their relationship. There was a spark between them, and finally Max felt it wasn't one-sided. He needed to be patient with Ginny and trust she'd come around in time.

"Yes, believe it or not, I don't live at the diner. I'm also not trying to murder you, so stop looking so horrified." He kept his hands on the steering wheel, which was no small feat at that moment. He wanted to reach out and take her hand, but he focused on the road. After last night's snowfall, he needed to keep vigilant. Got to love those Midwest winters.

As he pulled his car into the driveway, Max said a prayer that he'd cleaned the place up before he left. Ginny didn't wait for him to open the door, choosing instead to bolt out like the car was on fire. She nearly sprinted to the door, impatient as he took his time fumbling for his keys.

"Rushing me won't make the surgery go faster," he said.

Ginny rolled her eyes and stomped the snow from her boots. "I know that, but it makes me feel better."

Max turned the key and waited for the deadbolt to drop. "Then, by all means, stampede over me." He laughed.

Ginny shoved his shoulder playfully, and her touch sent an electric charge straight up his spine. He had to clear his throat and take a breath before he followed her inside.

He studied Ginny as she took in her surroundings. His house was modest, even by Midwest standards. He'd never wanted anything palatial, but now he wondered what Ginny thought of his little cottage. There was only one bedroom, but he'd renovated the kitchen to take up half of the first floor.

Not wasting any time, Ginny went into the kitchen and pulled out a stool, propping her elbows on the counter. Her attentive gaze swept over the space, from the six-burner stove to the stainless-steel fridge. "This is a great kitchen."

"Thanks. You should have seen it when I bought the place. It was barely a galley kitchen, which had horribly outdated appliances. The first time I tried to make dinner, I thought I would go insane." Max shuddered at the memory.

There were other reasons he nearly went insane back then. The wounds of their divorce were still raw, his heart bleeding more often than not. He had put all his energy into making the house his own, from the kitchen design to the masculine color scheme. Since Ginny occupied so much of his mental space, he wanted to erase her from his personal space. Were he being honest, Max knew it was impossible to wipe her from his memory.

"When did you move in?" she asked, tracing her fingers along the clean surface.

Without thinking, Max replied, "Just about two years ago." Barely after the ink was dry on their divorce papers. There was a part of him that had wanted to run away, leave Buckeye Falls and everything he knew. He felt worthless, utterly alone. Then Harold had made a comment about being grateful that Max stayed, how happy he was to still have family there. That had sealed the deal for Max, and he kept his promise and stayed put. Despite all the complicated memories tied to this town, it was his home. He wasn't going to run away.

"Oh," Ginny said, her mouth making a perfect *O*. She hesitated a moment before continuing. "Well, it's a great space."

"Thanks," Max said, opening the fridge to grab what he needed for the sandwiches. He was grateful that he remembered to keep his pantry stocked, because these sandwiches would be nothing without tomato soup for dipping.

While Max busied himself with making lunch, Ginny's phone rang. Both stopped breathing while she pulled it from her purse to see who it was. "Oh, it's my boss." She sighed with relief. "Do you mind if I take this?" she asked as she wiggled the phone in the air. Max shook his head and focused on grating three types of cheese.

Ginny tiptoed into the living room to take the call. Max wasn't eavesdropping necessarily, but he could tell Ginny was stressed from her tone. "No, Lana." She groaned. "I can't right now. Please, can't you just …" There was a break in conversation while she stalked around his living room. Her feet were stomping so loudly, Max feared she'd knock a picture off the wall. "I said this morning that …no … you're not … Lana!" Ginny's voice was practically a shout as she finally said, "I told you I can't. My father is in surgery right now. I'll check in tomorrow, but I'm unavailable today. Goodbye."

Max turned back to the stove so his back was to Ginny as she stomped back into the kitchen and plopped down on the stool. "Sorry about that," she said, smoothing down her sweater. Her hands shook as she attempted to flatten the mussed fabric.

"Everything okay?" he asked, placing the sandwiches into a pool of melted butter. The heavenly aroma of butter and bread filled the kitchen, and Max kept his focus on the stove. The soup simmered and he could not wait to dig in. Stressful day or not, this was his favorite lunch. "There are some seltzers in the fridge," he offered without thinking.

"Thanks," Ginny said, walking to the fridge. Max realized his mistake when she faltered and didn't open the door.

On the front of the fridge were some of his favorite pictures with Ginny. A candid shot from their wedding day, a picture of them in Columbus during the rib festival, a blob of barbecue sauce on her lips, and a shot of the pair with Harold on the last Christmas before she left. He knew he shouldn't keep photos of the woman who broke his heart, but they brought him such joy. Parting with all the evidence of their happier times didn't seem right.

Ginny ran a shaking finger over the festival photo, her expression hard to read. "That was a really nice day," she mused. "Didn't you win the barbecue sauce competition that year?"

He did, but that wasn't what Max remembered about that day. What Max remembered was how Ginny had held his hand during the voting, how she'd laughed and danced while a bluegrass band played by the river. Max remembered the feel of her as she jumped into his arms when they'd announced the winner, how she'd yelped when he spun her in a circle. That was the day Max knew he couldn't possibly be happier. He'd achieved a professional goal with the competition, but he'd also never felt closer to another person. Ginny completed him, plain and simple.

"Yeah, it's one of my favorites. Still use that recipe at the diner." Max plated the sandwiches and motioned toward the counter. "You okay eating here?"

Ginny nodded, opening the fridge to grab a couple of drinks. She slid one toward him and gaped at the sandwich. "Don't take this wrong, but you've come a long way with your grilled cheese. This could be on the cover of *Bon Appétit* magazine," she swooned.

Ginny's praise was a balm for his soul, and Max didn't fight the smile that took over his face. "Don't get too excited, I'm still using canned soup." He placed a steaming bowl in front of her and popped the top of his drink.

Ginny didn't wait for him, instead diving right into her sandwich. After one bite, she threw her head back and groaned. It was a sound that Max had heard her make in the bedroom, and he needed to take a chug of his water to cool down. "Max, this is amazing," she raved. "Are there two types of cheese?" She pulled the sandwich halves apart, leaving a foot-long trail of melted cheese.

Max dunked his sandwich in his soup. "It's three,

actually. Swiss, cheddar, and pepper jack."

Ginny slurped her soup and was silent for a moment, letting her attention stay on the meal in front of her. Max always enjoyed watching her savor food. She was an expressive eater, letting everyone know if she was merely eating to get through the meal or treating it as a religious experience. Right in that instance, she looked like she was on a spiritual quest.

"I hope you make these at the diner," she suggested, licking a trail of grease from his hand.

"Number twelve on the lunch menu. The only thing that varies is the cheeses. CeCe makes a tomato bisque, which is literally to die for. You need to come by and try it." Ginny flinched and put her sandwich down on her plate. Max noticed it wasn't the first time that mentioning CeCe brought a shudder, but now he wanted to know why. "What's up? You seem to have something against CeCe."

Ginny looked up and took a moment to school her features. She looked around the kitchen, as if the reason for her dislike was embedded in the walls. "Is CeCe your girlfriend?" she finally asked.

Max nearly choked on his seltzer. "W-what? N-n-no. Good Lord, why would you think that?" he spluttered. The notion of CeCe being anything but a friend and colleague short-circuited his brain. The only chemistry they shared was in the kitchen. Any other suggestion was laughable.

There was no hiding the fact that Ginny slumped with relief at the news. "No reason," she lied, trying to play it cool. She couldn't hide the flush that crept up her neck, or the fact that she was balling her napkin. *Busted!*

Max could not help himself, he beamed. "You're jealous." It was a statement, not a question. He couldn't believe he hadn't thought of that before. All the times Ginny tensed when CeCe was mentioned, and he hadn't put the pieces together. He felt like a goober. A smug goober, but a goober nonetheless.

Ginny shook her head. "Nope. I just wanted to know,

that's all."

Max slid his plate to the side and leaned closer, his appetite forgotten. "Are you seeing anyone in New York?" God, he didn't think she was, but now that he asked, he feared the answer. Harold kept up with what Ginny was doing, but he doubted the man would have shared this type of detail with him over their weekly dinners. No one, especially Harold, wanted to be the bearer of bad news.

"No, I'm not." Ginny dropped her spoon, her bowl now empty. Apparently the conversation had done nothing to her appetite.

Max slowly rose from his stool, taking measured steps toward Ginny. He treated her like a wild animal, afraid if he moved too quickly, she'd spook and run away. "That's good to know," he said quietly.

Ginny's eyes dilated, but she kept her gaze locked on his. "Is it?" she asked, her voice a little squeaky. She was adorable when she was nervous.

"Yes, it is." Max couldn't stop himself as he inched closer. Finally they were barely a foot apart. He could smell the mint of her shampoo and felt the heat radiating off her skin. "It's a very good thing," he mused.

Ginny angled her head up, keeping her eyes focused on his. "Why?" The question was so hesitant, Max wasn't certain she actually asked.

Before he could talk himself out of anything, he reached a hand up to swipe a lock of chocolaty hair off Ginny's cheek. Her skin flushed as he touched her, goosebumps erupting as he traced a finger down her skin.

"Because I want you all to myself," Max whispered.

Ginny didn't pull back, instead leaning into his touch. Their lips were now a hair's length apart. This was more than the night before; this was *the* moment. This was his shot, and he was going to take it.

"Max." She breathed his name like a prayer. Her tongue quickly darted out to wet her lips, and Max thought he'd faint.

Swallowing past the lump in his throat, he struggled to keep his cool. "Gin."

"Are you going to kiss me?" A hint of laughter tinged her question.

Max smiled, enjoying the familiar banter. "Is that all right?"

At first she was silent, and Max feared he'd overplayed his hand. Then Ginny leaned in, closing the distance between them. The feel of her lips on his overloaded his senses. It had been years since they'd kissed, but it felt like yesterday. He brought his hands to her face, cupping her cheeks as he deepened the kiss, holding her close. He cradled her gently, treasuring having her near again.

Max could have kissed Ginny forever, lost in nearly forgotten tastes and sensations. That is, until the shrill sound of his cell phone broke the spell. They both shot apart, a wild look in their eyes. Ginny's lips were swollen, her mouth slightly agape. She never looked more delectable, and he wanted to toss her over his shoulder and carry her to bed like the caveman he was quickly becoming. Any gentlemanly notions evaporated when their lips touched. Max was a goner, and he didn't give a damn.

Remembering the moment, Max cursed Alexander Graham Bell and the invention of the telephone. He pulled his phone from his pocket and saw the caller ID. "It's the hospital," he said.

CHAPTER 10

"Answer it!" Ginny barked, pointing at the phone like it was about to explode.

Max ran a hand through his hair, took a deep breath, and answered. "Hello?" Ginny watched his face, trying to decipher if it was bad news. Nodding a few times, Max let out a long sigh. "Great, we'll be there in ten minutes." He disconnected and shoved his phone back into his pocket. "Harold's fine. They are bringing him to a recovery room, and we can see him in about thirty minutes."

Ginny deflated. "Thank the Lord." Springing into action, Max gathered their lunch dishes and put them in the sink. Ginny took a moment to collect herself. "I'll be right back," she muttered, walking on shaking legs to the bathroom. Once the door clicked shut, Ginny braced herself against the sink and tried to even out her breathing.

From the fear over her father's surgery to what transpired with Max, Ginny felt her mind racing in her skull. There might as well have been a team of motorcyclists in a cage of death up there. Her temples pulsed, and she felt her stomach do a little somersault. "Calm down," she told herself, "just calm down. It's going to be fine."

For her father, yes. If he was out of surgery and going to

recovery, he would be all right. What wasn't all right was the fact that she'd kissed her ex-husband. Willingly and with her whole heart. Ever the gentleman, Max let her set the pace. He would never do what she didn't want, and the fact that he still had that much respect for her did nothing to calm her down.

Ginny reached for the faucet with trembling fingers, splashing cold water on her face. She checked her reflection and flinched at what she saw. Her lips were plump, the skin around them pink from Max's stubble. Rarely would she describe herself as appearing wanton, except for right now. She looked ready for a roll in the hay, not a ride to the hospital.

Fidgeting with her hands, she tried to center herself with another deep breath. When she opened the door, Max stood right in front of her. In one hand he held her coat, in the other her purse. "Car is warmed up. I'm ready when you are." His expression was kind, patient. Staring at his lips, she felt the lingering effects of their kiss.

"Thanks," Ginny replied, taking her coat and shrugging it on. Max held out her purse and she took it. Before her hand could fall to her side, he snatched it and held firm as he walked them to the car. Ginny didn't pull back, even though she felt like she should. She'd taken more than enough comfort from him, and she feared she was leading him on. Hell, she thought she might be leading herself.

Ginny slid into the passenger's seat, and Max waited until she buckled up before he closed the door. She watched him walk across the front of the car, his strides sure and his expression open. He was a good man, her ex-husband. Most men wouldn't stand by and help when their ex needed them, especially after how she left. The throbbing in her temples came back, but Ginny balled her fists in her lap so she didn't draw attention to her mind spiraling.

When Max got behind the wheel, he leaned across and opened the glove compartment. "Here," he said, taking a bottle of Tylenol out and placing it into her clenched hands.

"That tension headache isn't going to go away if you don't stop grinding your teeth." He was so casual, but the fact that he remembered her headaches and mannerisms did something funny to her heart. *This man still loves you, idiot!*

"Thank you," she whispered, swallowing two pills dry.

They didn't talk on the drive back to the hospital, and Ginny wondered what that meant. What was Max thinking? Should she say something? What did she even want to say?

"Here we are." Max pulled up to the front of the building. "You go in and check in with Janis. I can park the car."

Ginny reached for the door handle but stopped herself. Her feet barely moved, feeling as if they weighed a metric ton. "Wait, can I walk in with you?" She needed Max now more than ever. Despite the good news, she didn't want to walk into that building alone. "If you don't mind," she hurried.

Max smiled and reached out for her hand. He pulled it to his lips and kissed her knuckles. "I don't mind at all." Deftly kissing her hand once more, he reluctantly let go and drove toward the parking lot. He got out and ran around to get Ginny, who stood on shaking legs. "I've got you," he said, looping his arm around her waist and walking to the building.

When they made it to the reception desk, Janis was speaking to a familiar face. "Mona," Ginny blurted when she saw her father's … girlfriend? She still didn't know what to call Mona, but she was glad she was here. It was obvious she was quite smitten with Harold.

Mona turned when she saw Ginny and Max and sighed. "Oh good, I was hoping to find you. Janis won't tell me what's going on." Mona wrapped her arms around her middle and bounced on the balls of her feet; her eyes were tired.

Janis perched on her elbows, leaning closer to the trio. "It's HIPAA, Mona. You know I would give you information if I could."

Mona looked at Janis and shook her head. "I know, Jan; you're a doll. I'm just worried about Harold."

Ginny thought about what life would be like if her mother were around. Would she have been there, holding Ginny's other hand and worrying about her husband? After years of having these same what-ifs compete for space in her brain, she decided to stop overthinking and go with what made sense in the moment.

"Dad's fine, Mona. He's out of surgery, and we should be able to see him soon."

Mona pressed a hand to her chest. "He's okay?" she asked, her voice cracking as her eyes blurred with tears. "Harold is okay?" Mona lunged forward and pulled Ginny into the fiercest hug of her life. The relief washing off her was contagious.

"Oh no, is everything okay?" Natalie asked from behind them. She was holding a fistful of balloons in one hand and pushing a stroller with Otis in the other. Her cheeks were red from the cold. "I was dropping these off for Harold," she said weakly as she raised the hand with the balloons.

Otis decided he wanted a balloon and started fussing. His meaty little hands flexed as he strained against the stroller buckles. Max leaned down on his heels to talk to the toddler. "Hey, buddy." He waved his fingers in the air in front of Otis's line of sight and the boy was easily distracted. "What's all the trouble?"

Ginny never thought she'd see Max speak baby talk, but a lot was happening today that was unexpected. Natalie, unaware that Ginny's ovaries were combusting at the sight of her ex with a baby, stepped forward and frowned. "How's your dad?"

Mona dabbed at her eyes with a handkerchief that matched the pattern on her sweater, complete with a trim of tinsel. The woman's love for ugly Christmas sweaters knew no limits. "He's okay. I heard the good news."

Ginny nodded and took the balloons from Natalie. "Yes, he's in recovery. I'll make sure he gets these. Thanks for bringing them." Natalie gave her a one-armed hu

"You're welcome. I remember being in the h having the kids, and for some reason, balloons alw seemed like the best part of being in the hospital. I thought I'd share some of the fun." She shrugged, but Ginny was overly touched by her friend's kindness. The two had lost touch over the years, and it was yet another Buckeye Falls casualty that felt raw. Ginny wanted to stop discarding the people that mattered, but she knew she couldn't fix it all in one day. Right now, her focus was getting to her father.

When Ginny turned around, Max had Otis in his arms and was carrying him around the reception desk, a flurry of airplane noises coming from his mouth. The toddler giggled with delight and waved his arms in the air as Max knelt and dropped him down a couple of feet. When he shot back up and raised the boy to his shoulders, Otis nearly choked on his happiness.

Stealing the words from her mouth, Natalie whispered to Ginny, "He's amazing with kids. I had no idea until one night at the diner. Both the kids were tired, and not even the promise of cookies shut them up. As a table was complaining about the noise, Max came out of the kitchen with two little ice cream sundaes. He said they were for the sweetest kids in the diner, but they had to behave and eat every bite." Natalie smiled at the memory, and Ginny felt a knot tighten in her chest. In that instant, she didn't think her heart could handle one more charming detail about Max.

Just then he came forward and passed Otis off to Natalie. "Thanks for giving me a dose of Vitamin O." Max ruffled the boy's hair once Natalie perched the toddler on her hip.

"Oh please, Max. I should be thanking you. You're a sweetheart." She reached out and squeezed Max's arm before turning back to Ginny. "Let me know when your dad's home. If you're still free, I'd love to see you tomorrow night at the cookie decorating party. I'm saving you a seat."

Ginny had forgotten about the cookie party, and part of

her wondered if it was worth the effort after taking her father home. Mona must have read her mind. "She'll be there. I spoke to Harold last night, and I offered to get him settled in after Ginny brings him back." Mona turned to Ginny and offered a watery smile. "If you don't mind. I want to help."

It wasn't that Ginny minded, but she felt suddenly superfluous. The whole point of coming back to Buckeye Falls was to take care of her dad, not dash off to cookie parties and make out with her ex-husband. "Uh, yeah. I'm sure that's fine," she muttered half-heartedly. "But I want to go see Dad now; we can figure out the rest later."

Max looped her arm through his and stepped back toward the hallway. "You're all amazing for coming out. We'll tell Harold you were here."

Mona held up her hand and said, "Hold on, I brought a card for Harold." She rummaged through her overstuffed handbag and pulled out a red envelope. "Here," she said, tucking it into Ginny's coat pocket. "You're a dear."

Ginny merely nodded, too wrapped up in her head to say anything. Max tugged her down the hallway toward her father's recovery room. When they reached the doorway, Max paused. "Remember what Janis said, okay? He's going to look tired, but the surgery went well." He studied her face. She could feel him holding back, but she wasn't sure she wanted to hear what he had to say. "I'll let you go in first," he said, releasing her arm. "You should have time alone with Harold. I'll take a seat over here and wait until you need something."

It was pretty much the last thing Ginny expected to hear, and she felt the absence of Max's touch instantly. "Max, I …" Ginny licked her lips and tried not to stomp her foot in frustration. Her eyes welled up, and she knew she was going to lose it. She needed to be strong for her dad. There was a lot to unpack, and she didn't have the presence of mind right then.

"Text or call if you need me, but I'll be right here by the

vending machines." Max backed away slowly, pointing to where he'd be waiting for her. *He always seemed to be waiting for her.*

Finally, she knocked softly before opening the door. "Dad?" she asked, sticking her head inside. Her father was the only one in the room, laying in his bed with a blanket pulled up to his chin. His arms were on top of the blanket, with a series of IVs running from both hands. The rhythmic beeping of a heart monitor kept time with the racing of Ginny's own heart.

Despite Max's warnings, Ginny felt herself panic at how pale her father looked. All her life, he'd been a steadfast presence, completely unflappable. Now he looked like an old shell of the man she'd counted on her whole life. Ginny knew she'd have to be strong now for both of them.

Quietly, Ginny tiptoed to the side of the bed where there was a lone chair by the IV stand. Ginny pulled her coat off and sat on the edge of the chair, staring at her father's chest as it rose and fell with every breath. With a tentative hand, she reached out and grazed her fingers over her father's arm.

"It's bad form to tickle a man while he's down," her father croaked. His chest rumbled with a chuckle, but Ginny sprang back in her chair.

"Oh geez, I'm sorry." Her hands in the air, Ginny looked like she was caught robbing a bank.

"At ease, Ginnybread," Harold said. "I was trying to lighten the mood. You look like you're at a funeral."

Ginny raised an eyebrow at her father's casual attitude. "You realize you're in a hospital right now? That you're half-bionic and will set off metal detectors at all airports and courthouses for the rest of your life?"

Harold reached for a remote control on the side table, bringing his bed higher so he could meet his daughter's gaze. "Yes, I am part bionic, which means I'm stronger than before. Haven't you seen the *6 Million Dollar Man*? Have I failed you that much as a father?"

Resting her hands on her father's arm, Ginny shook her

head. "It's just hard seeing you like …" Her voice broke and she started to cry, heaving sobs that shook her body.

"Ginnybread." Harold reached for her, frowning as she continued to sob into her scarf. "There's a box of tissues over on the windowsill," he said with a wave. "It's going to be okay, I promise." He made a show of looking around the room. "Where's Max? I told him to stay by you no matter what you said." He winked at his daughter, but she couldn't stop the tears. "Didn't he do a good job with distracting you? I told him I was worried you'd be upset."

Ginny dabbed at her eyes with a fistful of tissues. "Oh, he distracted me all right." A bubble of frustration welled up inside her, and she had to take a moment to catch her breath. "I'm not going into that now, Dad. Right now, our focus is on you." She pulled the chair back to the side of the bed and took a seat.

"That's baloney and you know it. The hard part is over. I'm out of surgery and the doctor said I should make a full recovery over the next few weeks. Mona has offered to come by and take care of me when it's time for you to go back to New York. I have it all covered." Harold raised his bed another few inches and leaned slightly toward Ginny. "Now, tell me where Max is. I have a feeling that's a big part of why you're crying."

Ginny shook her head. "He's in the waiting room. I'm a little emotional because of you being here." To illustrate her point, she gestured to the wires and tubes currently nestled in her father's arms. "I like to see my dad outside hospital walls and preferably wireless." Harold didn't seem satisfied with her answer. He rested his head back and closed his eyes. "Are you in pain? I can call a nurse."

"I'm fine. They have enough pain meds in me to sedate an elephant. I'm going to wait you out." Harold peeked at his daughter before snapping his eyes shut again.

"Wait me out?" she asked, not following where her father was taking the conversation. "If you're too loopy, we can finish this conversation later."

"I'm not loopy. I'm perfectly coherent. My daughter is the one that needs to see a doctor."

Ginny scoffed. "For what?"

"Blindness," he deadpanned. "You can't see what's right in front of you."

Ginny leaned back in her chair, balling her fists in her lap. For the second time that day, she radiated with unanswered questions and feelings she'd let go dormant for years. "I don't know what you mean, Dad. We can talk when you're feeling better."

"He loves you," he said, his voice hoarse from dehydration. "That man loves you more than anyone, except maybe me, and I think you need to figure out what that means for you."

"This seems a bit philosophical, especially after you were just sliced and diced. Can we save this heart-to-heart for when you're home? Maybe when alcohol is present?" Ginny felt her fingernails digging into the flesh of her palms, leaving half-moon divots in her skin.

Now Harold's eyes were open, surprisingly alert and directed straight at Ginny. "I'm not saying I've had a near-death experience or anything, but a man gets to thinking when he's going under the knife." Ginny nodded but didn't interrupt. "One thing he realizes is that life is too damn short. I've spent too many years alone after your mother left. I spent too many years waiting for someone to come home who wasn't going to. It's a waste, let me tell you. Many hours I sat on the porch, some of them with Max, lamenting over the human heart. When you find someone who makes you happy, you want to be with them. Do you know what I mean?"

Ginny hardly wanted to talk through her divorce with her dad, but the pleading glint in his eyes told her she didn't have a choice. "What Mom did was …" She cleared her throat in an attempt to stop the next batch of tears. "What Mom did was horrible, to both of us. I know it wasn't easy on you."

"It wasn't, not one bit. But life has a funny way of making things right. I firmly believe that Mona came into my life at the perfect time. I'm finally done hating your mother." At his statement, Ginny's eyes flashed with rage, but he cut her off with a shake of his head. "I won't forget the pain she caused us, but I needed to let go of the anger. It was keeping me from finding happiness again. This may come as a surprise, but I love Mona. When I'm able to, I'm going to get down on one knee and ask her to marry me."

Ginny blinked twice, letting the news set in. Her father was in love and wanted to get married. While she never wanted her mother to come home, Ginny didn't know how she felt about the potential of a stepmother. "Oh," was all she could muster.

"Oh?" Harold coughed and patted his chest. "Is that a good oh or a bad oh?"

"It's a surprised oh, but not a bad one." She smiled as the news settled in. Her father wanted to settle down and start a life with someone. She'd never begrudge him that. Remembering the envelope, she pulled it from her coat. "This is from Mona. She was outside when we came back, and she wanted me to give this to you." Her father took it and placed it on his blanket. "Aren't you going to open it?"

Harold nodded. "I will, once you tell me what happened with Max. You're about to rip off your own fingers. Spill it before you are admitted for skin grafts."

Ginny looked down at her hands. A small trail of blood ran down her index finger from where she pulled at her cuticles. "It's nothing, we—"

"If it was nothing, you'd both be in here." Lifting one of his arms, he gestured around the empty room. "Now spill it."

"You're very bossy after surgery." Ginny sighed.

Harold grinned. "It's one of the few perks. Now talk. I have some nurses set to come back here any minute, but I want the dirt first."

Restless energy surged through Ginny, and she finally

gave up and paced the room. "He took me to his place for lunch and made grilled cheese sandwiches." Ginny took three steps toward the window, then pivoted and paced toward the door. "They were good sandwiches. You know how Max is—he can't cook something and not have it be perfect."

Ginny saw her father nodding. "He's an amazing cook."

"Well, of course he is. But emotions were high, and after last night at the ice cream parlor, everything felt all muddled. We had lunch, but after lunch we sort of …" Ginny raised one of her hands and twirled it in the air while the other stayed balled at her side. She was a nervous talker, and she was shocked to see her father was following along with her ramblings.

"You sort of what?" he asked, clearly waiting out his daughter.

"Kissed, we sort of kissed." She let the truth slide off her tongue and felt better and worse for having shared it.

Harold sat up and started applauding. "Thank the Lord!" His clapping shook the IV stand and caused an alarm to sound. Red, blue, and green lights flashed on the machines by his bed. Were they not in a hospital, the lights would have been festive.

Ginny raced to the side of the bed and full-on panicked. "Dad, stop. You're going to get in trouble." Images of stereotypical movie nurses roamed through her head, and she pictured a slew of terrifying characters coming to restrain her father. *Maybe he wasn't the only one being a little melodramatic?*

Harold waggled his arm, causing another alarm to beep. Cords and wires slapped against the railings of the hospital bed; the sound grating on Ginny's eardrums. "I don't care. You just gave me the best news I've had all year. Hooray!" Harold waved his arms over his head and hummed to himself, causing Ginny to go slightly insane. "I get a new hip and the best news in the same day. I'd say it's cause to celebrate."

How could her father celebrate something so emotionally draining and utterly confusing? Perhaps the Meyer family needed to swing by the counseling wing before discharge?

"Will you stop, please? There's nothing to celebrate," she snapped. Balling her fists at her sides, Ginny ground her teeth together. Despite the Tylenol Max gave her, her head pounded; a bomb ready to explode. "It was a mistake. A huge mistake. It didn't mean anything, just a low moment," she said, hating the way the light bled from her father's eyes. "Please don't look at me like that, Dad. It was foolish to kiss him, and it will only be harder when I leave again. It was a mistake."

Ginny wasn't sure if she meant harder for her to leave or for Max to watch her leave. In that instant, she didn't think the difference mattered. At least one of them would walk away with a broken heart, and her stomach flipped at the notion. The last few days had been nice—a lot more than nice. How was she supposed to turn away now when she remembered how Max felt beside her—remembered how tender he was when she was in his arms? *Yeah, she was already in trouble …*

Momentarily distracted by the bustle of the nurse's footsteps, Ginny turned toward the door. Harold's outburst had alerted half of the hospital staff to his alarms. Ducking her head to hide her embarrassment, she stepped back as a nurse strode toward them.

As if her father's expression wasn't bad enough, she turned to find Max standing in the doorway. The look on his face made her want to jump out the window and never come back to Buckeye Falls. His skin looked pale beneath his beard, and his eyes were downcast. He clutched the balloons in one hand, the other hung limp at his side. No one had ever looked this depressed holding a bunch of balloons. If the situation were different, she could laugh. Instead she felt her throat close and her stomach clench.

"Y-y-you're looking good, Harold," he stammered,

carrying over the balloons from Natalie. "N-n-n …" He stopped, trying to form the words, a frustrated expression masking his features. Max fumbled with his words for another moment, finally giving up and sighing. He hadn't appeared this tongue-tied in well over a decade. Not even the young man in the library struggled this much. She should be patient; she should be kind. Yet in that instant, Ginny felt too much of everything.

The dam burst, Ginny did something she hadn't done in years. She cut him off and finished his sentence. "Natalie and the kids brought these." Ginny took the balloons from Max's hands, then tied them to the edge of the bed, adding a spark of cheer to the dreary surroundings. Turning back to Max, she found his hand extended with his car keys. "What's this?" she asked, letting him drop them into her waiting palm.

"K-k-keys to my c-car." He stepped forward and shook Harold's hand. "G-glad to see you looking s-so good," Max said before turning and exiting the room.

Ginny started to follow, but another nurse entered with her hands on her hips. "Harold, what did we say about laying still? You're setting off more alarms than a game show contestant."

Harold chuckled at the nurse, but his eyes were on his daughter. Ginny held up the keys, terror causing her eyes to grow to comical proportions. "Go after him," he urged. The look on her father's face told her all she needed to know. She had to make this right—immediately.

With Max's keys still firmly in her grip, Ginny started for the door. When she made it to the waiting room, she found it empty. Jogging down the hallway, she saw Janis playing Candy Crush on her phone. "Where did Max go?" she asked, breathless and lamenting her forgotten jogging routine. If this were weeks ago, she'd be running laps around everyone without breaking a sweat. Now she felt like a wrung-out dish rag.

Janis startled and shook her head. "I'm not sure, but he

left that way." Janis hitched her thumb over her shoulder, motioning toward the exit.

Ginny didn't hesitate, running right out into the December chill without her coat. "Max!" she shouted but didn't see anyone in the parking lot. She ran the length of the building, doubling back in case he'd strode toward the far exit. How had he gotten away so quickly?

And more importantly, why had she lied like that to her father? Of course kissing Max meant something. It meant everything. Judging from his crushed expression and how he'd struggled to find his words, she knew she'd really hurt him. After everything he'd done for her, she was careless with his heart again. Worse than anything, she'd taken his words from him.

*

"Th-thanks for picking me up," Max said to Evan as he drove to his house.

Evan drummed his thumbs on the steering wheel, rocking out to the K-Pop blaring through the car's speakers. "No problem, boss man."

One of the many reasons that Max liked Evan was that he was always available. If you needed something, he was there to do it. No interrogation, just a lopsided smile and a helping hand. Evan was basically a golden retriever in human form.

"Can you take me to my place, p-please?" Max asked, knowing he was in no mood for CeCe and her never-ending questions. Having taken the day off to help Ginny and Harold, she would no doubt need a play-by-play of every reason he was suddenly back at work. She was a shrewd interrogator, and sometimes he thought she was better suited to a career in the CIA. Although he doubted agents could whip up a pavlova like CeCe could.

Evan turned left and hummed out the last line of the chorus. The music was upbeat and far too cheerful for

Max's current mood. Even though he couldn't understand the Korean lyrics, he was certain the song was not meant for his current situation. *Although what music is best when your ex-wife rips out your heart in a hospital?*

"I'll have you home in no time," Evan mused, making a turn onto a heavily trafficked back road. Compared to New York, the traffic in Buckeye Falls seemed laughable. Max remembered that day in New York when he'd gone looking for Ginny, feeling like every turn he'd made brought him closer and closer into the heart of a labyrinth. But that was Ginny's home, and much like a sword-wielding knight, Max knew he'd brave far worse to see her.

Max rubbed his face with his hands, trying hard not to make a scene in Evan's car. He was a sweet guy with enough on his plate. Watching his boss cry was a step too far. Hearing Ginny's careless dismissal of their kiss hurt worse than Max thought possible. He used to think that watching his wife load up a moving truck was worse, but he was wrong. Hearing her throw that moment away made him want to cry. He felt gutted, like she'd used his favorite boning knife to filet him from navel to nose.

Partly, Max was frustrated with himself. Ginny had a lot of distractions and frustrations to deal with, and he added to her stresses. He hadn't planned on kissing her at his place, but he couldn't fight the magnetic pull toward her. Discovering she was jealous of CeCe was too much, and it gave him a sense of hope he hadn't felt in ages. If Ginny cared enough to be jealous, maybe there was still something there between them. For years, Max had assumed it was all one-sided on his part, but now he wasn't so sure.

At least he hadn't been sure until he heard the truth from Ginny's own mouth. What a fool he'd been all those years, pining after a woman who didn't think enough to spare his heart once more. She had always been patient with his stammer, but she'd cut him off and dismissed him back there. She'd cut him down to his core.

Thankfully, Evan pulled up to Max's house as a lump

formed in his throat. Evan left the car running but kept his hand hovering over his keys. "Want me to help with anything?" he asked, clearly trying to read the moment. Bless his heart.

Max shook his head, swallowing a few times to get his mouth working. "No, thanks. I appreciate the ride, man." He clapped Evan on the shoulder and got out of the car. When Max reached the door, he remembered he gave Ginny his keys. Thankful for his extra pair, he pulled a spare key from a loose brick by his doorbell and let himself inside.

As soon as the door closed, Max slid to the floor and cradled his head in his hands. Back when Ginny filed for divorce, he'd made himself a promise. He would only cry once a week, and it had to be for a very good reason. When the notarized divorce papers arrived, that was a cry. Their first anniversary apart, that was a hell of a cry. The first time he met new people and stammered, he cried. Ginny had always been there to walk him through tense moments when his tongue couldn't keep up with his brain. Then suddenly he was alone to navigate through his stammer and all life could throw at him.

Max felt discarded, now more than ever, and he didn't know how to recover. How do you build a life around a missing person? Max knew Ginny hadn't come back to Buckeye Falls for him, but he'd let himself pretend it was their second chance. What a fool he'd been.

An hour after Evan dropped him off, Max heard a knock at the front door. He paused, not allowing his heart to hope it was Ginny. He kept silent, hoping whoever it was would go away. There was another knock, this time followed by a familiar voice. "I know you're here. Evan said he dropped you off." CeCe's voice came through the front door. Knowing it was cold, Max stood and opened the door. She stepped into the house and flicked on a light.

Max shielded his eyes with his hand and backed up toward his couch. "Geez, CeCe."

CeCe kicked the door shut and carried over a box,

placing it on the floor in front of the couch. "There's a quart of soup, a half loaf of sourdough I made this morning, a bottle of bourbon, and three slices of chocolate cake." She rattled off the contents of the box and didn't meet his gaze. "I don't need to know what happened, but can you confirm that Harold is all right?"

Max slumped back on the couch, draping his forearm over his eyes. "Yes, he's fine."

CeCe nodded, satisfied with the answer. "Works for me. Take tonight to do what you need to do. If you can't make it in tomorrow, we'll be fine. Evan wanted to work overtime, so he can help with the cookie event."

Max groaned at the mention of the event. Not only would Ginny be there, but so would most of Buckeye Falls, or at least the gossipy portion. "Let's see how I'm feeling in the morning," he moaned.

CeCe started walking toward the front door and paused. "You know I'd sooner gouge my own eyeballs out than talk feelings, right?" Max chuckled, the only response he could muster. "You're a good guy, Max. I don't know what is going on, but you deserve to be happy. Now I'm going to go back to the diner, but call if you need anything. You're my family, and family takes care of each other."

The conviction in CeCe's voice almost brought another round of tears for Max. After his parents moved to Florida and Ginny left, he only had Harold and staff in his life. He'd gotten very good over the years at pushing other people away when they got too close. Sure, he loved seeing people at the diner. They were on his turf, and he knew how to carry himself.

When CeCe blew into town faster than a bat out of hell, Max knew she'd be a perfect fit. Not only was she a fantastic pastry chef, but she craved the same type of solitude that Max did. They were both at home in the kitchen, where their feelings came out as rich stews and sweet confections. Even now, he knew CeCe would be there if he wanted to open his heart. But the words wouldn't come, and Max wanted to be alone with his thoughts … and that bottle of bourbon.

"Text if you need me," CeCe urged, opening the front door and letting a nip of the winter air inside.

Max pulled the cork from the bourbon and took a long swallow. "Why did you move here?" he asked, coughing as the amber liquid burned his throat.

CeCe hesitated a moment before closing the door. She dimmed the lights and walked into the kitchen, coming back with two glasses. "Helen's with Evan, they won't burn the place down," she assured him as she sat on the floor, her legs tucked underneath her. Max poured a shot into each glass, then placed the bottle on the floor between them.

CeCe shot back her bourbon, not even flinching. "I moved here to get away from a bad breakup." She sat back and stretched out her neck, taking her time with her story. "I dated this chef, Eric. What an asshole." She raised her glass and waited for Max to pour another shot.

"I thought you never dated anyone at work," Max asked, knowing that Evan had asked her out at least a million times. Poor kid.

CeCe shrugged and took her shot. This time she blinked as the alcohol burned its way to her belly. "Eric is the reason for that rule," she lamented. "Because it's a nightmare to work with an ex." CeCe handed her glass back to Max, her eyes now looking a little red around the edges.

Max nodded, although he never worked with an ex, he could understand the pitfalls. Bringing the person you love into your favorite space could quickly sour if the love was one-sided. "You want to talk about it?" he asked. He knew this would cross an invisible line between them. Not that their conversations were shallow, but they rarely shared specifics about their pasts.

"Not too much to tell. Eric was a creep, although a damned good pastry chef, but a creep nonetheless. We dated for a year until I found out that the reason he never had me spend the night was that he was married. I broke up with him, then he followed me around the city. He said he wanted us to be together, and I wouldn't understand how hard it was to be in love with two women." CeCe scoffed, leaning forward to grab one of the slices of chocolate cake.

Max was on high alert. "He stalked you?"

CeCe took a bite straight from the box and shook her head. "Maybe a little at first, but when I threatened to call his wife, he stopped. Then he started nasty rumors about me to blackball me from other restaurants. When I started struggling to find work, I packed up my car in search of somewhere new to live. I wanted to escape the drama for a while. Imagine my surprise when I stopped at this little town called Buckeye Falls for lunch. There was this cute diner, right off Main Street. The food was amazing, but the pie left something to be desired." CeCe's voice trailed off as she nibbled on her cake.

Max was content to drink more bourbon and wait for CeCe to continue her story. "So I tell myself I'm going to ask to talk to the chef, right? I figured, I'll tell this guy his meatloaf patty melt is the best damn thing I ever ate, but then I'm going to tell him his strawberry pie is the worst in the Midwest."

Max laughed at the memory of CeCe stomping up to the counter and barking at Helen that something needed to change. "I had literally just printed the help wanted sign for the door. Then I come out and hear someone yelling at Helen about the food. I thought 'what a jerk,' until I heard you offer to make a better pie."

CeCe swiped a crumb from her lips and laughed. "And two hours later, I had a job. The rest is history." She placed the box on the floor and sighed as the sugar hit her system.

Max took one more shot of the bourbon before falling back on the couch again. "I'm really glad you hated our pie," he said.

"I'm really glad you didn't tell me to pound sand." CeCe laughed. "I'd say it all worked out."

Max thought about his life through his bourbon haze. He had his own thriving restaurant and a staff he knew he could trust. He loved what he did—cooking for the town that had made him one of their own. Countless of people had it a heck of a lot worse.

CeCe stood, dusting more chocolate crumbs from her jeans. "Now, I realize I said Helen and Evan could handle things, but I should probably go back and make sure they aren't burning the place down, or worse, serving tomorrow's corn chowder." She gathered her empty box and carried it to the kitchen, coming back with a tall glass of water. "Drink this now, then I don't care how much more bourbon you have."

Max took the proffered glass, downing half its contents in one gulp. "Thanks, CeCe," he said, taking her hand before she could leave. "I don't say it enough, but you're a good friend."

CeCe squeezed his hand once before pulling back and resting her hands on her hips. "I won't say it again, but you deserve to be happy, Max. There are all sorts of reasons you're sitting here getting drunk, but make sure you know all the reasons before making any decisions." Max merely nodded as CeCe put her coat back on.

Absentmindedly, he wondered how he would get his car at Harold's house tomorrow. "Hey, do you think you could pick me up tomorrow and drop me off at Harold's? My car should be there in the morning."

"Yep, text me the time," CeCe replied as she stepped into the night. "Or you can just drive it from your own driveway." Max stumbled over to the door to investigate, his feet heavy and uncoordinated. "Is this some type of magic trick?" She smirked.

His car was parked in its normal spot, ready to go in the morning. CeCe stepped forward and grabbed an envelope that was flapping from his mailbox. "I'm guessing this will explain things," she offered, handing it to him. Max wasn't sure if he said anything before closing the door and falling back on the couch.

With trembling fingers, he opened the envelope, finding

a small note and his keys. *Thanks for your car, Max. I'll call you tomorrow.* It was written in Ginny's familiar scrawl, and Max wondered how she got home. If he wasn't already drunk, he'd go out and find her.

Max looked at the note again, noting there weren't any apologies or explanations. But there was a promise to call the next day. He didn't know how he felt about that, but he thought it was something. Kicking off his shoes and pulling a blanket over his lap, he turned his attention to a worn paperback on the coffee table and the rest of the bourbon.

CeCe was right; he didn't have to make any decisions now. Tonight he would hurt and lick his wounds, and he would be even more careful about opening his heart up to Ginny. He had to be smart and realize she wasn't going to stay in Buckeye Falls, but Max wasn't always known for his intelligence.

CHAPTER 11

Ginny woke to the now familiar sounds of breakfast being made. A clattering of a pan, the spluttering of the old coffee machine; it was a glorious symphony after a restless night's sleep. Ginny rubbed her hands over her eyes and stretched, already looking forward to the half dozen cups of coffee she planned to consume. All she had to do was get her father home, and she'd be able to relax again.

Pulling on her bathrobe, Ginny realized her father was still in the hospital. To her knowledge, Max didn't have a key and wouldn't be barging into her house anytime soon. The look of hurt on his face was burned into Ginny's brain, and she hated herself for putting it there. She felt lower than low, but her reflections on self-hate would have to wait until she found out who was in the house.

Carefully putting her slippers on, Ginny tucked her cell phone in her robe pocket and reached for the deadliest weapon she could find—her fourth-grade spelling bee trophy. Padding down the stairs, Ginny held her breath until she saw who was in the house.

"Oh! You scared me," Mona said, her hand pressed to her chest in surprise. Her other hand clutched a spatula, which hovered over a pan of sizzling bacon.

Ginny put the trophy on the table and sighed. "I won't lie, Mona. You scared me too. What are you doing here? Dad won't be home until this afternoon." She took a seat at the table and watched Mona turn a slice of bacon. She wore a blue sweater with dozens of sparkly white snowflakes attached—what Ginny now considered Mona's uniform of choice. Her hair was pulled back into a ponytail, which was held in place by a sparkling scrunchie.

Mona poured two mugs of coffee and joined Ginny at the table. "Here you go," she said as she slid the mug toward Ginny. "Two shots of cream and no sugar, right?"

Ginny was impressed. Mona had either paid attention or asked her father. No matter how she figured it out, Ginny had to admit she was touched by the gesture. "Thanks, this is perfect." She sipped from the coffee, collecting her thoughts. "If you don't mind me asking, how did you get in? I thought I locked the door."

Mona plated up eggs and bacon from the stove before grabbing two slices of bread from the toaster. Ginny watched her and quickly realized the woman knew her way around the kitchen just as much as Max did. Handing a plate to Ginny, Mona took the seat usually reserved for Harold. "Your father gave me a key a few months ago. I hope you don't mind."

Ginny shook her head. "No, not at all. You're both adults, and it's Dad's house, not mine." She hoped she didn't sound defensive, but yet again she felt like she missed the boat. Her father had a whole life she knew nothing about, with a woman who clearly cared for him. Judging from the delicious-looking breakfast, Mona was trying to make a good impression on Ginny. "Sorry, that came out wrong." Ginny sighed, placing her fork on the table and scooting back her chair.

Undeterred, Mona sprinkled pepper on her eggs and took a moment to respond. "This might seem strange to you—your father and I—but I want you to know I don't want to put you out. You are your father's family, and I don't want to replace anyone or get in the way. You say the word, and I'll leave." She took a bite of her eggs and washed it down with a swig of coffee. Her eyes were kind, but Ginny saw how tired she was.

Reaching out, Ginny rested her hand on Mona's forearm. The older woman looked up and smiled. "You really care for my father, don't you?"

"I love him," Mona said plainly. "Harold is kind and patient, and we enjoy spending time together." Her shoulders slumped as she continued. "I met Harold when I was at a low point in my life. We met a couple years ago, over at the community center. Did he tell you?"

Ginny didn't want to lie, so she told Mona the truth. She felt she owed it to both of them, to be honest. "Dad and I don't talk as much as we should. Being home again is showing me how much I'm missing."

"You're very busy with your career," Mona defended Ginny easily. "Harold doesn't fault you for that. In fact, he's very proud of all you're doing."

Never once had Ginny pondered her father's pride level in her career and recent life choices. Leaving Buckeye Falls was monumental for her. Not only had she left her husband, but she left her only family behind. It never occurred to her that her father would be proud of the decision, mostly because she felt like she had followed in her mother's shoes. One minute she was living the small-town life, and the next she'd pulled up stakes and left for greener pastures.

And very much like her mother, Ginny never reached out to Max. Of course, she kept in touch with her father, but never to the degree that she knew she should. Coming home was hard that first year. Not only was she afraid of seeing Max, but she hated to see the look of sadness on her father's face when she packed her suitcase and left all over again.

While she was gone, her father had found someone who loved him. Someone who looked after him and made him smile. "Tell me about how you met Dad," Ginny offered, taking joy in the happiness that radiated from Mona. It was in stark contrast to her own heartbreak.

"If you're sure it won't bore you," Mona said, spreading some jelly on her toast. "It's not much of a story."

Ginny laughed. "I highly doubt that. Any story that involves two people finding each other deserves to be told." Leaning in, Ginny ate her breakfast while Mona spoke.

"Well, I'd moved here from Cleveland. My ex-husband had decided he wanted to move out West. I'll tell you, I assumed I was invited on the move. Our two sons were grown and out of the house, so when he started talking about moving, I thought we'd do it together. Then one day I came home to a half-empty house and a moving crew taking half of our furniture. Douglas said he didn't know how to tell me our twenty-nine-year marriage was over, so he thought the sight of the moving crew would do it for him."

Ginny's fork clattered to the table, her jaw falling to her chest. "You're kidding, that's horrible! Mona, I'm so sorry." It didn't escape Ginny that both her father and Mona were unceremoniously dumped for the draw of the West. Both of their spouses left so cruelly. If she wanted to continue drawing parallels, Ginny knew her actions weren't much better. They simply took her in another direction.

Mona waved her off. "Thanks, dear, but you don't need to apologize. That was over five years ago, and I'm a much stronger person because of it. When Douglas left, I spent a whole year sitting in a half-empty house, just waiting for that dope to come home. When our youngest son, Tommy, came to visit for Thanksgiving, he showed me pictures of Douglas and his new girlfriend in San Diego. It was the kick in the butt I needed to get on with my life." Mona cleared her throat and sipped from her coffee. Ginny was too speechless to interrupt. She was impressed that Mona could discuss this so freely, without even the slightest tremble in her voice. "Then I came to visit my friend Elsie, who you might remember from the decorations debacle the other night."

If the circumstances were different, Ginny would have chided the other woman about that. But now anything connected with that night felt tainted. *Because I tainted it,* she scolded herself. What she wouldn't give for a shared ice cream cone and one of Max's smiles right about now …

Completely unaware of Ginny's internal dialog, Mona continued. "We went to grade school together, and she invited me out for a visit. After only a week, I knew this was where I wanted to live."

Shaking herself back to the moment, Ginny offered a grin. "It's nice you had friends like Elsie to look after you," Ginny agreed. "So when did you meet my dad?"

Mona nibbled on a piece of bacon, her eyes sparkling at the memory. "Elsie invited me to a town hall meeting to discuss the Christmas Jubilee. I was so excited to be involved, since Christmas is my favorite time of year." She gestured to her sweater as if that was all the proof she needed. "Over a plate of dry cookies, I bumped into Harold. He was there with Max, and the three of us got to talking. I gravitated toward them, really. They both seemed a bit lost."

Ginny shuddered at the notion that she made the two most important men in her life unhappy, even though she knew that wasn't Mona's point. "And the rest is history?" she asked instead, trying to keep her voice light. A belt tightened over Ginny's chest, threatening to steal her breath. Counting down from ten, she strived to look calm.

Mona ran her last crust of toast through a puddle of egg yolk, savoring the bite before replying, "Yes. We saw each other the next day at the diner, and just hit it off. We both like the same books, and I'm a huge sports fan. Raising two sons will do that to a woman." Mona smiled with the pride of a mother, and Ginny wondered if her mother ever thought about her and what they'd shared before she left.

Sensing where Ginny's mind had gone, Mona shifted to face her. "Your mother doesn't know what she's missing, if you don't mind me saying. This is a great little town, and your father is the sweetest man I've ever met. She's missing out on the best years of your life too. I won't pretend to understand why she left, but it's safe to say she's missed a lot."

Ginny looked around the kitchen and tried to remember the last time she had a positive memory of her mother. It scared her that she barely had any happy memories left. They were all tangled and tainted in her mind, the mind of a lonely daughter.

"I think you're really good for my dad," Ginny said, standing to clear the table. Mona tried to collect her dishes, but Ginny waved her off. "Nope, you cooked. I'll clean. Those are the house rules." She winked at Mona, who suddenly looked like she wanted to burst into tears. "Thanks for breakfast, and the talk." Ginny busied herself with dishes for a few minutes while Mona tidied up the living room.

Mona brought a few pillows and a new blanket, which she laid over the couch. She explained how the doctors wanted Harold to sit in a certain way, and that extra pillows would help with his pain while he heals. Ginny was grateful that Mona thought to ask these questions, as she hadn't thought much beyond the surgery.

Ginny's cell phone rang; another incoming call from Lana. Ginny looked at the phone but decided it could wait. She needed to coordinate when her father was coming back from the hospital with Mona. Just as she joined Mona in the living room, her phone chimed again. Lana was on a tear, that was certain.

"So I thought we could go over these last few email blasts and Facebook posts before we leave for the hospital," Ginny suggested, carrying in her notebook.

Mona fluffed a couple of pillows and patted a cushion. "Take a seat, we'll test out these new cushions." She took the notebook and pointed to one of Ginny's suggested posts. "I really like that one, by the way. I hope you don't mind, but Natalie told me what you were thinking. You clearly know your business."

Ginny flushed at the compliment. "Thanks." She took a few minutes to fill Mona in on her plans. During her downtime over the last week, she came up with a full social media schedule, plans for online contests to drum up interest for the vendors at the Jubilee, and even crafted a few descriptions for the email blasts Natalie wanted to send. She was pleased with what she'd put together in such a short period, especially with the distractions from her father's surgery and Max.

Max. Thinking about him hurt her heart. Absently, Ginny rubbed at her chest and sighed. "I think I need something to drink."

Mona patted her knee and stood. "Water or stronger?"

Ginny barked out a laugh. "That obvious, huh?"

Mona stopped in the doorway and shrugged. "I'm not a mind reader, but this is the first time I've seen you without Max by your side. I saw you two at the hospital together, but I haven't seen him all day."

"So it is obvious." Ginny sighed, falling back against the stack of cushions. Mona had done a good job, because they were incredibly comfortable.

From the kitchen, Ginny heard the cupboards open and close. Mona emerged a moment later with two glasses and an opened bottle of wine. "If we're pouring our hearts out, we need something to pour with it." She handed Ginny a glass and they clinked. "Ignore the fact that it's barely ten o'clock." She huffed a laugh.

Ginny took a sip and closed her eyes. If she pretended, she could see Max sitting with her, pulling her close on the couch. "I screwed up," she admitted, her eyes still tightly closed. "I screwed up and potentially broke his heart again." She took another sip and placed the glass on the coffee table. Looking at Mona, she saw she had the woman's full attention.

"Max is very forgiving and patient. I'm sure it's not as bad as you think," Mona said.

Ginny thought back to last night, dropping his car off at his house like a thief in the night. She'd called a ride share to meet her on the corner, too afraid that Max would offer to take her home if he spotted her. She'd even chickened out and suggested she'd call today, which she had no plans on doing in the light of day.

Ginny heard Mona talking and realized she'd missed part of her questions. "I'm sorry, what?"

Mona topped off Ginny's glass before responding. "I said, why do you think you can't fix this? If you don't mind me saying, that man is still smitten with you. I think you tell him you're interested and all will be forgotten."

Ginny wished Mona was right, but she knew it would never be that simple. "I said some pretty horrible things, and I think we're doomed to repeat the past. My life is in the city, and his is here. I'm not going to ask him to move for me—it wouldn't be fair."

Raising an eyebrow, Mona looked skeptical. "Are you certain? Sure, Max has the diner, but I think he'd give it all up if you said so."

Bolstered by the wine, Ginny shot down Mona's idea. "That's the problem though, it's always about me and my career. I couldn't ask Max to leave his life for mine. He wouldn't do it before the divorce, and now the diner is successful. He wouldn't leave it behind now."

"How do you know? Did you ask him?"

No, Ginny thought, she hadn't. She'd lied to herself about how she felt, then had verbal diarrhea in front of Max, spewing feelings that weren't even accurate. Of course she liked kissing Max. That had never changed. She was petrified for what that meant, so she threw up some roadblocks to protect her heart. Maybe she was trying to protect Max too?

Shifting gears, Ginny asked about the car she saw at Max's place last night. "Who do you know in Buckeye Falls that drives an old GMC pickup?"

Mona shrugged and finished her wine. "Was it black

with a little rust on the tailgate?" When Ginny nodded, Mona confirmed her assumption. "That's CeCe's truck. Why?"

Ginny strived to look casual but knew it was a losing battle. "No reason, just saw it last night when I dropped off Max's car." She picked at an imaginary piece of lint on her pants, but Mona wasn't buying it.

"Dear, there's no way anything is going on with those two. You might as well consider them brother and sister. Besides, CeCe would eat Max for breakfast if given the chance. You have no competition there."

That statement somehow made Ginny feel better and worse. "But why was she there so late?"

"Because they're friends. If you're having a rough time in New York, don't you have someone to call?" Mona made this sound so simple, but Ginny didn't really have a support network. Sure, her coworkers were always around, but never like that. No one would come over and dry her tears after a bad date, or give her confidence a boost after a rough client meeting. It was every man and woman for themselves, something she did not miss since being back in Buckeye Falls.

Mona looked at her phone and frowned. "Speaking of Max and CeCe, the cookie party starts in an hour." She looked at Ginny and shrugged. "One of us needs to pick up Harold and the other needs to make an appearance at the cookie party. The Jubilee planning committee needs to be represented."

Ginny felt as festive as a box of hair, but she knew Mona wanted to pick up her father from the hospital. "I'm guessing you'd like me to decorate cookies and share the final marketing plan with Natalie?" Ginny asked, smiling at how relieved Mona looked.

"If you don't mind," Mona wagered, "it would really drum up more interest if you're there. The town's talked of little else since you came home. I'm old news, I'm afraid."

Ginny thought about saying no, about chickening out

and running away from Max again. But she couldn't bring herself to disappoint Mona or Natalie that way. They were both counting on her to make the Jubilee the best one yet, and she wanted to prove she was up for the task.

Now the only problem was what to do about Max. Ginny didn't have the answers, but she knew she had to make it right. She couldn't end her visit to Buckeye Falls with Max ignoring her. It didn't sit right with her. Ginny needed to stick to her promise and go decorate some cookies. She knew her father would understand.

Pulling herself up to her feet, Ginny stretched and sighed. "Looks like it's time to get festive."

CHAPTER 12

Max was at the diner at the crack of dawn. Never much of a bourbon drinker, he was reminded of this fact as he lay on the couch feeling the world spin. A bottle of water, two ibuprofen, and a run later; he felt human. Rather than take the coward's way out, Max decided to face his issues head-on. He opened the diner's kitchen and started working on recipes for the Jubilee Ball.

Prepping for the Jubilee made him think about Ginny, and Max sighed. "No point going there," Max grumbled, sliding a cookbook to the side of the counter and cracking open another one. He had seven pots going on the stove. There was a pot of chicken pot pie, a tray of quiches ready for the oven, a pot of vegetable soup, and the beginnings of beef stew in front of him.

"Something smells amazing." He heard CeCe say from the back door. "I mean, other than me." She laughed at her own joke and hung her coat on the peg by the door. She didn't seem surprised to see Max at the diner so early, and he was just as unsurprised to see CeCe.

Part of what made their relationship work was that they were on the same page. Cook when the mood struck, whether it was a good mood or a bad mood. If either one wanted to cook at odd hours, that was fine by him. The only caveat was the meals they worked on ended up on the diner menu. The only exception being a lemon curd tart that CeCe let curdle. A rare miss by CeCe's standards, but not everything could be menu worthy.

CeCe snagged a clean tasting spoon from a drawer and joined Max at the stove. She dipped it into the pot pie filling and slurped. Her eyes fluttered closed as she hummed her approval. "You let me make the crust for that, and it's a winner."

Max gestured to the canister of flour on the counter. "I know you need to prep the cookies, but I thought …" He trailed off, knowing CeCe would read his mind.

"You thought I'd walk in here, get up in your business, and finish everything that needed baking? Wow, Max. It's like you know me or something." She rolled up her sleeves and started measuring flour and cubing butter. "I'll have this short crust ready before we open," she promised.

Keeping his attention on the vegetables he was dicing, Max said, "We should have plenty of time. Evan's still coming in. I tricked him into decorating duty."

CeCe laughed, working the dough with her hands. Crumbles of flour and butter stuck to her fingers. "Poor kid—he'll do pretty much anything you ask."

Max watched CeCe work and hedged his bets. "Evan does pretty much anything you ask too. Just saying."

"Different situations, and you know it." CeCe rubbed her forehead with the back of her hand, leaving a dusting of flour over her eyes. "He's a kid with a crush, that's all."

For nearly a year, Max had watched Evan fawn over CeCe. It was a poorly kept secret that he was in love with her, but Max pretended he didn't see it. "You know, he's only like five years younger than you. You make him sound like a toddler."

Slapping the dough on the counter, CeCe dug in with the heels of her hands, pushing until a strip of dough formed. She kept her eyes focused on her work, but Max could see her thinking. "What did I say last night? You don't mix work with pleasure."

Max was not deterred. "You look like you're enjoying work now. Why can't you humor the guy and take him out sometime? If it sucks, cut your losses."

"Says the man who won't confront his ex," she retorted, walking past him to put her dough in the fridge to rest. Once the door closed, CeCe spun around and crossed her arms. Max was surprised at how intimidating she looked covered in flour. "And don't you dare say it's different, because all matters of the heart boil down to the same thing." She held her hands up like a set of scales. "Someone gets their heart broken while someone else does the breaking. I'd rather avoid that messiness at work."

Max held his hands up in defeat. "All right, you win. I'll drop it."

CeCe narrowed her eyes at her boss. "Why don't I believe you?"

Max laughed. "Because you know me. I'll bring this up again soon enough, but I promise to drop it for now." He slid the cutting board's vegetables into a pot and added a sprinkling of salt. He hoped by playing nice, CeCe would help him today. It wouldn't be easy having Ginny in the diner, but it would be even harder if she stayed away.

Silently, Max continued working on his prep while CeCe got everything ready for the cookie party. She turned on Christmas music, which was very unlike her. She enjoyed the season as much as the next person, but she rarely donned ugly sweaters and sang carols. Humming, CeCe organized dozens of plastic cups with red, white, gold, and green sprinkles. She filled piping bags with white frosting and tied off the edges of the bags, lining them up on a tray.

Back when they opened the diner up for events like this, Max scoffed at the idea. He couldn't imagine his neighbors giving up their afternoons to decorate cookies or make gingerbread houses, but that is exactly what they did. The first Christmas they offered a party, the tickets sold out instantly. He had to turn folks away at the door, which only added to the allure of the event to begin with. There were even a few weekends when the diner would close early for birthday parties. He and CeCe had discussed expanding to more events, but they both forgot about it once the holidays ended. Standing there now, listening to the sounds of the season while his kitchen smelled like heaven, Max felt at peace. His heart was in pieces, but it would mend. It did before; he just needed to have faith.

"Did you guys start the party without me?" Evan asked from the doorway. He wore a heather-green sweater and a pair of jeans. He immediately flushed when CeCe came up and hip-checked him. The red blush gave him the perfect Christmas color scheme.

"We'd never start the fun without you," she teased, breezing past him with a tray of cookies. "If you really want to have fun, you can help me decorate the tables."

Max winked at CeCe when she walked past him with a box of decorations. They both knew Evan could handle it on his own, but it would make his day. "Sure," Evan breathed as he tripped over his feet to catch up to CeCe. "Let me get the door."

Before Max got too distracted, there was a knock from the back. A pull in his chest told him he wanted it to be Ginny, but he struggled to hide his disappointment when he found Natalie standing there.

Much like Evan, she'd gotten festive for the day. A pair of reindeer antlers sat on top of her blonde head, and red jingle bells chimed when she moved. "Hi." She waved, pushing past him without waiting for an invitation. She had a heaving tote bag slung over her shoulder.

Max stepped forward to take her bag, and she nearly fell over. "What is all this? I told you we have it all covered."

Natalie gave him a look like he'd lost his mind. "You have the cookie decorating covered, but I brought activities for the kids. Don't you remember last year? The Miller twins practically burned your diner down when they ran out of cookies to decorate."

Natalie pulled out three board games and a puzzle. She also retrieved three bottles of champagne. "Is this for the kids that won't calm down?" He laughed, checking the vintage of the bottle. This wasn't the cheap stuff he was used to.

Natalie giggled and moved the bottles to the edge of the counter. "Oh, Max, you always were a funny one."

Max smiled but didn't agree with her. While Natalie was never mean to Max, they were hardly friends when they were younger. Since her husband lived for teasing him, Max usually kept his distance from Natalie and her friends. The one exception being Ginny.

CeCe joined them in the kitchen and hugged Natalie. "Nat, you're early. Bless you. Evan doesn't have an eye for tinsel." She groaned.

Right on cue, Evan came into the kitchen covered in silver tinsel. Three clumps clung to his curls, and he fidgeted as he pulled a handful from inside his sweater. "Don't ask," he mumbled to Max, who could barely contain his grin. "CeCe had a great idea to hang this crap from the lights, but they wouldn't stick."

Natalie raised a manicured eyebrow. "It looks like we found the one thing this stuff does stick to."

Evan stepped to the corner and pulled his sweater over his head. Max heard both women gulp and turned to see what the fuss was about. Even in the fluorescent lighting of the kitchen, Max knew that Evan was fit as hell. The kid had at least two six-packs and arms that were honed from countless days lifting boxes and carrying trays. Max would kill for that metabolism again …

"Evan, dude. Put your shirt back on before the health inspector shuts us down," Max said, noticing how CeCe's face matched Natalie's red earrings. The only other time he'd seen that look cross her face was when she'd finally figured out why her blue cheese souffles were deflating. Yet her hungry expression had little to do with egg whites and a lot to do with the man standing before them—literally looking like a Christmas present.

"Good Lord," Natalie breathed, fanning herself with a menu. "I need to come back here more often." Turning to her friend, she added, "You've been holding out on me."

CeCe reached for her bottled water and took a healthy sip. Evan either didn't notice the women's reactions or was smart enough to school his features. Max envied the kid's physique. Between his hours at the diner and his appetite, Max hadn't seen a six-pack (outside a refrigerator) for more years than he cared to remember.

Natalie's phone chirped and brought everyone back to reality. Evan was now mostly tinsel-free, CeCe had rehydrated and composed herself, and Max had the pot pies in the oven. "All right, party people," Natalie crooned, "Anthony is dropping off the kids in a minute and he said there's already a few cars out front." She slid her phone back into her purse and caught Max's sour expression. "I told him he can't stay, especially if he's going to be a jerk."

CeCe gave Max a look he could read all too well before scurrying over to her prep station to grab her piping bags. "It's a shame the good mayor can't join us," she said.

Natalie rolled her eyes. "Oh please, none of us are disappointed. And by the way"—she turned and pointed at Max and CeCe—"whoever added the extra starch to his suit deserves a raise." Natalie stalked out to the dining room, the bottles of champagne clutched in her hands.

Evan took a tray from CeCe and followed Natalie to the dining room. CeCe waited until he was through the door before addressing Max. "Don't you say a word about—" She sighed, gesturing to her torso. "It was a weak moment."

Max tossed her a towel, which she caught midair. "You might want that for the drool on the corner of your mouth. Right here." He pointed to his face. CeCe mumbled a few choice profanities and stormed out of the kitchen.

Thirty minutes later, the diner was packed. Every booth had at least four people crammed in, with the available counter seats taken with winter coats and bags of gifts. Mona had called to share the news that Ginny would be representing her and the planning committee, which did nothing to calm the firestorm churning through Max. He couldn't decide if it was better or worse, knowing that Ginny would be there any second.

Under the ruse of keeping the lunches coming, Max stayed in the kitchen and focused on the night ahead. While mixing ingredients for salad dressing, Max looked up to see Evan sulking by the dishwasher. His shoulders were slumped forward and his head was bowed, a few loose curls falling into his face.

"What's up?" Max asked, coming over to check on his friend.

Evan looked up and shook his head. "Nothing, just checking on the dishes." Max looked over at the dishwasher, which was empty. Evan sighed and shoved his hands in his pockets. "I was going to ask CeCe to go to the Jubilee Ball with me."

Max's heart broke for the kid, whose eager expression hid the pain he was sure he felt. "What happened?" Max asked carefully.

Evan swept his hair from his face and huffed. "She said she doesn't want to go. Natalie was bringing up that everyone needed to get their dresses ready, but CeCe said there was no point. She didn't want to go."

Max considered his words carefully, as he didn't want to put either friend in a bad position. "Did you ask if she wanted to go with you?"

"No, I don't want to get shut down again." Evan leaned back against the dishwasher and groaned. "There's only so much rejection a guy can take, Max. I don't know if I can keep putting myself out there, knowing she's going to shoot me down."

That was a sentiment Max understood all too well. He battled with how to explain himself to Evan, when CeCe came back with two empty trays. "We need some more milk for the …" She stopped dead in her tracks and looked back and forth at the pair. "What did I miss?"

Max knocked his knuckles on the dishwasher and sighed. "Damn thing is acting up again. Evan was taking a look." He turned and saw Evan say a silent "thank you." "How's it going out there?"

CeCe put the trays by the dishwasher and adjusted the Christmas tree hat on her head. Natalie had shared the Christmas magic with everyone, regardless if they were feeling festive. "In case you're wondering, a certain New Yorker is here. She's at table five."

Max walked back to the counter where his salad dressing sat unfinished. "Good for her. I'm glad she made it."

CeCe threw her hands in the air. "You men." She exhaled. "Can't you go talk to her?"

Evan's face flashed purple. He opened his mouth and shut it twice before saying, "Whose side are you on? If Max wants to save what is left of his heart, then I say let him. What is the point of putting yourself out there if you're jerked around all the time?" Evan's voice went up to an octave Max didn't think should be humanly possible. "You women." He huffed as he stormed out through the back door.

"What's his problem?" CeCe asked, thrusting her hands on her hips.

"I want no part of this," Max said, measuring a cup full of olive oil. "But if I did want to get involved, I'd say maybe you should talk to him. He might have something he wants to ask you."

CeCe leaned on the counter, right over where Max was pouring. "Is this coming from personal experience?"

Max put down the bottle and pinched the bridge of his nose. "CeCe," he warned.

CeCe scoffed. "So we're allowed to dissect my love life, but not yours?"

"I didn't think either of us had a love life," Max offered, painfully aware of how parallel he and Evan's love lives were. Max had no right giving anyone advice if he wasn't going to take his own. Shoving the bottles back, he sighed. "I'll go talk to Ginny, but I need you to talk to Evan."

"About what?" CeCe seemed genuinely confused. "Did I do something wrong out there?" She gestured toward the dining room.

Checking to make sure Evan hadn't slunk back into the kitchen, Max lowered his voice. "He wants to ask you to the Jubilee Ball. He heard you say you didn't want to go."

CeCe smacked her forehead with her palm. "Crap, I wasn't thinking when I said it. I had no idea Evan was there." Max knew CeCe would never hurt Evan intentionally. It wasn't in her to be cruel.

"Answer me this, are you really not going to the ball?" Max asked, collecting his ingredients to put away.

CeCe joined in the cleanup and shrugged. "I wasn't planning on it. I thought after we got the food set up, I'd take a hike."

"Do you have anything against going?" Max really wanted to know because it wasn't worth pushing the issue otherwise.

Pondering for a moment, CeCe finally said, "No. Not really. I don't have someone to go with, so I didn't see the point."

"Then go with Evan. It'll make his freaking year if you do."

CeCe placed the last bottle away and poked Max in the chest. "Riddle me this," she urged, "are you going to ask your ex-wife? If you're going to play matchmaker, I want in on the fun." Max knew that look all too well. CeCe was digging in her heels, and there was nothing he could do to get away from her wrath now.

Evan's words rattled around his head. *There's only so much rejection a guy can take.* Perhaps this was Max's line in the sand. He'd opened himself up to Ginny, taking her into his home, and showed her what their life could be like. Her rejection cut just as deep as it did two years ago. Finally, Max was done being a doormat.

"Here's the deal," he said to CeCe, who stopped to watch him. His tone was more commanding than normal. "I'm going to go out and say hello to Ginny, but I'm done. Our boy Evan brought up a good point. There is only so much rejection a guy can take. If he asks you to go to the ball, make a decision, but stick with it." CeCe's throat bobbed as she swallowed hard, but Max wasn't going to let her interrupt. "I need to step back and focus on what makes me happy, what actually loves me back." Max paused, gulping in a lungful before continuing. "This place"—he motioned around them—"and all of you make me happy. It's been enough for the last few years, and it will continue to be enough."

CeCe gaped at Max, taken aback by his honesty. She looked around the kitchen for a moment and finally said, "You're on." She raised her index finger. "But if Evan doesn't ask, I'm not bringing it up."

Max nodded, pulling his apron over his head. Catching his reflection, he ran a hand through his hair and took a deep breath. "I'm going to get this over with. Can you please watch those pies?"

Feeling his throat tighten, Max merely nodded before walking past CeCe and into his future. He saw a flurry of activity in the dining room, with kids running around stuffed with sugary treats, and a few adults, who were slurring their speech after a couple glasses of champagne. But what caught his attention was Ginny, sitting at a table surrounded by children.

Her hair was tucked into an elf hat, and she looked adorable. Attention focused on the kiddos, she leaned in and pointed to a pile of edible glitter. Her voice was even as she instructed them on placing sprinkles on their snowmen cookies. "That's right," she cooed, "just like that. Awesome job," she praised one of the Miller twins. The kids raised their hands for a high five, which Ginny enthusiastically complied. "You two are decorating pros." The children beamed at her compliments before promptly running off to share their kudos with their mother.

Not wasting another moment, Max approached her table and plastered on what he hoped was a convincing smile. Judging from her expression, he knew he'd failed. "Th-thanks for coming out to represent the Jubilee committee. Mona said you were coming." Keeping his arms crossed over his chest, Max stared at the top of Ginny's hat. If their eyes met, his resolve would crumble faster than a gingerbread house.

Ginny slid across the booth and got to her feet. Max took a step back and bumped into Natalie. "Max, there you are. I was looking for you. This has been the best cookie party yet." She clasped her hands in front of her. "Thank you for hosting again. I can't imagine a better place for this event."

"You're welcome. You know I'm always happy to help."

Natalie opened her mouth to say something, but a frosting-covered Otis caught her attention. "Otis, what did Mommy say about frosting? It goes on the cookies, not in our hair." She sprinted off after the boy, who was giggling like a madman. Max smiled briefly at the kid before getting back to the issue at hand.

Hitching a thumb over his shoulder, Max made his excuse to leave. Ginny reached out and touched his arm. "Max, can we talk for a second?" she asked, her eyes hopeful.

"I really need to check on things," he offered lamely.

Ginny bit her lip. "I deserve that, but can I just have a second? I want to apologize for yesterday." Max's gaze was pulled from her ridiculous hat down to her fingers, which balled a napkin so tightly it turned into festive confetti.

"You really don't have to say anything, Gin. I need to get back." Max didn't wait for her to reply, instead stomping back to the kitchen. As soon as the door swung shut, he knew he'd been followed. CeCe looked up from the stove and dropped her tongs.

Ginny tugged on his hand, and Max was forced to stop. CeCe turned down the burners and cleared her throat. "I'm going to check on how things are progressing with uh …" She gestured toward the door. Throwing another glance over her shoulder at the pair, she finally stepped out into the festive chaos.

As soon as CeCe cleared the threshold, Ginny frowned. "Is that CeCe?" she asked.

Max reveled in Ginny's sour expression. "Yes, it is. I don't know why it matters. You can't be jealous and dismissive all at once." The crestfallen look on Ginny's face should have broken his heart, but he was done caring. "You really shouldn't even be back here. It's for staff only."

Ginny threw her hands in the air and followed Max toward his office. "So, this is how we're playing this? You're not even going to talk to me? We need to talk about this, not just ignore each other."

The pulse in Max's temple throbbed to life, and he counted down from five before turning to face his ex. "So you're upset that for once *I'm* ending the argument early? Should I let you get fired up and stomp off when it's good for you? Would that make this more p-p-palatable?"

His blind rage caused Ginny to fumble on her feet. "What's wrong with you?" she asked, clearly upset. "I've never seen you behave this way before."

Max shoved his hands in his pockets and rolled back on his heels. "Well, maybe this is the new Max. I think after all these years, I'm allowed to stand up for myself. I think my doormat days are finally over."

"Doormat? You think I treat you like a doormat?" Ginny looked as if he'd slapped her. Her jaw fell, and her eyes misted over. "Have I really been that cruel?"

Max felt his heart bang inside his chest. He'd sat on these frustrations for years, and dammit, it felt right to finally give them voice. "You kissed me and acted like it was a fate worse than death. How do you think that made me feel? I pine for you like a heartsick fool, and as soon as you're back,

I put my heart on the line for you, Gin. I would gladly do anything for you, and you exploited that."

"You think I exploited you?"

"I think you're going to leave again. I think you're not coming back from New York this time; at least not in a capacity to see me." Raking a hand through his hair, Max strived to keep his voice firm, his words sure. "I think I'm tired of always being the one left behind, so excuse me if I don't want to prolong the inevitable. It is brutal being taken for granted like this."

"You make me sound like a monster." Ginny sobbed, her hands pressed to her cheeks as the tears finally fell. "You make me sound like my mother."

Max knew he'd gone too far, stepped into painful territory that crossed a line. Just as his stutter was his soft spot, a part of himself he kept hidden, so was Ginny's mother. After years of bad-mouthing her mother's decisions, Ginny had fallen into the same pattern. He'd realized it long ago, but never said anything that mirrored her adolescent trauma.

Stepping forward, Max reached out for Ginny. "Gin, I sh-sh-shouldn't have said that."

As still as a statue, Ginny didn't breathe for a moment. Max watched in heartbreak as a single tear slid down her cheek, dissecting a constellation of freckles. With a shaking hand, she wiped away the tear. "You have every right to be angry. And you're right, I've taken advantage of your kindness. I'm sorry, Max." Ginny reached and fumbled with the doorknob until she finally broke out into the hot air of the kitchen.

Max watched her leave and felt rooted in place. Once again, his wife was leaving and he couldn't get his feet to move. At least he'd found his words this time, Max held onto that notion, that small point of pride.

He could still hear Christmas Carols from the party, but Max felt anything but festive. He felt raw, ripped open. It was not a new feeling for him, but he felt different this time.

It was like a nightmare you keep having, but you can't change the outcome. Arms flailing, reaching out to change the ending you know is coming. But now, he felt like this might have been the breakthrough he'd been waiting for. Sure, they were both upset. This time there was a difference; they both fought. They both said their piece.

There would be regret, probably sooner than Max cared to realize. But in that moment, locked inside his tiny office with the sounds of holiday cheer surrounding him, he knew he'd finally broken the cycle, broken free of his past pain. Because for once, he used his words to speak his own truth. If that's all it took to keep Ginny away, then it truly wasn't meant to be.

CHAPTER 13

"So …" Natalie said, her red lipstick dotted with white sprinkles. Otis tugged on her arm, clearly not wanting to indulge in girl talk when there were cookies to eat. Natalie ignored his whining and handed him a piece of cookie from her plate. The toddler took it, shoved it in his mouth, and fell back onto the floor, content with his sugar fix. "Why did I just see you run after everyone's favorite chef?"

Ginny stiffened, not wanting to draw any more attention than they already had. She hadn't thought twice before running after him and was caught off guard by Max's coldness. His words cut deep, but they'd hit their mark. A small part of Ginny was almost proud of Max. He called her out, and she knew she deserved it. What she also knew was her time with Max was likely over—for good this time. The notion sent a chill through her core.

"I had to check on a few things—no big deal." Not wanting to meet Natalie's assessing gaze, Ginny traced a line of dried frosting across the tabletop.

Natalie leaned forward, her elbows landing on the foot of a gingerbread man. "What's going on? And don't bother saying nothing, because you're a terrible liar." Ginny saw Madeline approach and thought she was safe from this line of questioning, but no such luck. Natalie never broke eye contact, reaching into her tote and retrieving a board game. She handed it to her daughter and instructed, "Find five children to play with. If you win, I'll get McDonald's for dinner." The girl yelped, snagged the game, and ran off in search of competitors.

"Does that always work?" Ginny asked, still hoping to avoid the third degree.

Natalie drained the last of her champagne and scoffed. "Like a charm. Now, stop trying to change the subject. My sub-par parenting isn't worth dissecting when I'm this sober. Your love life, on the other hand, is worth dissection. Spill it."

Glancing around to make sure no one was listening, Ginny sighed. "We had a fight."

Natalie motioned for Ginny to continue. "I figured that much. You look like someone just told you there isn't a S-A-N-T-A."

Against her will, Ginny laughed. "You know I can spell, right?"

Natalie looked undeterred. "Duh, but my toddler can't. Frankly, I don't want to have that conversation for at least another decade. Now, what did you fight about? You looked lovey-dovey at the hospital."

"A little too lovey-dovey," Ginny ground out. "If I tell you something, you promise to keep it between us?"

At her question, Natalie crossed her heart with a lacquered nail. "Much like Mrs. Miller's shortbread recipe, I'll take your secret to the grave," she promised. Against her better judgment, Ginny believed her. After all, Mrs. Miller's cookie recipe hadn't been figured out yet.

"Max and I kissed yesterday. It was a horrible mistake, which I told my father, and Max overheard. Now he's not talking to me, and I feel worse than I did when I left. On top of all that, my boss keeps calling and asking for help on projects I know she can do. Then I get mad at myself for not doing my job because I love what I do. But then I think of everything I'm missing here when I'm back in New York, and that has me feeling a little topsy-turvy. Especially since being with Max has brought up a lot of old feelings, and some of them are good, some of them are great in fact. Ugh, I don't know." Ginny let out a long breath and looked back to her friend. "There, that's everything."

Natalie didn't respond but blinked slowly and shook her head. The jingle bells on her headband chimed with the movement. "Yeah, you've literally made me speechless. There's a lot to unpack there."

Ginny reached out for the champagne bottle, grimacing when she found it empty. "Yeah, and now you know why I look like someone canceled Christmas. Because they kind of did."

Natalie shook her head. "We can fix this; I know we can. You just need a grand gesture to win Max back."

"Win him back? What is the point of that? I head back to New York after Dad's recovered."

Natalie shrugged and picked up the newly amputated gingerbread man. She bit off his head in one swift motion and washed it down with Otis's milk. "Do you have to?" Ginny opened her mouth to respond, but Natalie kept going. "You've looked really happy since you've been back. Max hasn't been this happy in years, and it's clear Harold and Mona love having you here. And if you'll allow me to be selfish, it's nice to have a friend here who isn't linked by our crazy children. Why can't you stay?"

Finally, Ginny cut in, "And what would I do for work? Wait tables? I have a career, Natalie."

"What happens if there are other opportunities in Buckeye Falls, beyond slinging cheesy bites at citizens?" Sensing a challenge, Natalie leaned into her argument. "Hear me out, Ginny. This place has changed over the last few years."

Ginny was dubious at best. The notion she could work—in her field no less—in Buckeye Falls was laughable. "And where would these opportunities be?"

Natalie leaned forward and lowered her voice. "With me."

Ginny shook her head. "I love your kiddos, but I'm not nanny material."

With a snort, Natalie waved off her suggestion. "Pfft, please. I have two sets of grandparents who cover that, thank you. What I'm talking about is for grown-ups. I'm starting an event planning business, and I'll need someone on staff who knows marketing and project management. I know I can't guarantee you the same salary, but that's the beauty of being here. The cost of living is in my favor." The expression on Natalie's face was nothing short of smug.

Now Ginny knew she was dreaming. First a fight with Max and now her friend offering her a job. It was all too surreal, and she couldn't fathom having a fulfilling job here. "But what kind of job is it? How do you know I'd be a good fit?"

Finishing off her cookie, Natalie stared at her friend. "Because you are one of the best in New York. Harold and Max brag about you all the time, so I did my homework. You've brought in major clients and are known for doing a lot with shoestring budgets. I know what I am offering will seem like small potatoes, but you'd oversee all marketing and deadlines. You'd be your own boss, and eventually I'd love to expand to a secondary location."

"But, Natalie, have you done your market research? Does Buckeye Falls need an event planning business?"

Natalie didn't appear concerned by Ginny's questions. "Yes, I've been working on this for a while. Believe it or not, I got a business degree before motherhood. The time has come to finally use it. Let me send you my specs, okay?"

It all sounded fantastical to Ginny. Being her own boss had long been a dream, and not just now as she struggled with Lana long distance. But would staying in Buckeye Falls be the right call? Even though she'd felt at home and relaxed since her return, there were reasons she'd left in the first place.

With the benefit of hindsight, those reasons seemed almost laughable. Ginny took pride from a job well done, and she knew the location of her work wouldn't alter her mindset. And What about the desire to live somewhere different, that need to spread her wings? Would she be happy here again? Was there a place for her?

Sitting in this cozy booth surrounded by friends and the holidays, it was easy for Ginny to picture herself back in Buckeye Falls. The question now was, what would Max think of her staying? Would her father even need her? Most importantly, what did she really want?

"Can I think about it?" she asked, hedging her bets.

Natalie beamed. "Are you kidding? I insist. Take the holiday, see how Harold is doing, and let me know. I'm not posting the job until I hear from you."

Just then, Ginny's phone chimed with an incoming text. *home and hihglly medicatedd*, her father's message read. She laughed at the typos and tucked her phone back into her pocket.

"That's Dad—he's home, and I want to check on him." Ginny stood and collected her coat and bag. Natalie slid out and handed her a platter of cookies.

"I saved these from my heathen children. Please give these to Harold and Mona." Ginny reached for the plate, but Natalie held firm. "And think about what I said, okay? That job is yours if you want it."

Ginny only nodded and left the diner. Her stomach was full of cookies, her heart was in pieces, and her brain was full of unanswered questions.

For the first time in nearly a decade, Ginny felt the holiday spirit. It was in the cookies she decorated, in the silly hat she wore to make her friend laugh, and in the way she stopped to smell the piney branches of the tree by her father's house. Christmas felt like a happy holiday again, and she knew Buckeye Falls was to blame.

Ginny smiled to herself as she got into her rental car. When she turned on the radio, a Christmas carol piped through the speakers. For three blocks, Ginny sang along with the familiar tune until she reached a stop light. Then her phone rang again. Assuming it was her father, she answered through Bluetooth with a smile on her face. "I'll be there in five minutes," she said.

"Thank God." Lana's voice boomed through the speakers. "That should be about as long as it takes me to strangle Morty."

The rental car lurched forward as Ginny's foot slipped off the brake. "Lana? I wasn't expecting you. I thought you were my dad." Ginny looked behind her and saw no one was waiting. She made a U-turn and parked in an empty parking lot, knowing she wouldn't be able to focus on driving with Lana barking in her ear.

A long sigh came through the speakers, and Ginny closed her eyes and braced for impact. If Lana was collecting her thoughts, it was never a good thing. "So you're not five minutes away from the office?"

Ginny went with the truth, no sugarcoating. "No, I'm still in Buckeye Falls. Dad got out of the hospital today." Realizing the music was still pumping, Ginny stabbed at the volume controls, silencing Bing Crosby.

"Sounds like you're having a festive time in old Iowa," Lana scoffed. Ginny opened her mouth to correct her on the state but thought better of it. "I thought I made it clear you were needed at the office, Ginny. There is too much on the line right now for you to be on vacation."

Finally, Ginny couldn't hold her tongue a moment longer. "This isn't a vacation, Lana. My father was in the hospital. I'm here to take care of him. I've mentioned this at least a dozen times." Very rarely was Ginny this insubordinate, but frankly she didn't care.

"You have a job to do. If he's at home, then you can come back to the office. Bring him with you if you'd like. Your place isn't far from here." In the background, Ginny heard rustling papers and mumbled profanity as Lana talked to her long-suffering assistant.

Ginny sat back in the driver's seat and gaped out the windshield. Lana wanted her to move her father, who just had hip surgery, to the city to sit alone while she worked a twelve-hour day. She pictured their home and what she was about to return to. Mona was cooking dinner, her father sharing colorful commentary of a basketball game on TV, the feeling of utter contentment that awaited her. Ginny could practically feel the warmth of the fire now.

"Are you even listening to me?" Lana snapped. "I have two client meetings booked for the next hour. You are needed here, now. Get your laptop and at least join the meeting remotely. I need to see your plans for the Haines account, and …" Ginny stopped listening after that.

For another five minutes, Lana droned on while Ginny thought about her life choices. When she left Buckeye Falls, she felt like she was breathing freely for the first time in years. She was making her way in the world, building a career she could be proud of. Now the thought of going back to her cramped apartment in New York, where not even a houseplant waited for her, seemed hollow, lonely.

Calls from Lana used to bring about a sense of urgency, a call to action to use her skills to craft brilliant marketing schemes. Ginny would get lost in the work, reveling in the feeling of creating something that people would see and rely on. But in that moment, sitting in an empty parking lot in Buckeye Falls, Ginny wanted anything but that. Maybe it was Natalie's offer growing roots in her muddled brain. Or perhaps it was the fact that Max and she had unfinished business. No matter the reason, Ginny knew things needed to change.

Finally, Lana realized she was having a one-way conversation. "Did you hear what I said? Morty is trying to send you the files, but he said you're not logged into the database."

Ginny put the car back in drive and took a cleansing breath. Her steady hands gripped the steering wheel as she eased onto the road. "I'm on leave, Lana. I'm not due back to work until late January."

Lana laughed, a humorless sound that raised the hairs on Ginny's neck. "No, your leave has been canceled. You're going to log into this meeting right now."

Before she could think better of her words, Ginny said, "No. I'm not. If you can't respect my need to be home with family, then I don't think I need to be working for you." The other line was silent for a long moment, and Ginny feared they'd been disconnected. She didn't think she had the guts to say that again.

"If you're not on this call in five minutes, you don't have a job," Lana said, her tone harsh.

"Then consider this my resignation," Ginny said, disconnecting the call and turning the Christmas carols back on. As she sped back to the house, Ginny sang the chorus to Rudolph as loud as she could.

*

"You're not seriously going to stay here all night, are you?" CeCe asked from the doorway, her coat slung over her arm. Her hair was pulled back in a ball cap, her eyes dark and tired. When the cookie party ended, the cooking for the Jubilee began. CeCe grated over ten pounds of cheese for her famous cheesy bites, while Max spent his night mixing the ingredients for the punch and packaging dozens of appetizers in paper boxes.

Rubbing the small of his back, Max stretched and groaned with his achy joints. "I'll head out in a minute." He yawned.

CeCe let the door close and stepped back into the kitchen. She surveyed the now-clean space, including all the boxes ready for Evan to pick up the next morning. She furrowed her brow and stared Max down.

"Why do I feel a lecture coming on?" he asked.

CeCe snorted. "Probably because you're about to get one." Max started to interrupt, but CeCe reached out and flicked his arm with her coat sleeve. "Now shut up and let me rant, then I'll leave you alone." Max made a show of rolling his eyes and leaned back on the counter. CeCe crossed her arms in front of her chest. "Something clearly happened today, and I don't want to hear about it. All I'm asking is that you don't spend another two years mending your heart. If you're truly done with her, then move on. If you're not, then make a move. Those are the options."

Max shook his head, as if the words didn't make sense. "And who died and made you the expert on love?"

"No one, but I pay attention. Since she's been back in town, you've been happier." Pausing, CeCe motioned toward his office. "The obvious exception being earlier today and last night. What I'm saying is, you have the power here, Max. You can decide what would make you happy and go for it."

"You make it sound so simple, but it's beyond complicated." How could Max possibly summarize their marriage and divorce to CeCe?

"Then un-complicate it. You two have a history, and judging from the looks you were swapping earlier, there's some chemistry as well."

Max scoffed. "And?"

"And? It's late, and I'm exhausted from grating a million pounds of cheddar. My point is, sleep on it and see how you feel in the morning. You might surprise yourself with your decision." CeCe pulled on her coat and headed toward the exit. She hesitated, picking up a reindeer tote bag from the floor. "Whose bag is this?"

Max slapped his forehead. "Natalie's. She told me to hold it while she loaded up the kids, but I got distracted. I can bring it to her place tomorrow."

CeCe nodded, satisfied that the solution was not hers. "Think about what I said," she offered as she closed the door behind her.

Max took a moment to wipe down the counters and lock up the safe. He was heading to the alarm panel when he heard a knock on the back door. Glancing at the time, it was far too late to be a customer. Evan and CeCe would use their keys.

For a moment, Max's heart soared when he pictured Ginny outside. Her cheeks would be pink from the cold, and her nose would be brighter than Rudolph's. Max smiled at the thought as he pulled open the door. The smile melted faster than a snowman in April when he saw who was knocking.

"Anthony?"

Mayor Snyder stepped past Max into the kitchen, shaking some snow from his mussed hair. "Max," he grunted his name in greeting. "Nat left a bag here or something."

Max was relieved this was a mere errand for his wife and not a time to dig up old issues. The very last thing Max needed tonight was a trip down Memory Lane with his least favorite neighbor. "Perfect timing," he said as he handed the bag to Anthony.

Anthony faltered when he realized how heavy the bag was. "What's in here, rocks?" He sighed, peering inside and finding an array of games and toys. "That's Nat for you, bringing the entire game cabinet on the road." Anthony took a step back but didn't walk toward the exit. He studied Max for a moment, his gaze steady.

"Something else I can help you with?" Max asked, privately celebrating his cold tone and crisp words. "Maybe you need something else dry-cleaned?" Max raised an eyebrow in challenge. While his exterior was still, he knew his heart was pounding. Confrontation was never his thing.

At first, Anthony shook his head and turned. But when his hand hit the doorknob, he stopped, mumbling something under his breath. He turned and looked at Max and shrugged. "Do you really think I'm that much of a jerk?" he asked, almost looking wounded.

Max scoffed. "You literally hate my guts, made a scene in my business, and tried to move the highway that would have killed my livelihood. Yeah, Anthony. Sometimes I do think you're a jerk." Max wished CeCe was still here, because no one in Buckeye Falls would believe he was standing up to Anthony. *Damn, this felt good.*

To his credit, Anthony didn't argue. Lowering the tote to the floor, he shoved his hands in his pockets and stepped closer to Max. "I shouldn't have overreacted with the spilled tea thing," he offered. For a moment, Max didn't think the other man would continue the apology. His expression was so sour, it looked like he'd eaten an entire bag of lemon drops. "I'm sorry, truly."

"Understatement of the year, but I accept your apology. You can share it with Evan tomorrow at the Jubilee." Max stood a little straighter as Anthony paled. "I think *he* really deserves your apology."

"Fair enough," Anthony agreed. "I know it's not an excuse, but since getting elected, it's been rough."

Max did not expect that level of candor from Anthony. During all their issues with the highway proposal, he hadn't paid attention to the mayor or his appearance. Standing so close now, it was impossible to miss the dark smudges under his eyes or the frown lines etched on his cheeks. "I'm sorry, man. I didn't think of it that way."

Anthony lifted a shoulder and sighed. "Following in my father's footsteps isn't what it's cracked up to be, but I'll figure it out." He took a moment, looking around at the kitchen. Max was grateful he'd taken the time to clean up, so it looked its best. "Nat said you hosted a great party. The kids loved it too."

Max preened at the compliment. "Thank you. That means a lot coming from you. And I mean Anthony, not just the mayor."

"You do good work, Max. There's a reason this place is a local institution."

There was a history between the pair, and Max wagered neither one truly remembered why they had a falling out. One day they were on the football team, and the next Max was the target of everyone's ridicule. Back then he was an easy mark, a late bloomer with a stutter. While not excusing their behavior, he could see the appeal of hassling the newest kid in town.

Perhaps it was the holiday spirit, but Max hoped this was a turning point. He adored Natalie and the kids, so it only made sense that he and Anthony mended their broken fences. Now that he understood the stress the mayor was under, Max could approach their interactions with a little more tact. He tried to take the high road, and this relationship was a good place as any to practice what he preached.

Anthony leaned down to pick up the tote again, clearly done with discussing their emotions. "If I can change the subject," he said, wilting under the weight of the bag. "Do you think Ginny will take Natalie up on her job offer?"

Max flinched like he'd been sucker punched. "Job offer?" Suddenly he felt lost, like he was joining the conversation halfway through. "What are you talking about?"

Anthony frowned, clearly surprised that Max wasn't already in the know. "Nat offered Ginny a job at her new events business. We bought that old storefront downtown near the library. She asked Ginny if she'd be interested in staying here and helping. Sorry, man, I thought you knew." He held up his hands in front of him, now easing back toward the door, as if Max would pounce. "She asked her today, at the cookie party." He was backpedaling, and Max appreciated the effort.

Of course Max didn't know. Just like before, he and Ginny were not communicating. He rubbed the back of his neck, feeling beads of sweat forming as his pulse kicked up. Why couldn't she have told him? Why did he hear about this from the last person he expected?

"Thanks for telling me."

Anthony hoisted the bag over his shoulder, clearly ready to go. "I'm sure if she accepts, Natalie will tell the whole town. She'll probably make me put it in the town's newsletter." Both men smiled at the mention of Natalie's tenacity. "I hope for both our sakes, Ginny takes the job. Something tells me it would be just as nice for you."

Max was taken aback by Anthony's sincerity. "I figured you didn't care what happened to me or my ex-wife."

"Wow, man, you really do think I'm an asshole." Anthony chuckled. "We might not see eye to eye most of the time, but I know that you are good for this town. Frankly, it sounds like you've been a lot more fun to be around since Ginny came back. Maybe it'll all work out."

Max barked out a laugh. "Have you already gotten into the eggnog? We haven't opened up like this since the football retreat sophomore year."

Anthony's honey eyes brightened at the mention of high school. Despite making good in Buckeye Falls, he clearly missed his glory days more than he'd admit, especially to Max. "Maybe it's the holiday spirit? Or maybe I am a selfish jerk who wants your ex to move back to make my wife happy. Happy wife, happy life."

Not quite ready to agree, Max walked with Anthony to the door. "I'll walk you out," he said, punching in the alarm code and locking the door. He stood and watched Anthony pull out into the chilly December night, the taillights of his expensive SUV fading as he crested the hill to Main Street.

Max couldn't process what Anthony had said. Ginny got a job offer to stay in Buckeye Falls. What did she think? Was she even entertaining the idea? Knowing Ginny, probably not. She was so dead set against this town, Max would not be surprised if she'd already shot down Natalie.

But then a brand-new thought came to Max. What if she did take it? Would she want to be with him if they were both in town? Max's scrambled thoughts were interrupted by the sound of a car pulling into the diner's parking lot. He zipped his coat up to his neck and walked toward it, waiting for Mona to step out.

She wore a bright green hat in the shape of a Christmas

tree, complete with twinkling lights. Max gestured to the hat as he joined her. "You should save all that sparkle for tomorrow. It'll be perfect for the Jubilee."

Mona reached up to touch the hat. "Oh dear, I thought I turned it off." She pulled it from her head, shook her hair back into place, and tucked the hat under her arm. "I came to see you. I'm glad I caught you."

Max hitched a thumb over his shoulder. "I just locked up. Did you need any of the food tonight?"

Mona shook her head and sighed. "It's Ginny … I wanted to talk to you."

Max didn't know if his heart could stand the roller coaster ride that was the topic of his ex-wife. "Did something happen? Is she okay?"

Mona shrugged. "Yes, as far as I can tell. She seemed a little off when she got back to Harold's place. Of course, she was happy to see him. But …" Mona twirled her hand in the air, searching for the words. "But she said she wasn't planning to go to the Jubilee Ball. That seemed odd, especially since Harold told me she has a dress and everything. Did something happen? You didn't come by tonight—what's wrong?"

Ah, the dress. The dress he bought for Ginny when they weren't making time for each other. She'd seen it on a walk down Main Street, oohing and awing over the cut and the color of the beading. Max knew she'd look like a walking Christmas present in it. Once she'd left for work the next day, he'd driven to the shop and bought it for her. He'd planned to take her to the Jubilee, planned to start making more time for them. Foolishly, Max had thought a few yards of sequins and silk could save his marriage.

Bless Mona and her optimism. Max knew Harold was a lucky man to have someone so caring in his life. "I got busy here, helping CeCe for tomorrow. I'll swing by Harold's this weekend." It was a lame lie, and Max could tell Mona wasn't buying it.

"Did you two have a disagreement?"

Max chose vague honesty in his reply. "She's my ex-wife, it only makes sense we'd have a few disagreements." For starters, they disagreed that the divorce and their kiss were mistakes. Max would gladly give up his entire knife collection for just one more minute with Ginny. Reaching up, he scratched his beard and wondered when he'd stop feeling the ghost of her lips on his. Probably not for the rest of his life, he lamented.

Mona splayed a hand across her chest and sighed. "If anyone understands disagreements with exes, it's me. Which is why I know you two aren't finished."

"It's not that easy, Mona," Max said, hating the defeated tone in his voice.

"Matters of the heart never are. It's Christmas, Max. Don't you think you two are due a miracle?"

Max wanted more than anything to agree with her. But this was life, not a Hallmark movie. He and Ginny would not magically come together in a whirlwind of tinsel and mistletoe. There was history they needed to traverse. Plus, they needed to communicate. While he wanted Mona to be right, Max knew it was hopeless.

Either reading his mind or sensing the moment, Mona stepped close and pulled Max in for a hug. He savored the moment, especially since it had been over a year since he'd hugged his own mother. Mona and Harold had become his surrogate parents. Most men in their thirties would laugh at Max for feeling the need for more family, but to Max, the people in his life were precious.

"I really appreciate you coming out here, but the damage is done. We both said some hurtful things to each other and—" Max's words were cut off by Mona's sweet laughter.

"Oh, Max, you really are a sweetheart. What do you think apologies and grand gestures are for? Tomorrow is the Jubilee, anything can happen. You get the food to the Jubilee, and I'll take care of getting our girl to the ball. How does that sound?"

Max soaked up Mona's optimism like a sponge. "How

do you know she'll even listen to you?"

Mona waved his words away. "Are you kidding? I'm bringing my secret weapon."

"Do I even want to know?" Max laughed.

"It's Natalie. Need I say more?"

Max barked out another laugh, knowing that if anyone would get Ginny to the ball, it would be Natalie. "This might sound crazy, but I think you're onto something."

They walked to Mona's car, and Max opened the door for her. She slid in and tossed her hat on the passenger's seat. "Remember, text Harold in the morning. We'll take care of the details."

Max looked at Mona's hopeful expression. "I hope you're right about all this." He sighed.

"Max, dear, how quickly you forget. It's Christmas, the season for miracles." Mona turned on her car and headed back into town. Just like he did with Anthony, Max stood in the winter air and waited for her car to disappear from view.

The thought of seeing Ginny tomorrow at the ball warmed him from the inside. He was feeling more hopeful than he had in days, hopeful that he and Ginny could finally communicate, finally reconcile. Anthony's mention of the job only fueled that fire of hope.

Keeping his thoughts and feelings inside didn't help anyone, least of all Max. Perhaps tonight, his three visitors were his ghosts of Christmas, showing him the way forward. Max exhaled into the night and got into his car. He wanted to get home and rest because he had a big day ahead of him. Tomorrow is the day he would get his wife back.

CHAPTER 14

Ginny couldn't sleep a wink. Between worrying about her father's recovery, to the flashes of pain in Max's eyes, her mind could not rest. Padding down to the kitchen, Ginny quietly turned on the coffee maker and started pulling out ingredients for breakfast. From the living room, she heard her father's snores on the sofa. Last night as Mona was leaving, they'd debated trying to get him upstairs but decided to keep him comfortable on his cushions. Mona was a lifesaver, that was for certain.

It never escaped her notice that Max would have been wonderful. He was excellent company for Harold, but also would have been a support for her. She missed his flannel shoulders and strong arms holding her steady, holding her firmly in place when she faltered. Why had she reacted the way she did? Why did she think she could live without him in her life?

Max was really finished with her now, and who could blame him? Even someone with so sweet a disposition has their breaking point. His ex-wife returning home at the holidays, wreaking havoc in his personal life, and embedding herself in his turf had to hurt. *Why, why, why* did she have to be such a flake when it came to Max and his heart?

At the start it was easy to play the blame game, looking back on the last year of their marriage. Max was always at the diner. He'd never made time for her—the list could go on. Yet this visit home brought the truth into sharper focus. Ginny had been as bad, maybe worse, when it came to the reasons behind the divorce. When Max was working, so was she. She'd been just as invested in her career as Max had been in his. What should have brought them closer together ended up tearing them apart.

Ginny realized two important things: Max deserved better, but so did she. Ginny wasn't her mother, and Max wasn't Harold. They could make things right; they could talk to each other and figure it out. There was still something between them, and she wasn't going to lose it again.

Sliding the butter dish toward the toaster, Ginny busied herself with other thoughts, other concerns. One concern that did not rear its ugly head was her recent unemployment. Throughout the night, the only thing that didn't keep Ginny up was the fact that she quit her job. She expected a pang of regret or a moment's sanity when she would call Lana and beg for her job back. But there was nothing. After more than two years of working herself into a stupor, she had nothing to show for it beyond a sense of relief to be done.

Ginny pulled a carton of eggs and started cracking them into a bowl. She used such force that the shells splintered inside, leaving Ginny to fish them out with her finger. "Come on." She groaned as the fifth egg nearly exploded in her hand.

"Are you making crunchy omelets this morning?" Harold croaked from the doorway. His salt and pepper hair stood in every conceivable direction, and he leaned against the wall for support.

Task forgotten, Ginny rushed to his side and let him lean on her. "Let's get you some coffee," she said as she guided him toward his chair. Before Harold could settle into his seat, Ginny brought over his coffee and the morning paper.

The Jubilee was the front-page story, and seeing the details made her chest ache.

Harold smiled at his daughter and patted her cheek before she could step away. "You're so sweet taking care of me, Ginnybread."

Pausing by her father's chair, Ginny bit her lip and let his words sink in. "It's no trouble, Dad. Anyone worth a darn would help." Even though her mother rarely haunted their conversations, Ginny pictured her clearly in that moment. Never a nurturing woman, Ginny always went to her father when she needed some TLC. Harold was warm and giving, and it never escaped Ginny that her mother made a mistake. How could she have walked away from a man who had so much love to give?

Suddenly Ginny felt uneasy. The parallels between her and her mother were too much, and she needed to clear her head. "What can I make you for breakfast?" she asked, turning back to the mess of eggs and shells.

Harold studied his daughter for a moment, taking in her tense shoulders and the abused eggs clenched in her hand. "You want to talk about it?" he asked, his voice light and his tone reassuring. "I happen to have all morning free," he teased.

Ginny shook her head, keeping her gaze on the massacre in front of her. Deciding it would be easier to start from scratch, she dumped the bowl into the sink and wiped her hands on her bathrobe. "How about oatmeal?" she suggested, nearly throwing the half carton of eggs back into the fridge.

"How about coffee first? Frankly, I don't have enough oatmeal for you to toss in the sink. And stop that, we don't have a garbage disposal." He winked, but Ginny blanched at the statement. She sat back in her chair and placed her coffee cup in front of her. Keeping her eyes downcast, she poked at a hole in the tablecloth. Harold didn't say anything, just watched his daughter with interest. He knew he could wait her out.

Less than a minute later, Ginny leaned forward and rested her elbows on the table. She looked up into her dad's earnest expression and nearly burst into tears. "I messed up, Dad." She sobbed, wiping at a stray tear with the sleeve of her robe.

Harold eased himself forward and sipped from his cup, careful not to put too much weight on one of his sides. "Well now." He sighed, undoubtedly upset to see his daughter in distress. "Let's start at the beginning." Ginny tugged at the sleeves of her robe and mumbled to herself for a moment, struggling to find the beginning of her recent path to self-destruction—or self-enlightenment if she was feeling generous.

"I guess it's two things, although one isn't really bothering me like it should."

"Start with that then. We will work our way up to the bigger issues at hand." Harold nodded at his own suggestion, pleased when Ginny licked her lips and shared her thoughts.

"I quit my job," she blurted out. Her shoulders lifted with the admission. "On my way home from the cookie party. My boss, Lana, called, and it sent me over the edge. Her work-life balance policies are a joke, and I'd had enough."

Harold didn't wince at the admission, keeping his eyes locked on Ginny's expressions. "You don't seem very upset about this. When did these policies change?"

The question threw Ginny, and she paused to collect her thoughts. "Never, really. I guess my opinions on the policies changed," she offered. Millions of examples of these previous imbalances raced through her mind now that she thought about it. There was her birthday last year when she worked nearly until midnight finishing up an account in Japan. Then there was the Valentine's before when she'd inadvertently stood up a Tinder date after she'd lost track of time in a staff meeting. The latter didn't really bother Ginny, especially now, but the memory of the lonely birthday eating a Lean Cuisine was the perfect example.

Her father waited for Ginny to find her words and share her thoughts, as he had done so many times before. Ginny supposed this was where she and Max had found their communication patterns, back when they communicated. Ginny borrowed her father's patience, while Max found his words; then the pair would talk and come to common ground. Looking down at her slippered feet, Ginny wondered if there was any common ground left to stand on.

"Penny for your thoughts? You seem a million miles away." Ginny looked up and blinked back into focus. "I won't pretend to understand your field, or what the current job market is like." Harold cleared his throat before sipping his coffee. "You will find another job, and in the meantime, you have a roof over your head. What's really bothering you, Ginnybread?"

The childhood endearment tightened Ginny's throat, and she tried to swallow past the fresh bout of tears. Giving up the ghost, she hiccupped as the tears escaped. Harold reached for a tea towel draped over the other chair and handed it to his daughter, his eyes turning red as he watched her collect herself. "I think I'm like her. It scares me to death." Ginny cried into the damp towel.

Fully understanding the situation, Harold rapped his knuckles on the table to get her attention. "I'm only going to say this once, all right?" This was the business tone, the tone Harold used when Ginny was in trouble or something major happened. Squaring her shoulders, Ginny waited for the impact of his words. "You are absolutely nothing like your mother. I cannot stress that enough."

"How can you say that with a straight face?" Ginny lamented.

"Watch me," Harold ordered, circling his face with his index finger. "You are not like your mother." Sensing she didn't believe him, he tried another tactic. "Can you tell me how you think you're alike? Maybe that will help me prove my point."

Ginny tensed but didn't shy away from the question. "I'm not very nurturing, and I throw people away."

Holding up a hand, Harold interrupted her examples. "I'll stop you right there on your first point. You left your job and came home to help me recover. Plus, you've been working on the Jubilee. That is selfless and very caring. We both know your mother wouldn't have done any of that, even when she was living at home. When I really need you, I know you'll be here. Don't you see how that's already a major difference?"

The clock on the kitchen wall ticked with Ginny's racing heart, ticking away her fears as she watched her father's kind expression. She felt a little more grounded knowing that her father believed in her so much, and better yet that she met his expectations. "That's all well and good, but what about the fact that I threw Max away?"

Harold thoughtfully scratched at his graying beard. With the anticipation of his surgery, his usual grooming habits had flown out the window. "I've said this before, and I mean it. No one knows what goes on between a husband and wife except for the husband and wife. You need to talk to Max about this and see where you kids stand."

Ginny's finger tensed around the cuff of her sleeve, the terry cloth bending into submission. "I don't think Max will ever speak to me again."

"That's baloney. The man worships the ground you walk on. When you see him tonight at the Jubilee, I'm sure …" Harold clamped his mouth shut, his cheeks blazing crimson. "I mean, whenever you see him again. I'm sure you'll talk and work things out."

Raising an eyebrow, Ginny watched the flush on her father's cheeks run down his neck. He couldn't quite meet her gaze, and she knew something was up. "What's going on?"

"You're telling me why you think you're like your mother. I'm telling you now, she wouldn't have worried about throwing anyone away, husband or otherwise." His words stung harder than Ginny wanted to admit, but she knew they were true.

Her mother had never reached out to her after that day, and Ginny knew it was why she had trouble trusting anyone beyond her father. If the woman that gave birth to her didn't want her in her life, then why would anyone else?

"Do you think she ever thinks about us?" she asked, watching her father's face fall.

"I'm usually an optimist, but I really don't know. I'd like to think deep down, she's proud of you. With that darn internet, she probably knows more about you than I do." He chuckled half-heartedly. "Your mother was a complicated woman, but I'll forever be grateful that she gave me you. She gave me my family."

Ginny crossed over to her father and leaned in for a hug. She cried into the neck of his favorite hoodie, savoring the scent of his skin. "I love you," she said, feeling a sense of relief and content at sharing her fears with her father.

"I love you too." Harold held his daughter, barely grimacing as she leaned too much into his embrace. "You're going to be fine. If there is anyone I know who can get their life together, it's you."

Finally Ginny felt herself smile. "You seem awfully certain, considering I just told you I was unemployed and persona non grata with my ex-husband."

Harold smiled at his daughter's statement. "I have it on good authority that you got a job offer recently."

Ginny scoffed. "There really aren't any secrets in Buckeye Falls, are there?"

"Haven't been before. Why start now?" Harold shrugged, holding Ginny's hand until she rose to her feet. "Now that we've poured our hearts out, could I have another cup of coffee?"

Sniffing, Ginny took both their cups and strode toward the coffee maker. "I think I can muster up some breakfast now. You hungry?" Harold nodded and patted his belly. Before she could start, there was a knock at the door. "Who could that be? I didn't think Mona was coming by until lunch."

Harold shrugged, but his eyes sparkled with mischief. *Oh boy …*

When she pulled open the door, Ginny saw Natalie carrying two enormous tote bags. "Morning!" she chimed as she pushed her way into the house. She headed straight to the kitchen without a backward glance, her heels clicking across the hardwood floors.

Ginny started to close the door when a foot poked in through the doorway. "Thanks for holding that," Mona said as she waddled past, her arms weighed down with boxes. "Who knew donuts were this heavy?" Hot on her heels was another woman, and pretty much the last person she expected to see at the house—CeCe.

"Thanks," CeCe said on a huff as she followed Mona and Natalie inside. Gobsmacked, Ginny didn't move for a moment, trying to figure out why she was here. Unless she wasn't alone?

Ginny stuck her head out to see if anyone else was waiting in the cool December morning. Unfortunately for her, there was not a Max Sanchez in sight. "Damn." She sighed as she closed the door. Walking into the kitchen, she found Mona starting a new pot of coffee while Natalie covered the table with the contents of her bags. CeCe had her head in the fridge as she stacked plastic containers.

"I've labeled these by dates, so eat in order," she instructed from inside the veggie crisper.

"What is all this?" Ginny asked, picking up a stack of papers that were next to a curling iron.

CeCe waved but stayed by the refrigerator. "Max and I offered to bring some of the Jubilee foods to Harold since he can't make it."

"That's really sweet," Ginny said, meaning it too. Now that she knew CeCe wasn't competition, she really could see the appeal of the woman.

"The food is usually the best part," Mona agreed as she

strode to Harold and gave him a chaste kiss on the lips. Ginny was pleased to discover the sight didn't surprise her anymore. In fact, she relished seeing her father being cherished like that.

Turning back to the stack of supplies on the table, Ginny knew Natalie was up to something. "Do I even want to know?"

Natalie took her cup of coffee and sipped thoughtfully. "Probably not, but you're about to find out." Mona plated up donuts for everyone and took the empty seat next to Harold. The pair leaned closed and shared a quiet chuckle while Natalie finished setting her things. "All right, let's start with business before we go to pleasure."

Ginny raised an eyebrow at her friend. "I have a feeling none of this is going to be pleasurable," she deadpanned.

Natalie waved her off with a manicured hand. "Not for you, for me. I'm going to enjoy the next few hours."

Mona took a bite of her donut and said through a mouthful of jelly. "I don't doubt it, Natalie. You scare me sometimes."

CeCe pulled out a chair and sat down. Her gaze was locked on Ginny, but it wasn't unkind. "Nat is a force to be sure." She took a donut and ate half of it in one bite. "Damnit, these are actually pretty good."

Mona snorted. "I told you to give that new bakery a shot. They aren't real competition for you and Max." Harold swiped a blob of jelly from Mona's cheek, and Ginny felt her heart pang at the sight. That was true tenderness.

"Here," Natalie said as she thrust a stack of papers into Ginny's hands. "This is the job description, salary range, and business plan. Take these and review them. I thought we could meet up after Christmas to finalize our plans." She winced at her words and amended, "That is if you *like* the plans."

Glancing down at the sheets in her hands, Ginny saw a very generous salary and a job description that was comparable to her job in New York. Sure, there were some differences, but the core parts of the job were there. She could be creative but manage a smaller client base and forge more relationships on her own. Held in her sweaty hands was a job that could make her happy, in the town that suddenly felt like home again.

Before she could talk herself out of it, Ginny squared her shoulders and stepped right into her new life. "I'll take it. Let's start mid-range on the salary and we can negotiate a raise after the first year's appraisal. How does that work?"

Natalie blinked. Her jaw hit the table as Mona patted Harold's hand. Ginny didn't miss the look those two shared, and she knew there were a lot of cooks in this kitchen. "I know I should make you wait, but I'm not looking this gift horse in the mouth." Natalie leaned across the table to embrace her new employee. "This is against everything in the employee handbook, so you'll just have to sue me." She laughed as Ginny pulled back.

"That went better than I thought." Mona beamed as she dabbed at the tears in her eyes. "Congratulations to both of you."

Ginny was excited, truly looking forward to starting something new with Natalie. She turned to CeCe and grimaced. "Can you please not share this with Max yet? I want to talk to him myself."

CeCe dusted donut crumbs from her hands and nodded. "I'm a vault. He doesn't even know I'm here."

"He doesn't?"

CeCe huffed out a laugh. "He's a friend, but we don't tell each other everything. If I'm being honest, I wanted to make sure you were as nice as everyone says you are."

Ginny snorted. "I'm sure you heard I was wondering the same about you."

CeCe chuckled. "If you promise not to use Max's heart as a punching bag, then we have no issues." She crossed her heart with her index finger. "I mean it, Ginny. Nat's one of my best friends, and if she wants to work with you, I trust you're good enough for Max."

Ginny, her chin wobbling, felt a sense of relief wash over her at CeCe's assessment. She didn't realize it, but she was banking on the other woman liking her. Max made no effort to hide how important CeCe was to him as a person and a chef. The last thing Ginny wanted was to make things harder for him.

Suddenly, Natalie took Ginny's hand and pulled her to her feet. "Okay, now that we're all best friends and employed, the fun part can begin."

"Do I want to know?" Ginny asked with a groan.

"Like I said, probably not."

CeCe gathered the empty donut box and chuckled. "Buckle up," was all she said as she retreated toward the trashcan.

Harold took the donut from Ginny's forgotten plate and took a bite. "Just remember to be nice to your new boss, Ginnybread."

"What does that mean?"

Natalie took Ginny's hand and tugged her toward the stairs, the curling iron clutched in her other hand. "It means it's time for Cinderella to get ready for the ball. CeCe, grab that last tote bag!"

Ginny couldn't help but laugh as Natalie practically dragged her up the stairs. "You're forgetting a very important part of that fairy tale." Ginny grunted as she pulled her arm free. "I don't have a dress."

Natalie plugged in her curling iron and sat it carefully on the dresser. Turning, she flung open the closet, retrieving the red dress from the back. "This is all you need, plus my makeup magic. I'm your freaking fairy godmother." Natalie smirked as she tossed the dress on the bed. "CeCe, can you find that tube of concealer?"

CeCe made a face, her nose wrinkling in confusion. "Nat, when was the last time you saw me wear concealer? Isn't that like shapewear?"

Natalie let out a huff and pointed to her friend. "You're next on the makeover train." CeCe snorted but didn't argue.

"How did you know about this dress?" Ginny asked, turning the conversation back to her Cinderella moment.

Mona joined them in Ginny's bedroom, a tote bag in one hand and her coffee in another. "Your Prince Charming. He let it slip that you might need it someday."

Tears threatened to fall again, and Ginny sniffed. "Max bought that for me?"

Natalie stopped pulling her makeup out of her tote long enough to smile up at her friend. "He sure did, so let's not keep him waiting. It's grand-gesture time, girl!"

And with that, Natalie plucked up her curling iron and went into full fairy godmother mode. CeCe stood smiling, nibbling at the last donut Mona had shared. All three women went to work on turning her into a Buckeye Falls' princess, and Ginny was all too happy to play the part.

*

"That should be the last of it," CeCe said as she slammed Evan's trunk closed. "I'll bring the extra utensils after I get ready.

Max patted Evan on the back and smiled when he saw how early it was. The old saying was definitely accurate, many hands make light work. "You're the best. Thanks for making all these trips."

Evan flushed at the praise, his skin getting dangerously close to the color of Santa's suit. "No big deal. What's the point of owning this beast if I can't use it?" Evan rapped his knuckles on the car door and smiled at his beat-up hatchback.

For a moment, no one spoke. They were exhausted from days of cooking, baking, boxing, and packing. The Jubilee was the highlight of the holidays, but few people realized how much work really went into an event that half of Buckeye Falls attended. "I should go home and become more presentable." CeCe gestured at her flour-speckled jeans and her ball cap.

"Not on my account. I don't mind if you show up as you are." Evan smiled at CeCe, his skin officially the color of cranberry sauce. "Pick you up at six?"

Max watched CeCe soften a little. "I'll meet you there at six-fifteen. How's that?"

Evan wasn't deterred. "No point driving two cars. I'll pick you up. I can take you back whenever you're ready. I swear." He held his hand up, giving CeCe the Boy Scout salute.

Max bit his lip, dying to interject on Evan's behalf. The kid was trying so hard to please CeCe, it nearly broke Max's heart. She rolled her eyes and finally gave in. "Fine, pick me up at six. But remember, this is not a date-date."

Now Max couldn't help himself. "Date-date? I know I'm out of practice, but what the heck does that mean?"

CeCe looked to Evan for support, but he merely crossed his arms in front of his chest and waited for her explanation. "I wouldn't mind a definition myself, seeing as how I'm part of this non-date date."

Max hid his smile behind his hand as CeCe stomped her foot. "This was a bad idea." She groaned. Holding up her hand, she began defining the nuances of non-date dates. "First, no touching."

"But it's a dance. How will we not touch?" Evan scoffed.

"Amendment to point one—touching only on the dance floor. And no funny business or shenanigans." CeCe waited until Evan seemed content before continuing. "Next, no mistletoe or romantic gestures. Lastly, this doesn't mean anything. We are two friends going to an event together. That's it."

Max couldn't hold it in another second. "So, it sounds like you two are going to have a magical evening," he surmised. "Make sure you stomp on CeCe's feet at least once during a slow dance." He winked at Evan, who looked surprisingly upbeat.

CeCe pointed at Evan and sighed. "You look too happy for a man who just found out he's not going on a date. Why are you so happy?"

Evan shrugged; the gesture carefree. He took a moment before he answered. "I'm looking forward to spending time with you outside the diner. If that means we don't touch, laugh, or generally enjoy ourselves, I'll take it." Stepping into his car, Evan shouted through the open window. "Pick you up at six." He drove away, leaving a slack-jawed CeCe behind.

Max gave the guy credit. Evan was taking what he could with a smile. Max envied the kid's resilience; it was in short supply with Max. "I think it's great you two are going together," Max offered a confused CeCe. "You'll have a great time, I'm sure."

CeCe shook her head as if she could loosen the cobwebs cluttering her brain. "It's going to be a disaster. I'm leading the guy on; don't you see that?"

Max shook his head. "You told him, in very vivid detail with bullet points, how this isn't a date. I don't know if you could have done more explaining without getting a whiteboard and drawing the portions of your heart that were off-limits. Give the guy some credit; he knows the score."

CeCe clamped her hands on her hips and stared Max down. "Speaking of men who know the score, what are your plans with Ginny?"

Rubbing the back of his neck, Max fought against the tide of nerves churning through his stomach. He had no idea if, yet again, he'd be alone and heartbroken on Christmas. "We'll see. I'm working on my Hail Mary. I'll either be the happiest guy in Buckeye Falls tonight, or I'll be drowning my sorrows with Evan at the punch bowl. Either way, tonight is a shift for me."

CeCe was intrigued. "What kind of shift?"

"I'm either going to get my wife back, or I'm going to cut ties and start over. I cannot stay in this constant state of limbo, not knowing if she'll ever change her mind. If Ginny's happiness isn't with me, then I hope she can find it. And it will mean I need to find mine."

CeCe smiled, an honest smile that made it to her eyes. "That sounds surprisingly healthy."

Max laughed. "Don't be fooled. If she turns me down again, I will be calling you for more bourbon and a shoulder to cry on."

Thrusting her hand out to Max, CeCe shook it and said, "Deal. I'm here if you need me." She bit her lip and continued, "I wouldn't count your girl out just yet. Have a little faith."

Max pulled CeCe into a hug, a completely foreign act, and both were silent for a moment. "Thank you, CeCe. I know I don't say it enough." Max heard a sniffle, but he knew better than to bring it up. CeCe would kick him in the groin if he brought up any more emotions.

Pulling back, CeCe wrapped her arms around her torso to stave off the chill. While the skies above were cloudless and blue, there was a nip in the air that even a down coat couldn't keep away. "I better go become presentable for this thing. Take care of yourself, and let me know what you need." Max nodded and watched CeCe get into her truck and back out of the parking lot.

Normally Max liked to have a plan in place when he had something to accomplish. Need to revamp the menu? Time to survey the customers for what they wanted. Even his time with Harold was carefully scheduled. It was a trick Max had learned back in school when his stammer had gotten the better of him. If he knew what was coming, he'd have time to practice and plan his words.

Now he was mere hours away from seeing Ginny, and he had no idea what he would do or say to get her attention. All he'd managed so far was texting Harold to confirm she would at least be at the Jubilee, but that fact did little to calm his nerves. "Get it together, man," Max said to himself as he locked up the diner and headed back to his house. Plan or no plan, he couldn't show up tonight in his soiled apron and jeans. He needed to get decked out, and fast. He was also going to take some of CeCe's advice and have a little faith. After all, it was the Christmas Jubilee. Anything could happen.

CHAPTER 15

"I'd like to thank you all for attending tonight's Jubilee." Anthony's voice boomed over the crowd. The mayor looked sharp in a tailored black tuxedo. "Before we kick off this year's ball, we have a few other folks to thank. I'd like to start with Mona and my lovely wife, Natalie, who co-chaired this year's planning committee." He paused and smiled as the room applauded.

Max yanked at his own bow tie, remembering why he preferred flannels and T-shirts to formal wear. He felt like a fish out of water. Mona materialized at his side, looping her arm through his and whispering, "You look very dapper tonight."

Turning, Max found Mona in a green dress with little glass ornaments dangling from the neckline. "Thanks, Mona. You look gorgeous. I'm sure Harold is devastated he couldn't make it tonight." After texting his friend, Max discovered Harold didn't have the energy to leave the house, but he'd insisted Mona attend.

"He'll get an eyeful later," she teased. "Recovery is key right now; romance can wait."

"Still," Max agreed on a laugh. "I'm sure he wishes he was here."

Mona nodded. "He's at home with the Cavs and a bowl of cheesy bites. He'll survive."

Just as Mona was about to continue the reasons why Harold would survive, Anthony's speech continued. "And finally, I would like to thank Max and CeCe and the team at the diner for catering tonight's festivities. I know I speak for all of us when I say I cannot wait to dig in." Everyone whooped and clapped at the mayor's words, giving Max a warm feeling of accomplishment. He knew Anthony was being diplomatic, but it still felt good to have his neighbors support him and his team. All his time toiling away in the kitchen, all his dedication to making the diner his were worth it.

Max leaned toward Mona. "Is it bad that I'm enjoying this year's remarks?"

Mona smiled and said, "Just you wait. It's only going to get better."

Max was intrigued, but he didn't have time to respond. His words escaped him when he saw who was taking the microphone from Anthony. "Gin." Her name came out as a breath, and Max felt his heart rattle in his rib cage.

Ginny was transformed and practically glowed from the makeshift stage. Her red gown sparkled, catching every scrap of light in the crowded venue. That dress waited two years for her to come home, but it was worth the wait. It hugged every curve and made her look like a Christmas Princess. Whether it was her big-city weight loss or her recent dive back into Midwestern fare, the dress looked like it was made for her. Tendrils of her chocolate brown hair framed her face, with the rest piled in curls on top of her head. Her makeup was tasteful, yet bright, with her eyes popping and her lips a delectable shade of apple red. Max's mouth watered.

Reaching out with a shaking hand, Ginny took the mic and smiled nervously at the crowd. It could have been Max's imagination, but he felt her gaze combing the crowd for him. "Thanks, Anthony—I mean, Mayor Snyder. You'd think I'd be used to calling you that by now." She laughed and the room joined in. "Some of you know me. I'm Ginny Meyer. I've been back home in Buckeye Falls to help my dad." She paused and added, "Who is home and recovering well." A few folks clapped at the update on Harold's health, and Max saw Ginny gulp in air before continuing. "When I came back, I didn't expect to do much beyond playing nurse while Dad recovered. But when a few friends mentioned this event, I had to jump in and help. I'm so happy that I did."

Ginny glanced off stage to where Natalie and Madeline were waving and grinning like goofballs. Both wore red dresses, matching their counterparts' red ties. Anthony held Otis, who looked bored with the festivities but pleased to have a cheesy bite in his mouth. A trail of drool slid down his chin as he chewed. Very few people could pull off that look, but Otis mastered it.

"Doesn't she look lovely?" Mona asked, pointing to Ginny, who had continued her thanks to the planning committee.

Lovely didn't even start to cover how Ginny looked. For the first time in years, she looked at ease, at home in her surroundings. Her usual smile was firmly in place, lighting up her face brighter than any Christmas tree. "Sh-sh-she looks st-stunning," Max finally offered.

Mona patted his hand. On his other side, CeCe and Evan joined them. CeCe wore a simple black dress with jingle bell earrings. Evan cleaned up nicely in a suit that might have been his dad's, but Max was not about to ask. True to CeCe's date-date rules, he stood a respectable six inches apart and didn't touch her, but the look he gave her spoke volumes. He was beyond smitten with CeCe. Max said a prayer to Saint Nick that they would find their own happily ever after, regardless of what happened with his own love story.

Ginny's voice pulled him back to the moment. "In addition to thanking all our supporters and sponsors tonight, I would like to thank *you*, Buckeye Falls. You showed me the true meaning of the holidays again. It's about family and being surrounded by the people you love." Her gaze swept across the room until it finally landed on Max. Her voice didn't falter as she continued. "And there's someone else I'd like to thank tonight. Max Sanchez." It could have been his imagination, but Max felt a hush fall over the room. "Max, you have shown tremendous patience, love, and understanding with me. I apologize for how I behaved, because I truly am sorry." Her voice caught on the last word, and Max's feet propelled him toward the stage.

Pushing through the crowd, Max kept his eyes locked on Ginny as her bottom lip trembled. "I'm coming," he said as he passed his friends and neighbors. When he got to the stage, he took the stairs two at a time. "Gin, what are you doing?" he asked when he was by her side.

Ginny blinked back tears and said, "Making a grand gesture." Max shook his head, trying to take in every detail in front of him. From the look on Ginny's face, to the way she reached out for him, clutching his hand in hers, Max wanted to catalog every minute detail. Continuing to speak into the mic, Ginny said, "I'm so sorry for everything. You've shown me nothing but patience, kindness, and love since the day we met, and I haven't always returned the favor. Now that I'm back, I'd like to make it up to you." Collected murmurs threatened to drown out Ginny's speech, but she carried on. "Will you let me make it up to you?" She squeezed Max's hand at the question, her gaze hopeful.

"You're back?" It was near impossible to believe what he was hearing.

"Yes, if you'll have me. I don't think I can live without you another second, Max. We will still have a lot to talk about, but I'd like to—"

Ginny's words were cut off when Max pulled her toward him for the best kiss of their lives. The feel of holding his wife in his arms nearly brought Max to his knees. He was faintly aware of the cheers from the crowd, but he was focused on Ginny. Ginny, who was real and in his arms. Ginny, who said she was not leaving Buckeye Falls. Surely, this had to be a dream, a candy-cane-induced hallucination.

"Can we continue this somewhere else?" Max asked in between kisses. He cradled her face in his hands, afraid to pull back for even a second.

"You mean outside Buckeye Falls? I think it'll be hard to have our privacy after this." Ginny laughed as Max scooped her up and placed the mic back on its stand.

Before he stole his wife away, Max stopped and said, "Thank you all for a wonderful Jubilee. I'm selfish enough to say this is, by far, the best one yet. Now, let's party!" He heard the audience erupt into cheers as they poured out into the wintery night.

Big, fat snowflakes fell, clinging to the grass, making the town look like a snow globe. When they were outside and out of sight, Max eased Ginny back to the ground. Her heels slid on the concrete, but he had no plans of loosening his hold. The town was deserted. Everyone was at the Jubilee, leaving them in peace. The falling snow dampened the sounds around them, and all they could hear was each other breathing.

Ginny held on to his forearms as she steadied herself. Once she was on terra firma, she reached up and swiped a lock of hair off his forehead. The familiar gesture sent a charge through him.

"I meant every word I said back there, Max. I'm so sorry. I didn't mean what I said to Dad at the hospital, and I hate myself for taking your words. I know it's going to take more than me continuously apologizing …" Her words faltered, but she looked determined. This was clearly hard for her, but he was proud of Ginny for making this right—he was proud of her for saying what she needed to say. "I'd like us to try again."

Max took her hand in his and tugged her closer. "Are

you sure this is what you want? Because I won't be able to let you go again, Gin. This is it for me." Ginny smiled and nodded, her hairdo bobbing on top of her head. Max cupped her face and kissed her gently. She greedily returned the kiss, and he felt his heart swell. "Gin, this is all I ever wanted. *You* are all I ever wanted."

Ginny's hands glided up to his shoulders where she smoothed his lapels. "You are all I've ever wanted, Max. I am sorry it took me this long to realize that."

Time had no meaning now that Ginny was back in his arms. Max knew he would have waited until his dying day for her. There had been a million scenarios in his head on how he'd ask for her hand again. Each was carefully planned and crafted, but none of that seemed relevant now.

Ginny was here and ready to give them another shot. Throwing caution and the best laid plans to the wind, he reached into his tuxedo jacket and retrieved a small black box. It was a box he'd had at the ready since the day the moving truck pulled away.

"What's this?" Ginny asked, holding the small box in the air.

Clearing his throat, Max collected himself. Emotion clawed at his throat, but he wanted this to be perfect. Despite having practiced this moment in his head countless times, he felt completely unprepared. She stepped closer, their toes touching, and looked up into his eyes. Her expression was bright, and a smile cracked her lovely face.

"Max?" She twisted the box in the air, careful to keep it in his line of sight.

Max reached out and took her hand, clasping it gently in his. "Gin," he said clearly, his mouth and brain in sync. "I'm not going to pressure you into anything. But when you're ready, I'm going to put this back on your finger."

Max pulled one of Ginny's hands free and kissed her knuckles. Like always, she'd forgotten her gloves, and her fingers were little icicles. She shivered, from the cold or Max's kiss, he wasn't sure. Leaning closer, she placed a kiss on his cheek. The tender gesture nearly brought the man to his knees. "Max," she whispered into his ear. "What happens if I want that ring now?"

Max stilled, not even breathing in case it broke the spell. Even in his wildest dreams, he never expected a reconciliation to be this simple. "If you want it now; it's yours. It's always been yours." Opening the box, he held it closer so she could see it in the fading light.

The ring had been his grandmother's, and Max always knew it belonged on Ginny's hand. A simple white gold band; it was studded with three diamonds that caught the light and sparkled like stars. During that first year of their marriage, Ginny would walk around their house at night, and Max could see her sparkle. He used to call her his little homing beacon. She gasped when she saw the ring again, as if she wasn't sure it was real. Just as she reached out for the box, he pulled back a few inches.

"What's wrong?" she asked, studying his face.

Max hated what he was about to ask, but he couldn't help himself. He needed answers. Frankly, he deserved them. "You're sure you want it? Like I said, t-this is it for me, Gin." After thirty-plus years on this planet, Max had never felt so vulnerable. His future happiness was in Ginny's ungloved hands.

Max watched Ginny swallow, then step back into his space. "I'm sorry, Max. I'm sorry for everything that happened with the divorce. I've been thinking about us a lot lately, and I wish I could …" A tear slid down her cheek as she fought against a wave of emotion. He wiped the tear away with his thumb and kissed the trail it left behind.

Ginny wobbled on her heels a bit, so Max steered them toward a bench on the sidewalk. "If you're not ready to talk about it, we don't have to now. Tonight has been perfect, and I don't need anything you're not ready to give."

Ginny pulled a tissue from her purse and blotted her eyes. The sequins on her dress scraped against the bench as she leaned closer and rested her head on Max's shoulder. It seemed so natural, sitting with her in the cool night air, his arm pulled tightly around her. He knew things were shifting, but he didn't want to get ahead of himself.

Finally, Ginny spoke. "I've been thinking about my mom since I've been back. Thinking about how she left, how I hated her for it, and how I vowed never to do anything so cold, so callus." Her voice hitched on the last word, and Max felt her shudder. He pulled her closer to him but didn't interrupt. Ginny didn't often open up, and when she did, it was best to stay quiet.

After a moment, Ginny continued. "She left us without looking back. I never understood how she could do it, but then over a decade later, I did the same damned thing. When I got the call from the New York office, I felt like I'd made it. My career was so important to me. I wanted to get out into the world and make my mark. But the trouble was, when I signed the divorce papers and started my new job, it all felt wrong. I dove into projects, accomplishing my professional goals. All the while, I knew something was missing."

"What was missing?" he asked, his voice barely a whisper, coming out in a puff of frozen mist. For a moment they were both silent, and Max feared his question was lost to the night.

Finally Ginny responded. "You were missing, Max. I was missing my support system, my best friend, my soul mate. I'd be walking home at night, starving since I hadn't eaten yet, and I pictured you in the house. You'd be wearing that old blue apron with the elephant on it, and you'd be making me grilled cheese sandwiches. I knew you'd pull me into a hug as soon as I walked through the door."

Now it was Max's turn for waterworks. His eyes clouded over at all the wasted time, all the words they should have said years ago. "I never knew you thought about me, or that dumb apron," he said. Hesitating a moment, he added, "I never meant to be so apathetic."

Ginny snorted and covered her mouth with her

crumpled tissue. "You always looked ridiculously adorable in that thing," she mused, leaning back to meet his gaze. When she saw the tears glistening in his eyes, she took a deep breath. "And you're not the only one who had blinders on in our marriage. I let a lot of things slide, but that was before. I want to come home, Max. I've been falling apart lately, and these last few weeks are the first time I've felt like myself in ages. I miss you, I love you, and I want to come home to Buckeye Falls."

She gestured to the ring box, still clutched in Max's hands. He shook his head, still absorbing her confession. "I haven't stopped thinking about you, worrying about you, loving you since the day you left. You've always been the one for me, Gin. Always."

"Max, I never meant to hurt you like I did. There's no excusing it, but I want to make it up to you." She swiped at her cheeks, her hands still bare to the elements.

Max stood and eased down to his knee in front of her. This was not where he'd planned to make his grand gesture, his bid for her heart, but it was going to have to do. Right in that moment, he couldn't imagine a better place.

"Gin, I'm going to ask you something, and I want your honest answer." He looked up and saw she'd lost the battle of tears, as her cheeks were damp and her makeup smudged. She'd never looked lovelier.

"It's honesty from here on out." She laughed.

Max nodded sagely. "Good, then we're on the same page. Gin, I love you, and I want you back in my life. I want to go through life with you, be here to support the highs and lows. I promise to make you enchiladas and grilled cheese sandwiches and keep you smiling after stressful days. I promise not to let the diner take over and be mindful when you need your own space." Max paused, the cold from the sidewalk seeping into his suit pants. "What I'm rambling on about is … Gin, will you marry me … again?"

Fortunately, she didn't make Max wait for her answer. "Give me that ring," she huffed impatiently, her lips tipped up in a gorgeous grin. Without breaking eye contact, she took the ring from the box and slid it onto her finger. Despite the cold, it fit perfectly. "Yes. Yes, Max. I will marry you again."

He couldn't wait. He pulled her to him and kissed her like his life depended on it. No matter what happened next, he knew he had Ginny back in his life. His girl had finally found her way home.

EPILOGUE

Three Months Later

"I know this is your bachelorette party, but can we take a minute to celebrate our first successful event?" Natalie asked through a mouthful of grilled cheese sandwich.

CcCe snorted with laughter as Mona tried in vain not to get tomato soup on her sweater. Since the holidays were over, she was back to wearing colorful sweaters that didn't have a Santa stapled to the front or twinkling lights that could blind a person. This sweater was white with "Mother of the Bride" embroidered on the front in pink lettering.

Ginny had purchased the sweater as a gift when she saw it on Main Street. Mona had been nothing but supportive. Ginny wanted to celebrate the woman who had brought love back into her father's life, as well as her own. Ginny knew her father was going to pop the question, and she couldn't wait to officially call Mona family.

Ginny handed Mona a napkin and smiled. "I think we can celebrate whatever we want because it's my party." She raised her champagne flute and cheered. "To our new business, our friendships, and falling back in love."

Mona raised her glass and beamed. "I'll drink to that."

CeCe downed her glass and clapped. "I just have to say," she said as the room fell silent. "That I have never seen my boss so happy, and it has made work even better than it was before. And let me tell you, I've always liked working at the diner." Everyone chuckled and started refilling their glasses. "You and Max, you belong together. I'm so happy you came back home."

Ginny was touched by CeCe's words and struggled to keep from crying. For some reason, falling back in love had turned her into a faucet. "Thanks, CeCe."

She waved away the praise. "Don't thank me, just keep Max happy." She winked, and they all burst out laughing.

While Mona cued up their next rom-com, Natalie returned from the kitchen with a tray of cheesy bites. "I hid these for last. It is the end of our cheesy feast," she proclaimed, placing the tray on the coffee table.

Ginny felt her mouth water as she snagged a bite and popped it into her mouth. "CeCe, no matter what you do, never stop making these." She covered her mouth with her hand, her ring sparkling in the firelight.

Mona asked, "So where is your other half tonight? What is the bachelor party plan?" She nibbled from a cheesy bite and rested back on the couch.

Ginny wiped her mouth and sat next to Mona. "Max picked up Dad, and they were going to pick up Evan and meet Anthony at the tavern in Elm River."

Natalie sighed. "I still want to know how you got my husband to be human again. Did you threaten bodily harm, CeCe? Or did you threaten him with unflattering social media pics, Ginny?"

"How do you know it wasn't me?" Mona asked, her tone even. "I can be very persuasive if I want to be."

"Mona, I have no doubt," Natalie teased.

Ginny was skeptical. "How did Anthony get talked into a night of fun with the boys?"

CeCe took a sip of her champagne and laughed. "I may have told him Natalie would bring me all of his suits, and that I'd take them to Green's for extra starch."

All four women burst into laughter, Natalie nearly falling off her chair. "It's been months, and he still complains about that suit. I don't have the heart to tell him I brought it back to Green's after his outburst."

Ginny looked at these three friends she'd made since coming home. She couldn't imagine not having a support system like them in her life. Even though Natalie was technically her boss, she was a friend first. And she damn near fell in love with CeCe that first day at the house. Mona was thrilled with the news that she was moving back home and quickly jumped into her mother-of-the-bride duties.

Max and Ginny found a cottage off Main Street that was between Natalie's office and the diner. It was also barely ten minutes to Harold's house, which would soon be Mona's house as well. Ginny felt her heart grow at all that had transpired. Love had found its way back to Buckeye Falls, and she couldn't wait to remarry Max in the morning.

Her phone buzzed from her purse, and Ginny walked over to grab it. "Hey, we said no boys tonight," Natalie scolded.

"I'm making sure it's not an emergency," she chided. "Hold your horses."

The text was from Max. It had several heart-eyed emojis and an *I love you.* Then another text came through that simply said, *why did I invite Anthony?*

Ginny smiled and responded, *because you're a nice person?*

Max replied right away, *no, it has to be something else.* He included a winky face this time.

After three hours, the movies were done, and the women were filled with champagne and enough dairy products to clog all their arteries. Mona helped clean up before excusing herself to drive a very tipsy CeCe and a very drunk Natalie home. "We'll see you at the community center bright and early," she said. "Make sure you get plenty of rest. I'll take care of these two."

Natalie and CeCe mumbled their congratulations as they

stumbled to Mona's car. Ginny stood on the porch long after their headlights faded over the hill. Spring was nearly here, and Buckeye Falls felt like it was coming back to life after such a cold winter. She knew the community center would be lovely tomorrow.

Agreeing to have it someplace low-key, Ginny and Max planned a simple ceremony followed by cake and cocktails—both courtesy of CeCe and Evan. The pair even agreed to go to the wedding together, but only after it was established as a non-date date. When they couldn't decide on flowers for the centerpieces, Max suggested oranges in big glass bowls—unsquished of course. Who could argue with that?

Just as Ginny turned to go back into the house, she heard tires crunching on the driveway. Expecting to see her father, she was pleasantly surprised to see Max's car. He held up his hands in defense when he stepped out. "I know we're not supposed to see each other before tomorrow, but I had to see you."

Ginny warmed at his words and jogged down the porch steps to meet him halfway. "I'm so glad because I couldn't wait to see you too."

Max pulled her into a bear hug and kissed the top of her head. Ginny felt so at home in his arms, she couldn't imagine how she'd managed to walk away in the first place.

"Have I told you recently that I love you?" she asked, resting her head on his shoulder.

"Not in the last two hours," he teased, kissing the top of her head once more for good measure. "I cannot wait until tomorrow. You're going to be Ginny Sanchez again."

Ginny leaned back to meet his gaze. "I think I've always been Ginny Sanchez, I just didn't know it."

She got on her tiptoes and kissed Max in the moonlight. With nothing but the sounds of crickets and the wind in the trees, Ginny felt a calmness settle around her soul. She'd fallen home. Even with stumbles and setbacks, Ginny knew she was where she needed to be—right here with Max.

The End

ACKNOWLEDGEMENTS

Let me start out by thanking the team at Inkspell Publishing—specifically Melissa, Yeza, and Shel. This book would not be possible without your guidance and support. Thank you!

To the team at BH Writing Service—specifically Jessica and Judy. Thank you for your help getting this story to where it is today.

To my writer friends, both in Ohio and Indiana, who listened while I droned on about this and other stories racing through my head. I appreciate your insight and willingness to share in the crazy craft of writing.

The biggest shout-out to my family and friends. Thank you for being the first to pre-order my books. I could not do this without cheerleaders like you in my corner.

Last, but certainly never least, to my husband for your relentless support of this dream of mine. I could not write sappy stories without you in my life. I love you.

Happy reading, everyone! 😊

HERE'S A SNEAK PEEK AT THE SECOND BUCKEYE FALLS NOVEL… Falling for You

Chapter One

CeCe LaRue was wrist-deep in a mound of bread dough when she heard her cell phone ring. Mumbling a few choice profanities, she lifted her hands and attempted to answer the phone with her elbow. Max's smiling face beamed from the taunting device. After one more attempt at elbow poking, the phone went silent. "Come on," she groaned, knowing the reason her boss was calling.

"He's calling off again, isn't he?" Evan Lawson asked from the doorway. He shrugged off his jacket and dusted a few snowflakes from his blond curls. Walking over to the table, he picked up her phone just as Max called again. "Hey, Max," he answered, watching CeCe roll her eyes from her spot at the table. She tried to push her hair back with her forearm and ended up covering her nose in flour. "Yep, it looks like sour dough this time."

CeCe could hear both men laugh at her morning routine. It wasn't her fault she wanted the diner to have fresh bread every morning. "Put him on speaker," she ordered while thrusting her hands back into the blob of dough.

Evan shrugged and didn't put the phone on speaker. "Sure thing. We'll get everything ready to go. See you soon." He disconnected and put her phone back on the table. Evan's blue gaze finally met CeCe's, and he smiled. The guy had an unnerving ability to disarm her with just one of his goofy grins. Darn him.

"I could have taken that, you know." She huffed, turning her face down to her work.

Undeterred, Evan walked over to the sink and washed his hands. Within a minute, he donned an apron and started cracking eggs for the breakfast rush. "I know, but watching you flail around entertains me," he said, smiling through his egg cracking.

"Ugh." CeCe grumbled as she formed loaves of bread and covered them in a towel to rise. No matter her mood, CeCe trusted the bread-making process. Life was complicated, but she knew that flour, yeast, water, and salt made terrific bread every time. "What's his excuse this time?"

Evan pulled down a few frying pans from above the stove and lined them up by the grill. "Does he need an excuse? He's been with Ginny every waking moment since Christmas." There was no malice or accusation in Evan's tone; the kid was a born romantic.

Their boss, and friend, had finally gotten his ex-wife back over the holidays. While it was certainly heartwarming, it threw their usually predictable boss off his game and into the arms of love. Sure, Max was still devoted to the diner, but he'd found the work-life balance he'd been missing for years.

"No. You're right. He doesn't need an excuse." CeCe wiped her hands clean on a towel and started icing a tray of cinnamon rolls. The rolls were still warm, and the cream cheese icing oozed into the cinnamon swirls. Like clockwork, Evan joined her side and leaned in for a closer look. His eyes practically sparkled as she handed him the pallet knife. "You can have the rest, but don't eat it near the counter."

Evan scoffed, but took the proffered knife. "I'm not a kid. I know not to drool over the customer's food." He took his prize and backed away to the sink in the corner. CeCe attempted to ignore the sinful noises Evan made as he licked the knife clean.

Pulling at the collar of her tunic, CeCe tried to cool herself down. "Must be the ovens," she muttered as she ambled into the walk-in fridge for the rest of the breakfast ingredients. As she opened the door with an armful of trays, Evan was there to take them. He reached out and took the load without even a grunt, carefully placing everything on the counter. "Thanks," CeCe said as she handed him the second round of trays.

Following a familiar routine, the pair stood side by side at the counter and chopped, mixed, and prepped what they needed for breakfast. CeCe used to do this routine with Max, but Evan had been taking more of an interest in cooking over the last year.

CeCe had been at the diner for nearly four years, the longest she'd ever been at one job. She was weeks away from her thirtieth birthday, and she wasn't too proud to say it was getting to her. Time never meant much to CeCe, who traveled around the Midwest finding kitchens where she could use her pastry chef diploma. A stint in Chicago, and a stop in Ohio's three-C's, and CeCe had somehow found her peace in the small Ohio town of Buckeye Falls.

The peace of their morning prep work was interrupted when Helen, their waitress, barged in through the backdoor. "Did you see?" she practically shouted as she ran over to the counter, the local paper clutched in her meaty hand.

Evan hurriedly moved a bowl of eggs to the side so Helen could thrust the paper onto the counter and slapped her hand over the headline. "What's up?" Evan asked, craning his neck to see what all the fuss was about. Helen was usually more sour than excitable.

"He's coming to Buckeye Falls this summer for a food competition," Helen exclaimed; her excitement was contagious until CeCe finally saw the 'he' in question.

Glancing down at the paper, CeCe felt her hands go clammy as she dropped her whisk. It clattered across the floor and landed next to Evan's sneakered feet. Without saying a word, he retrieved it and tossed it in the sink. He pulled another whisk from the utensil holder and tried handing it to CeCe, but she was lost in a slew of emotions.

DON'T MISS ANOTHER AMAZING STORY BY LIBBY KAY

The slopes are heating up this holiday season!

Skiing's golden girl finds love this Christmas when she falls for the sport's bad boy.

Christmas is Sienna Markum's favorite time of year. From the tinsel and traditions to the down time with family, all Sienna wants is a break from training. The Paralympics are months away, and she's set on winning Alpine gold.

Connor Shoemaker has no plans for Christmas, other than train for the Paralympics. A motocross accident took one of his legs – and all of his confidence. Connor doesn't think anything can get his old mojo back, until he meets Sienna.

Sienna was told her training would be private, but soon, she starts to warm up to her new training partner. Bad boy Connor is more than meets the eye. When her Christmas plans fall through, Sienna finds the best present under the tree – Connor.

But is Sienna willing to balance her training with a shot at love?

Can Connor find his confidence again, off and on the

slopes?

Together, these two will learn there is more to life than skiing. And it looks a whole lot like love.

Fans of sports romances like Icebreaker by Hannah Grace, and The Wall of Winnipeg and Me by Mariana Zapata will love the enemies to lovers and forced proximity tropes in Libby Kay's books. SNOW IN LOVE will have you snuggling up and enjoying hot cocoa by the fire. A perfect cold weather read!

EXCERPT:

"Hey, Golden Girl!" Sienna heard Connor's voice as he slid to a halt in front of her. He used his wrist to pull up his goggles, dazzling her with his blue eyes. They literally sparkled like a character in her favorite vampire romance novel. Damn him.

Sienna bristled. "Don't call me Golden Girl. Do you happen to see Bea Arthur around here?" Sienna assumed he wouldn't get the reference, but she wasn't that lucky.

Connor shrugged before stabbing his poles into the snow. He put his hands on his hips and said, "I'm more of a Betty White fan."

Sienna slid toward Connor and lifted her chin. "Betty seems a little too sweet for you. Aren't you more into the Blanches of the world?"

A glorious grin cracked Connor's face as he chuckled. "Nice to know you're worried about my type. Frankly, I'm surprised you have enough time to pay attention. Don't you have a daycare center to dedicate, or a puppy to rescue?"

Mentioning her beloved dog, Roscoe, brought Sienna's blood boiling. Throw in the fact that he mocked her charity work, and Connor Shoemaker was officially on her last nerve. "I'll have you know, I like helping people." She hesitated, worrying her bottom lip. "And I like animals. Who doesn't love puppies? Roscoe is a very good boy." She hated how lame her argument sounded, but she wouldn't have anyone dissing her doggo.

Now Available In Ebook And Print Where Books Are Sold

ABOUT THE AUTHOR

Libby Kay lives in the city in the heart of the Midwest with her husband. When she's not writing, Libby loves reading romance novels of any kind. Stories of people falling in love nourish her soul. Contemporary or Regency, sweet or hot, as long as there is a happily ever after she's in love!

When not surrounded by books, Libby can be found baking in her kitchen, binging true crime shows, or on the road with her husband, traveling as far as their bank account will allow.

Writing is a solitary job, and Libby loves to hear from readers. Reach out and review her stories anytime. She'd love to hear from you.

Website: https://www.libbykayauthor.com/

Facebook: @LibbyKayAuthor

Goodreads: Libby Kay

Instagram: https://www.instagram.com/libbykayauthor/

Bookbub: https://www.bookbub.com/profile/libby-kay

Made in the USA
Monee, IL
09 March 2023

29509294R00156